TELL

ME

MY

NAME

TELL

ME

MY

NAME

ERIN **RUDDY**

DUNDURN
TORONTO

Publisher: Scott Fraser | Acquiring editor: Kathryn Lane | Editor: Allison Hirst
Cover designer: Laura Boyle
Cover image: shutterstock.com/Anki Hoglund

Library and Archives Canada Cataloguing in Publication

Title: Tell me my name / Erin Ruddy.
Names: Ruddy, Erin, 1972- author.
Identifiers: Canadiana (print) 2019016512X | Canadiana (ebook) 20190165146 | ISBN 9781459746152 (softcover) | ISBN 9781459746169 (PDF) | ISBN 9781459746176 (EPUB)
Classification: LCC PS8635.U345 T45 2020 | DDC C813/.6—dc23

We acknowledge the support of the Canada Council for the Arts and the Ontario Arts Council for our publishing program. We also acknowledge the financial support of the Government of Ontario, through the Ontario Book Publishing Tax Credit and Ontario Creates, and the Government of Canada.

VISIT US AT

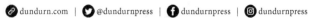 dundurn.com | @dundurnpress | dundurnpress | dundurnpress

Dundurn
1382 Queen Street East
Toronto, Ontario, Canada
M4L 1C9

For my loves
Brad, Nate, and Cohen

PART ONE

TELL ME MY NAME

CHAPTER 1

Ellie opened her eyes. Tried to move but couldn't. It was dark, and her vision was cloudy. She was able to make out the square case of a window. Curtains drawn, flaccid. A single wooden chair. She was lying on a wrought-iron bed.

She lifted her head, felt a wave of nausea roll through her. Remembered the noxious cloth. She wiggled her wrists and ankles. Something was binding them — something sharp and unyielding. Plastic cable ties.

She tried to scream, but the sound came out as a muffled moan.

Where am I? Who did this?

Light splashed the wall as someone entered an unseen door.

"Hello, Ellie," a deep voice said. "Do you know how long I've been dreaming about this moment?"

She knew she couldn't respond, not with the gag filling her mouth. But she tried anyway, releasing a series of stifled sobs.

"There, there," the man said, stepping into view. The bed frame shifted as he eased himself next to her. "You'll have your chance to speak soon enough. But first I'd like to get properly reacquainted. It's been so long." He paused, gazing into her eyes. "Man, what a surprise it was to see you driving by after all these years … you, of all people. I recognized you instantly. Still as beautiful as ever. Then, that shower routine you put on the other night … what a show, Ellie, what a show …"

Ellie stiffened. Remembered the feeling of being watched the night she'd tested the new outdoor shower. The man was crazy, or he'd made a mistake. Once he removed the gag, she could explain to him that he'd mixed her up with some other woman. Surely then he'd let her go. Otherwise, Neil would return with the groceries and he'd find her missing from their cottage. He'd call the police and she'd be saved.

"Ellie, Ellie, Ellie … the things you do to me," he continued. "Neil is a lucky guy. But it seems his luck has finally run out. You see, I have a little game in mind for the three of us. Hey, don't look so worried, I promise it'll be fun. You just have to follow my rules. Rule Number One: no screaming. Rule Number Two: no flailing, no fighting, no trying to escape. And finally, Rule Number Three, the most important one of all …" He paused and stroked her hair. "It's easy. All you have to do … is tell me my name."

The man got up and looked down at her. With a surprisingly delicate touch, he leaned over and removed her gag, brushing away the tear that had trickled down her cheek.

"Please, you have me confused with someone else!" Ellie cried, anguished. "I swear to God. This is all a mistake —"

"Oh, spare me, Eloise. Do you really think I'd have gone to all this trouble if I wasn't sure it was you? Look, I'm not saying it'll be easy. It has been a while, and the truth is — well, I didn't always look this good. I've made a few changes to impress you. But I want you to try to see past all the superficial details, see me for who I really am … for the man I've always been. Now, look at me, Ellie. Look at me really closely, and think."

Ellie was sure she didn't know the kind of sicko who'd abduct a woman from her own kitchen, surgery or not. The room was spinning so wildly she thought she was going to be sick. She closed her eyes and tried to calm down, tried to think of a plan to get free.

Her eyes snapped open as a sound caught her ear, the sound of a car passing outside. She could hear it slowing, then pulling into a driveway a little farther down the road. *Their driveway.*

"Hear that?" the man said. "That's the sound of our game beginning. Time to put that pretty little head to work. Just say my name, Ellie. Say it, or your husband loses a toe. See you soon."

The door clicked shut behind him.

CHAPTER 2

Two Days Earlier

Neil and Ellie were full of nervous energy as they cut across the northern landscape, temporarily untethered from their adult responsibilities. In the back of the car, their retriever mix, Hamish, panted happily. They'd just dropped their kids off at Camp Metawe, a self-described "Wilderness Adventure Retreat for Budding Explorers" located in the middle of nowhere.

Ellie had put on a brave face, smiling and waving as Beth, nine, had scampered off, hauling an oversized duffle bag and a bright-orange life vest. Michael, six, had needed some extra coaxing. He was more like her, timid — overwhelmed by the bedlam of the sprawling campgrounds, a field of chaos overseen by teenagers wielding clipboards and megaphones, shouting inaudible instructions that echoed through the trees, largely unheeded.

And then they were alone. Just the two of them. About to embark on their first extended holiday *sans children* in ten years.

"When we get there, I'll start prepping to build that outdoor shower," Neil said, scratching his neck. He was already chomping at the bit to delve into a new project. Ellie could see the familiar spark in his eye. Neil was always happiest in his own world, tinkering with a broken bike or repairing an old motor. While he focused on the plumbing project, she'd get some other chores done — like contending with the boxes of knick-knacks that had somehow trailed them from their primary home. Pretty, decorative objects that only added to her stress level.

Marvin Gaye's "Sexual Healing" came on the radio, interrupting Ellie's reverie. She wondered if it hinted at things to come — a reawakening of her languorous libido.

Then, two hours later, they arrived at their brand-new cottage on the outskirts of Maplewood, a two-storey structure with vaulted windows nestled on the shore of Euclid Lake. Pulling into the driveway was a cathartic moment, the two of them acting like giddy teenagers. For years, they had dreamt of owning a small cabin off the beaten path — simple, rustic, nothing fancy — but this place was beyond their wildest dreams. It would be a while before they could afford to furnish it completely, but that didn't matter. They'd make do with an expanse of bare walls and whatever bedraggled furniture the previous owners had left behind.

Turned out the previous owners had good taste.

//////////////////////

Shirtless, Neil rummaged through his toolbox on the back deck, where the outdoor shower was to be installed. His shoulders were smooth and muscular. Watching him from the kitchen, Ellie thought he looked much younger than his forty-four years. She felt a twinge of desire triggered by the sight of his flexed biceps, the way his skin glistened in the hot July sun.

"You want a beer?" she called through the open window.

"Thanks, babe," he said, wiping sweat from his forehead.

Ellie pulled a bottle of Stella Artois from the fridge, then tipped some Chardonnay into a glass for herself. She traced her fingers along the edge of the table, a rustic slab of rich, dark oak, and imagined it filled with platters of food. One day it was sure to become a cherished family heirloom, despite having been donated to them by complete strangers.

Holding both drinks, she pushed open the screen door with her toe and went outside to the picnic table. She could see the lake shimmering in the distance, hear the water lapping on the pebbly shore. She closed her eyes and tried to let the soothing sound unwind her; to centre her in the moment.

No squabbling, no whining. Just the gentle waves …

When she opened her eyes again, she spotted an enormous brown box propped against the side of the cottage.

"Surprise!" Neil said, beaming. "You're looking at our brand-new, state-of-the-art Napoleon Prestige Pro gas barbecue. Happy tenth, eleventh, and twelfth anniversaries, sweetheart."

"Babe, you shouldn't have."

Though she loved a good barbecue as much as the next person, Ellie had hoped their upcoming tenth anniversary would warrant something a little more sentimental than an oversized gas grill.

"I have another surprise for you." Neil approached her with a rascally grin and opened his hand, revealing a small ball of Kleenex.

"What's this?"

"You'll see."

She unravelled the wad of tissue. Inside were two semi-translucent capsules. "What on earth …"

"This is the modern version of weed. Cannabis in pill form, with just the right balance of THC and CBD. Eddie gave them to me. Said it might help us spice things up."

"Spice things up?"

Neil nodded. "No Netflix tonight, my dear. Tonight we are rediscovering our old adventuresome selves."

Ellie squinted up at him. Gnawed on her bottom lip. "I don't know. Pot makes me paranoid."

"Come on, Ellie. Don't you remember the good old days, back when we were young and madly in love? We've got two weeks to find that spark again. Think of it as therapy. The chance to shed some of that built-up mommy angst."

The twinkle in Neil's eyes reminded her of the moment they'd first met back at that smoky, seedy dance club. It was a moment that felt like a hundred years ago.

"So, what do you say … later tonight, we make ourselves a little nest over there by the fire, settle in, and see where the evening takes us?"

He kissed her on the mouth, and her stomach did an unexpected dance. It had been a while since a kiss from her husband elicited such a powerful reaction.

"Okay, maybe," she conceded, swatting away a mosquito.

Neil's eyes lit up, and Ellie took a sip of wine.

////////////////////

The night was warm, oozing humidity. Ellie lay stretched out on the grass. She couldn't remember the last time she'd looked at the stars and really taken them in, all their celestial glory against the infinite backdrop of the sky. Out here, they looked too brilliant to be real. The grass tickled her thighs and neck, but she didn't care — not about the ants crawling in the dirt around her, nor the twigs getting caught in her hair.

Neil was by the fire, poking at the glowing embers with a stick. Only the snap and sizzle of flames pierced the silence, until he said, "What did I tell you? Nothing but good, happy vibes."

Ellie sighed her agreement. She was still too captivated by the night sky to speak. The universe was pulsing and flaring, its vastness incomprehensible. Her skin felt clammy, her mouth and limbs full of cotton. If she'd had to sum up how she was feeling in one word, *gelatinous* seemed to describe it.

Neil dropped his stick and drifted toward her, then got down on the dewy grass by her feet. He grabbed her big toe, gave it a twist. "Hey, let's take off our shirts. Let our skin breathe."

"Hmm, not a bad idea."

She sat up and attempted to pull off her T-shirt, becoming entangled in the navy-blue fabric. Strands of hair came loose from her ponytail and fell in wisps over her eyes.

"You're beautiful," Neil said. He wriggled out of his own shirt. "Now, what about the bra?"

Ellie looked down at the tired garment she'd been wearing for the better part of a decade. She snapped the worn strap and said, "Nah, I don't think so. You never know who might be lurking in those woods besides the coyotes."

"Hey, if that old couple next door want to spy on us having a little fun in the privacy of our own lot, let them. It'll make one hell of a first impression."

"Maybe for an exhibitionist. You forgot you married an introvert." Ellie flopped back beside him like a rag doll, extending her bare limbs in all directions. She felt a pleasant pulsing behind her eyeballs and inhaled deeply, taking in the aroma of timber smoke. "I've never actually seen them," she went on. "It's been dead quiet over there every time I've walked by. No sign of life, like no one's ever at home."

"Thank God for that … and for the acre of forest between us. I like my privacy, too. Now take off that bra." He pawed at her bare arm like a dog clawing at an empty food dish.

Ellie could feel the heat from her husband's skin, his warm breath grazing her neck. An urge to shed layers, to free her inhibitions, was undeniably building inside her, yet she still couldn't shake the feeling that they weren't entirely alone.

"I'd like to, but can't we go inside?"

"Hell, no!" Neil countered. "I spent all day imagining you naked under that shower. I'm not stepping foot in the cottage until you strip down and enjoy my craftsmanship. Go on, try it out. It'll feel great, I promise."

He flashed a lascivious grin. He was clearly swept away in the same pleasurable tide that she was. *Cannabis-infused oil ... a conduit of good vibes, indeed.*

She glanced over at Neil's handiwork. At the moment it was nothing but raw plumbing and a chrome faucet secured to the trunk of a tree. No privacy walls or curtains of any kind. The night was dark, but the campfire cast warm light onto the marble step where she'd have to stand buck-naked under the shower head. Beyond that stood a tall bank of trees. No one could possibly see her unless they wandered up the driveway and came around the side of the house.

"All righty, then," she said, surprising herself as she sat up and brushed herself off. "A cold shower on a hot night? Bring that shit on!"

Neil's eyes shone in the darkness as Ellie peeled off her shorts and bra, pulled down her undies, and stepped into the fire's golden light, her body tingling and her mind unbound.

CHAPTER 3

The morning light sliced through the blinds, sending blistering pain right to the centre of Ellie's skull. Payback for the excesses of last night. "Rock 'n' roll, pay the toll," she muttered to herself, rubbing sleep and ash from her eyes.

Hamish was whining at the foot of the bed, wanting to get out for his morning pee. Neil was a lump under the sheets beside Ellie. She pushed him, evoking a muffled moan. "I'll take him, you sleep," she said, as if it would have gone any other way.

She stood up and yanked on the only articles of clothing she could find: Neil's boxer shorts and faded Supertramp T-shirt, circa 1980, featuring the *Breakfast in America* album cover. Neil loved his rock nostalgia.

Ellie felt woozy as she went downstairs. She was aching in unusual places from their long night of adventurous sex. There was no doubt she'd unleashed her sensuality and attained a blissful state of abandon that was rare these days.

When she slid open the back door, Hamish pushed past her, a blur of golden fuzz, and hoofed it toward his favourite new tree. She watched sleepily as he relieved himself without so much as a millisecond wasted.

After he was done, she slapped her knees and beckoned him back, but he ignored her, his attention caught by something in the trees. He tore off toward the neighbours' property, then vanished. Ellie felt a surge of disdain for her dog. *Neil's dog, the one he'd insisted on getting.* Then she slipped on her flip-flops and grudgingly started after him.

Separating the two lots was a thatch of scrubby forest that acted as a natural barrier, blocking both sight and sound. Until now, Ellie hadn't ventured into it. She zigzagged through the maze of branches until an enormous grey house came into view. It was set back from the road, the property line clearly marked by bright-red posts. The real estate agent had told them that the neighbours expected those posts to be respected. "The Palmers are not social people," she'd warned them.

The dog was nowhere in sight.

"Hamish!" Ellie called in a loud, scolding whisper.

She fought her way through the foliage and eventually emerged at the edge of a flawless lawn trimmed with ornate planters and cast-iron lampposts. At last she glimpsed Hamish standing over what looked like a small animal carcass in front of a double-door garage. Just the thought of it repulsed her, but clearly Hamish wasn't so squeamish. He was nose deep into investigating the furry mound, seconds from initiating the dreaded drop and roll.

"Hi there!" a man's voice called out.

Ellie shrieked and spun around. At first, she couldn't see anyone in the harsh contrast of the trees and the sun. Then she was able to make out the broad shoulders of a man standing about ten feet away, his face hidden in the shadow of his hat brim.

"Oh, hi there. I'm really sorry for coming onto your property. My dog, he must have caught a scent. Let me just grab him and I'll be off in a jiffy."

She hurried over to retrieve Hamish, dragging him away by the collar despite his stubborn resistance. He was growling, too, which was unusual for the sweet-natured mutt. Ellie suspected that the dead thing, whatever it was, had tapped into some wild instinct.

The man sauntered toward her with a laid-back swagger. He looked about fifty, with rugged, attractive features. His eyes, dark and brooding, were set in a distinguished-looking face with characterful wrinkles that reminded her of George Clooney.

"Jake Palmer," he said, offering his hand.

Ellie became uncomfortably aware that she wasn't wearing a bra under the threadbare Supertramp T-shirt. *Tramp is right*, she thought, as she awkwardly accepted his handshake. "I'm Eloise Patterson, your new neighbour. We just bought the place next door. Sorry for trespassing. Hamish here is overwhelmed by all the marvels of nature, particularly the decaying ones." She indicated the carcass.

"Ah, I see," Jake said, eyeing the grey-brown lump. "A dead raccoon. Distemper's likely what got it. It's spreading around here like wildfire. I'll call animal control. But in the meantime, you should really keep Hamish there on a leash. The coyotes are fierce around here, too. Something to keep in mind, especially at night."

"Thanks, I'll remember that," Ellie said, grabbing Hamish and holding him tight. "Well, it was nice to meet you. I've been meaning to come over and introduce myself to you and your wife."

"My wife … I'm afraid she's not with us anymore. She died a few weeks back. It was a long time coming, though. I'm glad she's in a better place now, but I miss her to death."

"Oh, I'm sorry to hear that. My condolences," Ellie said. Hamish squirmed in his collar.

Jake lowered his gaze, kicked at the rocks with his heavy beige boots. "It's all part of life, I guess."

"Hey, would you like to join us for dinner sometime?" Ellie asked, spurred by empathy but immediately regretting the invitation. "My husband, Neil, and I, we …"

"I'd love to. I'm free tonight, as a matter a fact."

"Tonight? Um, okay, I think that would be fine. Say around seven?"

Jake nodded. He nudged his broad-brimmed hat and said, "You know, you can leave by the driveway over there. No need to get all scratched up in that inhospitable bush."

"Right ... thanks." Ellie smiled. She felt her cheeks burn as Hamish leapt from her hold, forcing her to strike out from the shadows into the direct sunlight — boxer shorts, free-hanging boobs, and all. "See you tonight," she said.

"Indeed, you will," Jake said, watching her go.

CHAPTER 4

Nancy Booker, their real estate agent, had made out the neighbours to be a pair of cranky old geezers, reclusive types who despised kids, dogs, laughter, music — any audible expression of merriment. So, when Ellie had returned from her walk that morning to inform him that George Clooney's doppelganger would be coming over for dinner, Neil was intrigued.

Sure enough, the guy now standing in the doorway did resemble the A-list actor. Oddly, though, he was squeezed into a butter-yellow T-shirt that was clearly too small for him; the thin fabric was pulled so tight around his thick neck and torso that Neil wondered if the seams might split.

"You must be Jake. I'm Neil. Come on in."

"Hiya, Neil. It's a real pleasure to meet you."

"Likewise," Neil said, shaking Jake's hand. He led the way into the kitchen, where Ellie was busy arranging a cheese platter. She was dressed in jeans and a red plaid shirt, her hair pulled back in a loose ponytail. She looked pretty but casual, and Neil took silent comfort in the fact that she hadn't worn something alluring for this buff Clooney look-alike.

"Hi, Jake. Thanks for coming," she said.

"Real nice spot you've got here," Jake replied, ignoring the lack of furniture and the barren white walls. "I really appreciate the invite. It's been a quiet few weeks since ... well, you know."

"Yes, Ellie told me about your wife," Neil said. "I can't imagine what you're going through."

Jake shrugged, offered a wan smile. "Life and death are inseparable. For some of us, the death part happens a little too soon, though."

"That's the sad truth," Neil said.

An awkward silence followed, broken when Ellie asked Jake if he'd care for a beer.

"Oh, yes please," he said eagerly.

While Ellie fetched a round of drinks and tended to the food, Neil led Jake over to the screen door and ushered him out onto the back deck. The sun was setting on Euclid Lake, and Neil didn't want to miss it.

Left alone in the kitchen, Ellie pulled a plate of raw steaks and two craft lagers from the fridge, then retrieved a stemless wineglass and a bottle of Merlot from the hutch. She figured they'd need to let the meat stand for a good half hour before sparking the grill, which meant a considerable amount of small talk. She sighed, mentally kicking herself for not trying harder to delay this social engagement. *The sooner this is over, the better.*

"So, Jake," she heard Neil say through the window, "how long have you been living up here? Ellie and I have been admiring your house."

"It's a real beauty, isn't it?" Jake's voice drifted into the kitchen. "We've had it for quite a few years now. Can't remember exactly how long."

"Any kids or grandkids?"

"Nope, never had any kids. Never felt the need to complicate life with noisy little rug rats. I gather you and Eloise don't have any, either?"

"Actually, we do. We have two noisy little rug rats," Neil said. "A girl and a boy. I'm surprised you haven't heard them before. They can be … *exuberant*, let's say. They're off at camp right now, so we've got two weeks of peace and quiet."

"Sounds like it'll be a nice break for you two."

"Sure will, and a long time coming."

Ellie slid open the door and stepped outside, carrying a tray full of refreshments.

"Let me help you with that," Jake said, jumping to his feet.

His assistance proved less than helpful, with a nearly toppled wine bottle and a dropped cheese knife to recover. Still, Ellie appreciated the effort as Neil looked on.

She sat down opposite Jake at the picnic table and poured herself some wine. The first sip tasted good. A little too good, considering the previous night's excesses. But it was a Saturday night in the middle of

July, after all — *why not numb the hangover with a little hair of the dog?*

"So, Eloise," Jake said, "Neil tells me you have two kids. I never would have guessed it."

"Oh, why is that?"

"Well, just the way you cut through that obstacle course of a forest this morning like an Olympic athlete."

Ellie released a shrill laugh and nervously gulped her wine. In her bleary state, she'd half expected him to say that he'd caught sight of her dancing for Neil under the outdoor shower.

"Yup, Ellie's very athletic," Neil said, folding his arms and beaming proudly at her. "She's very hands-on with the kids. Takes them to all their practices and helps with their training, whether it's soccer, basketball, or gymnastics."

"Gymnastics, eh?" Jake interjected. "Well, that explains everything."

"Ha! No," she replied, blushing at the fleeting image of herself in a leotard. "Our daughter is the gymnast, not me."

"*Was* the gymnast, you mean," Neil said forlornly. "She's lost interest now. At nine going on nineteen, she's not our little acrobat anymore."

Jake smiled. "As a parent, I imagine sometimes you'd like to put them in a bottle and preserve them. Protect them from all the unforeseen hazards of life."

"Absolutely," Neil said. "Especially the girls. They mature way too fast. These days they're caught up in Snapchat and makeup when they oughtta be playing with dolls. Freaks me out. But what are you going to do?"

"Embrace the changes, I guess," Jake said. He turned to Ellie. "We all change, don't we?"

She nodded. "Hopefully for the better."

By the time they went inside and sat down for dinner, Ellie was feeling a tad more relaxed. The men had locked on to a shared passion for sports cars, allowing her to take a back seat to the conversation about V12 engines and turbochargers. After dessert, Ellie got up to clear the dishes and shot Neil a look to signal that it was time to wrap up their little fiesta. She had a warm glow on from the wine, and the only person she wanted to share it with was him.

Neil caught the sign and let out a perfunctory yawn. "Maybe it's the alcohol, but I seem to get tired a whole lot earlier these days. Hardly ever make it past ten anymore."

"Now, now, let's be honest here," Jake said. From her position at the sink, Ellie could see the man leaning in toward Neil, his eyes compressing into two dark slits. "Why the hell would you want to sit here talking with me when you could be all alone with your beautiful wife?"

There was an uncomfortable pause, then Jake chuckled in a way that diffused some of the tension. He rose to his feet and wiped his mouth. "I'll leave you to it, then. Thank you for a delicious meal."

Neil and Ellie saw him to the door. Jake hesitated before turning and smiling at Ellie.

"A wonderful evening," he said, bowing his head. "Until we meet again."

"Until then," was all she could think of to say.

CHAPTER 5

Hamish was whining at the door, scratching at the glass with his claws. Ellie rubbed her eyes. She must have fallen asleep on the couch. She looked at the clock. It was closing in on 5:00 p.m.

Neil had gone into town about twenty minutes ago to fetch some dinner supplies. She'd heard him rummaging for his wallet, his phone, the reusable grocery bags, once the inactivity of the rainy afternoon had finally gotten to him. Unlike Ellie, Neil did not take to sedentary Sundays.

As she traipsed over to let the dog out, Ellie noticed Neil's iPhone half-buried under a newspaper. She rolled her eyes and tugged it into view. Clearly Neil was not on top of his game after two days of copious alcohol and late-night bedroom activities. *Sexual healing also has its cons*, she thought.

She was about to put the phone down when it buzzed in her hand, its screen lighting up with an incoming text.

> Hey, you never got back to me. You know I
> hate to be kept waiting.

The name above the message was MJ. Ellie wracked her brain, but couldn't recall any MJs. *A colleague?*

Then came another text.

> :'(Miss you

A cold feeling crept through her, and she felt woozy.

She stared down at the two words, trying to convince herself that they meant nothing. But they *did* mean something. They were personal, intimate words. MJ, whoever she was, missed Neil — missed Ellie's husband. There was no way a work associate had sent it.

Ellie took a breath, tried to think rationally. Was she jumping to the worst conclusion? Neil didn't have any sisters, and his mother had passed away from cancer nearly three years ago. As far as she knew, he didn't have any female friends who weren't couples friends — and even supposing he did, who would send a message like *miss you* in a platonic sense to a married man with two kids? The more she grappled with the obvious, the angrier she became.

She typed in Neil's password, *HAMISH*, but the phone refused to unlock. When had he changed his password?

Behind her, the dog's whining had escalated to desperate yelps; if she didn't let him out soon he'd have an accident all over the floor. She unlocked the door and nudged open the screen. Hamish wiggled past her and shot off across the lawn and into the trees.

"Damn it!" she shouted, tears filling her eyes. "Not again!"

She slipped on her flip-flops, hiked up her pajama bottoms, and darted out into the uninviting elements.

"Hamish!" she called, approaching the same prickly treeline he'd vanished into just yesterday. "Hamish, come back here right now!"

But there was no sign of him. To avoid looking like a trespasser again, Ellie opted to take the road. She didn't get very far, though — just as she was leaving the flag-stone path, she ran into Jake. He was bent over Hamish, who aggressively snarled and bucked like he was feral.

"Looking for this guy?" Jake called through the pelting rain. Water trickled down his forehead, his nostrils, and the square line of his jaw. "Didn't I tell you to put him on a leash?"

"Sorry, he just escaped on me," Ellie said, grabbing hold of Hamish's collar. She knelt down and rubbed his ears, held him close in an effort to subdue him. "Honestly, these raccoons are really stirring him up."

"Good thing I happened to be coming this way," Jake said. "Wondered if you'd mind sparing some of those delicious spices you used to dress up our steaks last night. My wife always used to handle that stuff, you see."

The last thing Ellie wanted to talk about was steak seasoning. But rather than let on to a complete stranger how upset she was, that she might be on the edge of a marital crisis, she swallowed her despair and said, "Of course. Come on back to the kitchen and I'll grab you some."

She kept a firm grip on Hamish's collar as she tugged him along the slippery flagstones to the back deck.

"Thanks again for inviting me over. Neil seems like a great guy," Jake bellowed after her.

Yeah, real great, Ellie thought, yanking open the screen door and ordering Hamish to stay put. Then she turned to Jake. "Why don't you wait here while I grab you that steak mix? That way you won't have to take off your shoes."

As she entered the bright light of the kitchen, she noticed that her pajamas were soaked clear through and her hair was a wet tangle of knots. She wondered what sort of impression she was giving Jake — likely that she was a lazy slob who couldn't be bothered to get dressed. *First boxer shorts, and now pajamas.* He'd probably think it perfectly reasonable that Neil was having an affair.

Miss you … The words swirled in her mind as she walked over to the cabinet, dazed and fighting back tears. She looked inside the top cupboard, but the seasoning wasn't there. Where might Neil have put it? Likely on the Lazy Susan in the corner cabinet, even though she hated that thing and had asked him to remove it. In her mind it was a finger-breaker waiting to happen.

With the feeling of betrayal heavy on her chest, she bent down and spun the round shelf like a roulette wheel, eventually arriving at the coveted item.

"I love your ass."

Ellie stopped cold. The jar slipped from her fingers as she turned. Jake was standing right behind her, his eyes flashing wildly.

"What did you say?"

"You heard me. Now come to Papa."

His hand shot up, covering Ellie's mouth with a damp cloth. It was emitting an acrid smell, and she knew right away it was soaked with some kind of chemical, something that would knock her out. With every ounce of strength she had, she struggled and flailed, fighting desperately to get away from the intoxicant.

But when drowsiness finally took hold, she fell into what felt like a bottomless hole, and there was nothing she could do to prevent it.

///////////////////

Neil pulled into the driveway and switched off the engine, the view before him spellbinding. Their cottage was picture-perfect. A level or two above their means, but seeing as it would someday be their retirement home, and lakefront properties were growing scarcer by the second, Neil rationalized their current financial strain as the price of long-term happiness.

He felt a surge of warmth thinking of his future, his family. He hadn't always been so lucky, so charmed in life and love. The only child of overachieving, under-nurturing parents, he'd spent his younger years lonely and yearning for approval, in constant fear of disap-pointing his cold, surly dad, who threatened Neil with military school whenever he fell out of line — which wasn't often, apart from that one year of his life when rebellion had taken hold and made him do a few stupid things, like stealing beer and sneaking the car out for the occasional joyride. Some of those stupid things still haunted him late at night, or in his dreams, but for the most part, he didn't think about that wayward period of his life, choosing instead to live in the present.

Neil smiled, recalling how he'd first laid eyes on Ellie twelve years ago, a moment that had been etched in his brain ever since. He often reflected on the sequence of events leading up to that fabled moment — how someone had anonymously sent him a pair of VIP dance club passes. Suspecting they'd been a gift from his co-workers to help him get over his recent split from his girlfriend Vanessa, he'd come close to tossing them aside. But eventually he decided to use them, accompanied by his good friend Eddie. At the club, Eddie had cajoled him into chatting up some yappy redhead, which Neil had quickly regretted. As he was mentally forming an exit strategy, the bartender had poked him in the back, handed him a Heineken. And when Neil turned and saw the bright-eyed angel who'd sent it, both the redhead and Vanessa instantly became figments of the past.

That legendary beer had sparked everything that followed — moving in, marriage, kids — and they'd been happy. But things had been rough in the relationship over the last few years. That was undeniable. They'd grown distant. Cold. After the small press Ellie had launched went belly-up, she seemed to lose her sparkle, her chutzpah. In her mind, it was an epic failure, and it ate away at her soul. Neil knew she blamed him for a lot of it, too: For not being supportive enough. For not being more involved with the kids. For being so occupied with his own demanding career. The list went on.

Fortunately, they'd turned a corner during these past three months. Neil attributed the improvement to the cottage. It gave them focus, a shared goal. A fresh setting, detached from the past, where they could start over. Fall back in love.

He got out of the car, gathered up the groceries, and trudged up the steps to the front door. The rain had calmed to a mild drizzle, and he was glad that their newly planted geraniums had gotten the soaking they'd needed.

He proceeded inside, kicked off his shoes, and went into the kitchen. Hamish was whining and pacing with agitation alongside the sliding door. He wanted out.

"Ellie?" Neil called, glancing at the empty couch. He noticed the door to the Lazy Susan cabinet was open, and a spice jar had fallen open on the floor. He plodded over and picked it up, then fetched a rag to wipe up the mess.

"Just a sec, boy," he told Hamish.

As he rinsed out the cloth, he spotted his cellphone on the kitchen counter. Wiping his hands, he grabbed it and unlocked the screen. What he saw made his heart seize. Mia had texted.

Hey, you never got back to me. You know I
hate to be kept waiting.

:'(Miss you

"Ellie?" he called again, his palms already sweating. Had she seen those telling words pop up on the screen?

He closed his eyes, swallowed hard. Felt his bowels clench in anxiety. Was this the beginning of the end? Was his marriage, his life, all about to be ruined over a drunken mistake at that tech convention in San Francisco three months ago?

It had been nothing more than a fling, a worthless roll in the hay with an American colleague he barely knew. He'd intended to confess to Ellie right away, accept the bitter consequences. But when he got back, she'd greeted him with such warmth, such unbridled old-school-Ellie elation, because she'd found an online listing for a cottage. "The cottage of our dreams," she'd said.

He hadn't seen his wife so happy in ages. Couldn't stand the thought of ending her joy, of shattering the world they'd created. But he should have been truthful and bared his soul in the first place. With urgency, he headed for the stairs. He needed Ellie to understand that it had meant nothing, that he'd suffered a momentary lapse of judgment caused by too much alcohol and raging hormones, having not had sex in the five months prior. He needed to tell her that he would do anything to make things right and that he deeply regretted not having told her sooner. He regretted giving Mia his damn phone number, too.

Neil was halfway to the landing when he heard a knock at the door. Annoyed, he turned and stormed back down to the entranceway. Hamish darted over to his side, a guttural snarl escaping his clenched teeth.

"Hey, buddy, relax," he said, patting him on the head. "It's nothing to worry about, I promise."

He opened the door to their new neighbour, Jake, and forced a smile. Jake returned a friendly grin ... and then the grin turned into something sinister. Neil recognized the Louisville Slugger he'd purchased last month for his son's birthday in the brief second before the wood made contact with his skull.

CHAPTER 6

Ellie struggled to wrap her mind around what was happening. Tried to think rationally through the sequence of events that had led her to this unfamiliar place. She'd been kidnapped by the man who'd presented himself as Jake Palmer, a man now claiming to be someone from her past. Someone who had changed his face. He'd captured her in her kitchen, and now appeared to be holding her hostage at the Palmers' house next door. *Where are the Palmers?*

Ellie grew frantic. She screamed and flailed, her mind inundated with gruesome images of her dead neighbours and of Neil's toes being chopped off.

After a moment, she stilled. She knew her only hope was to figure out his real identity. In retrospect she should have caught on to the deceit sooner. He'd hardly been the cranky, antisocial old geezer described by the realtor. In fact, he'd been the opposite of aloof, practically inviting himself over for dinner, for God's sake. And now she was a prisoner on his bed, challenged to a game with unthinkably grisly consequences.

She had to figure out who he really was. She had to remember. She didn't believe this man was someone she'd known very well, much less slept with. Before Neil, she'd only had one serious boyfriend: her college sweetheart, Mitchell Lowry. Even then, Mitch had been dull beyond his years, a real pushover without a single ounce of aggression in him. It had to be someone else, someone obscure. But dredging through the past to identify some murky figure in her forty-year lifespan wasn't going to be easy. Unless he'd made one hell of a bad impression.

Ellie's earliest childhood memories were of people who smiled and waved hello. Of decent, caring folks who'd shovelled each other's walks, pruned each other's hedges. That was life in the suburbs.

The third eldest of four girls, Ellie always knew she was loved, even though sometimes she felt that she lived in the shadow of her sisters — the older ones, Laura and Bethany, in particular. While Laura was the family jewel, an extraordinary beauty with the flawless features of a model, Bethany was the athlete, a promising competitor in every sport she tried.

The Blakely house was a red-brick postwar bungalow amid a maze of homes that looked just like it. It backed onto a glorious ravine, but the girls were never allowed to venture down there after dark. Ellie's father was a caretaker at the local high school, and he knew from snippets of gossip he heard that bad things often happened in that ravine. Boys would lure their innocent girlfriends into the cover of the trees and feel them up. Some of them bragged about popping a girl's cherry.

Besides wanting to be pretty or athletic, Ellie's childhood worries had been few. But all that changed in the spring of 1986, when disaster struck the household.

One rainy afternoon, Bethany and her best friend, Tamara Kendall, were heading to an out-of-district skating tournament, driven by Tamara's mom, Enid. Tragically, another vehicle collided with their minivan, and the culprit fled the scene. Both Tamara and Enid were killed instantly. People said it was a miracle that Bethany had survived, that God had spared her. But Ellie wasn't convinced. A severed spine, permanent brain damage, and a life confined to a long-term care facility didn't seem like God's grace, and she secretly wondered if death would have been a blessing for Bethany.

Ellie still remembered her parents' agonized cries that terrible night, as well as their grief in the months that followed. It had been a summer of endless heat waves. A real scorcher, as she recalled it. Somehow she'd ended up in charge of her little sister, Evelyn, while her parents were tied to the hospital. Evelyn was three years younger and a royal pain in Ellie's ass. To avoid the heat, they'd spent most of their time hunkered in the basement, building forts out of sofa cushions and watching back-to-back soap operas on TV. Sometimes they'd get creative and re-enact the juiciest scenes from *The Young and the Restless*, using pillows if a scene required kissing.

Of course, Laura, the eldest at fifteen, should have been the one in charge, but as their parents put it, Laura just wasn't the helping type — and that trait only intensified after Bethany's accident. Laura rarely came out of her bedroom except to sneak off with her friends at night. Ellie did hear Laura crying at times, but only when she thought no one was at home.

Ellie also remembered that summer as being the first time a male acquaintance had made her feel uneasy. That boy was Morris Denkworth, their geeky next-door neighbour. Morris was sixteen and didn't have any friends — or so it appeared to ten-year-old Ellie. Any time she and Evelyn ventured outside to play, Morris would be creeping around in the adjacent backyard or leering from an upper window of his house. Her parents had told her to be kind to Morris, that he was just different, like his folks. Ellie's dad knew Morris from the high school and felt sorry for him. Said the other kids were cruel, including Laura, who called him "Egghead" and made fun of his unfortunate looks. Morris had big front teeth and a long, narrow face. The worst part, though, was the inflamed acne that covered every inch of his skin, like a topographical map of red, oozing pimples.

One day near the end of the summer, Laura had invited some of her friends over to sunbathe in the backyard. She'd banished Ellie and Evelyn to the house until after all her friends went home.

Ellie thought this was unfair. With the first day of school nearly upon them, she wanted to soak up the last of the sun, too. She also wanted to eavesdrop on the older girls, listen to their teenage blather and find out who was kissing whom.

"Let's sneak out the front, climb the Denkworths' fence, and hide in their garden so we can hear what the girls are saying," Ellie had proposed. Evelyn was hesitant, so Ellie added, "If you do it — and keep totally quiet — I'll give you one of my favourite dolls."

"What about Jessica?" Evelyn pressed.

The prospect of giving up Jessica, her well-loved Cabbage Patch Kid, stung Ellie more than she thought it should at her age — which meant, maybe, it was the right time to pass the relic on. "Fine … Jessica," she said.

The two sisters shook hands in an official pact, then crept out the front door, as quiet as kittens.

The fence between their lot and the Denkworths' was about five feet tall, made of solid wooden slabs. Ellie would have no problem getting over it, but featherweight Evelyn didn't have the strength or ability to scale it on her own.

"Stand on my knee and I'll help you get over. Remember to keep quiet."

Evelyn obeyed, allowing her sister to launch her over the fence like a beanbag. But Ellie applied too much force, and Evelyn thudded to the ground with a wince. Ellie scrambled over the fence to find Evelyn with two scuffed knees, on the cusp of unleashing one of her notorious ear-splitting wails. She quickly reminded Evelyn about their deal. Miraculously, the prompt worked, and the two of them carried on toward the cover of the neighbours' unkempt garden.

"Hello." A croaky voice startled them.

Morris Denkworth was standing there, his two buckteeth looking outlandishly yellow in the sun.

"We, uh, we were just going to spy on our sister," Ellie tried to explain. "She's in the back with her friends, sunbathing."

"Yeah? Which friends?"

"Anne, Nikki, Amy, Lisa. You know them?"

"Of course I know them!" Morris barked, rolling his eyes at the insinuation that he didn't know the high school's upper ranks.

"You … wanna spy with us?"

Ellie hoped that if she included Morris in their secret mission, he would be less inclined to rat them out. To her immense relief, he finally nodded. Ellie felt a rush of nervous excitement as she navigated the way trough the overgrowth and found them the perfect shady place for eavesdropping. They could hear the girls babbling on about some cute boy named Jason, could see Laura fanning her face with a *Seventeen* magazine, her long hair billowing behind her svelte shoulders. She was wearing a hot-pink bikini, and her legs looked impossibly long and tanned. But Ellie soon became uncomfortably aware that Morris wasn't gazing at her gorgeous older sister. He was looking at her, ogling her flat chest in a way that made her flesh crawl.

///////////////////////

"Hello, darling, I'm back … and I brought you a visitor," Jake said, barging into the dark room. He was dragging something behind him. Ellie strained to see what it was, and a surge of sickness nearly overcame her at the realization that it was Neil.

"Please, Jake, don't do this!" she cried out.

But Jake ignored her and continued to pull her unconscious husband along, heaving him roughly onto the chair and binding his wrists together and his ankles to the posts. Neil's head slumped forward, and he was gagged, but Ellie could tell from the way his eyes fluttered and rolled that he was beginning to come to.

"Stop calling me Jake. He's gone, and so is that haggard old wife of his. Now, have you been thinking, Ellie? Have you been putting that pretty head of yours to work, like I told you to?"

He let go of Neil and came toward her with a deranged look in his eyes. Ellie could see that whether she named him or not, he would likely hurt them anyway. At least by playing his game, she could buy them some time. A chance …

"Yes, I've been thinking," she said, suppressing her panic. "I've been trying to remember you, but you said that you've changed. How am I supposed to know who you are if you look different now?"

"Oh, Ellie, I'd remember you, no matter how much you changed. In fact, I've spent many years imagining how time might have altered you — a few extra pounds on that ass, a few grey hairs on that head. Yet here you are, hardly any different."

"Any different from what? When? Please," she pleaded. "Just give me a time period. Some sort of reference point …"

"Nope, no hints. I believe in you, Ellie. I know you can do this. Now think."

Neil let out a moan, his head bobbing as he struggled to regain consciousness. When his eyes finally opened and he focused on Ellie, on her form splayed across the mattress, he began wailing and thrashing so hard that he and the chair fell over sideways.

"Neil, stay calm! You have to stay calm!" Ellie cried out, unable to see him now that he'd fallen on the floor.

"Listen to your wife. You're not going to help matters by losing your shit, got it? Just accept that this is your fate, your punishment. Truth is, Neil, I don't really know you from Adam. But I've never liked you. In fact, I despised you from the moment I saw you. I know for a fact that you don't deserve to have Ellie as your wife." He paused and leered at her on the bed, his thirsty gaze sweeping over the length of her. "She's such a little peach, isn't she? We go way back, me and Ellie, except … well, she doesn't seem to remember me, and that just hurts. So, we're going to play a little game. Ellie gets three chances to say my name. If she gets it wrong, you lose a toe. The second incorrect guess costs you a finger."

He addressed Ellie. "And don't even think about dragging it out all night. If you take any longer than half an hour to make a guess, I count that as wrong."

Then he turned back to Neil. "And if she guesses wrong the third time, I'll have to kill you. Sorry for your luck."

Ellie could hear Neil writhing madly, trying to shout past his gag, but she knew his efforts were futile. They were completely at the whim of a madman. For now, all she could do was play along, follow his rules, and think.

Keep calm, and try to remember …

CHAPTER 7

Jake, for lack of a better name, got down on his knees and peeled off Neil's shoes and socks. There was something in his right hand: a gleaming chef's knife. Neil started to sob, but Ellie fought to remain calm. Her mind raced to come up with something, anything she could say to make this psychotic man stop.

"I think … I think I remember you," she said in a quiet, shaky voice.

Jake went still for a moment, then he stood up and approached the bed. He took her tear-streaked face in his hands and stared at her longingly, his gaze lingering on her mouth as though he wanted to kiss her. "Are you sure about that? You remember what happens if you say the wrong name."

Just the thought of this motherfucker using that knife on Neil tore her apart. It didn't matter whether Neil had cheated on her or fallen in love with some other woman — she wouldn't just sit by and watch him be tortured and mutilated.

Was it possible that this man was her old neighbour, Morris Denkworth, otherwise known as Egghead? Could he have changed that much since adolescence? Morris had been a beanpole, whereas the man before her now was a serious specimen, perfectly fit and handsome. It would have taken a huge amount of surgery — a complete face transplant — not to mention one hell of a workout regime to achieve such a radical improvement.

Morris had come off as a pervert, but he'd been a harmless one all the same. He'd gawked at her and made her uncomfortable, but that was the extent of it. Unless he'd become considerably warped after high school. Unless he'd allowed those sexual urges to fester into something darker, meaner …

"What's my name?" Jake breathed in her ear. "Tell me my name, Ellie. I've been waiting all these years to hear you say it."

Ellie said a silent prayer. Then she turned to her captor and regarded him fiercely. "Your name," she whispered, "is Morris. Morris Denkworth. You're my old neighbour. Our backyards used to share a fence. We spied on Laura once — you, me, and my little sister, Evelyn."

Jake's face dropped, his eyes flooding with disappointment … then rage. "Wrong, Ellie," he said, running his fingers through his hair. He balled his fist and planted it in the mattress next to her face. "You are so fucking wrong. I'm disappointed in you, you know that? I really thought you'd remember me, after all I've done for you, all the sacrifices I've made and my efforts to set things right."

He had tears in his eyes. Ellie felt tears pooling in her own eyes, too.

"Please give me another chance," she pleaded.

"Oh, you'll get another chance. Two more, to be exact. But in the meantime, Neil here has to pay for your mistake. We'll just go ahead and lop off that little pinky toe. As far as I can tell, it doesn't have much use, anyway."

He got up and went over to the fallen chair. Pale with fear, Neil was completely quiet, but Ellie shrieked hysterically.

"I said, no screaming!" Jake roared, coming back and cuffing her hard on the cheek.

After that, Ellie closed her eyes as tightly as she could. She wanted to cover her ears, too, but she couldn't do that with her hands tied. Couldn't block out the sound of the knife slashing down on her husband's bare foot, or his gasping and wailing. And in the deadly silence that followed, Ellie began to pass out.

/////////////////////

In college, Ellie had been the serious type — shy and bookish, keeping to herself. She favoured loose-fitting sweaters and baggy jeans, garments that downplayed her attractiveness and allowed her to drift about mostly unnoticed. Never attended any keg parties. Never smoked a cigarette or missed a morning lecture. All she ever dreamed about was a career in publishing. To make a living working with words. To support herself and make her eternally wounded parents proud.

During her freshman year, Ellie had lived in an all-female dorm. Stacy West, her roommate, was a self-professed "wild thing" with bright-pink hair and ADHD. Half-Korean, all-Calgarian, Stacy was small as a mite but had as much lusty energy as a frat house. She was also quick with comebacks, hence her nickname, "Zesty Westy." Though the two roomies got along just fine, Ellie was far too reticent to keep up with Stacy's social agenda. When Ellie met Mitchell on trivia night at the local pub, the rest of her university experience was framed by the safety of having a boyfriend.

In retrospect, those days had been tame to the point of dreary. While Stacy hit up every party she could and slept her way around the small university town, Ellie opted for trivia nights at the Pig's Ear, tucked in a booth with Mitch and their fellow nerds, trying to come up with the right sports legends and pop culture icons. Eight years had passed since Bethany's accident, but Ellie still suffered from a fear of the unknown, meticulously structuring what should have been carefree college days around a predictable, safe routine.

However, after graduation, something in Ellie started to burn: a desire to break free. To shake off the doldrums of her own making and apply a little zest to her humdrum life. And so, in one whirlwind week, she broke up with Mitchell Lowry and quit her job at Williams-Sonoma. She spent what remained of her dwindling savings on some trendy new outfits and hit the town with Stacy, then experienced her first three-day hangover.

But when Stacy left the country that fall to go back-packing through Europe, Ellie found herself floundering alone in her parents' partially finished basement suite with no money, no direction. That's when her restless-ness shifted into something different: a pining for pro-ductivity. And so began her quest to land herself a "real" job. But after weeks of hopeful searching, Ellie grew dis-couraged. Outside of retail, she had no work experience so she was consistently turned away by employers who were looking for just that.

On the heels of each doomed interview, she'd head home and mope in the basement, only sur-facing occasionally for food and a shoulder to cry on. Throughout this draining process, her parents remained supportive. They housed her, fed her, and reminded her daily that the Lord had a special plan for her — one that only He could guide her through — and, lo and behold, eventually they were right. Ellie, however, suspected it had something to do with her rapidly declining standards.

In late autumn of that year, she accepted an unpaid internship at a downtown marketing firm called Buzz, a "beehive for creative thinkers and branding strategists with a gift for cultivating meaningful messaging." Ellie saw it as a stepping stone to her future, a doorway to her publishing dreams. But getting there wasn't easy. The commute from the boonies was tedious at the best of times, let alone during rush hour. So three weeks in, Ellie decided that it was time for another milestone: flying the coop. Leaving the comfort of her suburban home and settling in the city. Luckily, her older sister, Laura, was well-equipped to put her up until she could squirrel away enough money to rent a place of her own.

Laura was a high-fashion model, earning big bucks walking the runways of distant meccas, like London, Tokyo, and Madrid. She was gone a lot for work, and Ellie loved having her big sister's lavish King Street condo all to herself. She hated the pretentious decor that filled it, but knew better than to comment, for fear of jeopardizing her tenuous living arrangement.

The first friend Ellie made at Buzz was a young project coordinator named Paige Zimly. Tall, black, and fiercely pretty, with close-cropped hair and ever-present earphones, Paige seemed calm and centred in that claustrophobic setting, where staffers were constantly gossiping and backstabbing, throwing hissy fits and accusing each other of laziness or incompetence. Turned out Buzz was dog-eat-dog, and Ellie knew that sticking with cool, unflappable Paige was her best chance at survival.

Overseeing the mayhem was the boss, Harold. Handsome Harold, the women called him — or just HH, when discretion was called for. He was tall and tanned, with piercing blue eyes and lustrous brown hair that smelled like Aveda's cherry almond shampoo. He was ten years married, or so they'd heard, but that didn't stop anyone from crushing on him.

The first H also doubled for Handsy, which Ellie had discovered one day when he appeared behind her and began nonchalantly kneading her neck. "What are you working on?" he asked, leaning in so close his minty-fresh breath glanced off her cheek.

"Uh, just that copy for Marshall's website," she said, trying to hide her tension and show that she was cool with whatever was happening, even though she wasn't sure physical contact in the workplace was permitted, particularly from the boss.

"Good stuff." With that, Harold straightened up and flounced away as though back rubs were just part of the daily grind.

"You shouldn't let him do that," a voice remarked.

"Sorry?" Ellie rolled her chair back and peered around the fabric partition. A young man with a mess of frizzy hair was slumped in front of a computer, ardently working the keyboard as though he hadn't uttered a peep.

"Excuse me, did you say something?" she asked again. This time the young man paused in his work.

"He shouldn't be touching you like that."

It felt rude, the way he didn't even look at her when he spoke, particularly given the loaded subject matter. But she ignored the comment and rolled back to the privacy of her own cubicle.

"I'm Austin … Austin Pert," he carried on through the partition. "If you ever need any updates made to that shitty desktop computer, I'm your guy."

The next day, at Paige's insistence, Ellie invited the IT specialist to join them for lunch. Male staffers were rare at Buzz, and they were both curious to know if this one had anything interesting going on under that mop of unruly hair.

But even in the dimly lit sushi restaurant, he avoided eye contact, preferring to stare at dead space as he spoke sparingly about his past. The atmosphere was a little tense and awkward as Paige and Ellie tried their best to keep the stagnant dialogue going.

"So, where are you from?" Ellie asked, as their server arrived with a platter of assorted rolls.

Austin tossed his hair, unwrapped his chopsticks, and mumbled, "Austin."

The two women glanced at each other.

"Wait," Paige said, leaning in, "are you saying your name is Austin and you're actually *from* Austin … as in, Austin, Texas?"

"Yup."

Paige giggled. "Well, that's practical. Handy when you're renewing your passport."

"Go ahead, mock me. But it could have been a lot worse. My mom's maiden name is Powers," he said, with deadpan delivery.

He raised his pinky to his lip in an impression of Doctor Evil, prompting Ellie and Paige to crack up with the kind of uncontrolled belly laughs that twist one's abdominal muscles into burning knots. It was the ice-breaker they'd needed, and just like that, a new friendship was born.

The following weeks at Buzz were a blur of laughter and lunches, taglines and tech talk, and unofficial tutorials about the emerging opportunities of the internet.

Austin was obsessed with the digital universe, and he was most in his element when he was coding, his eyes pinned to his monitor. He and Ellie often chatted through the divider, breaking up the monotony of the day with humorous repartee. It wasn't flirty, per se, but something was building between them. An undercurrent.

But that undercurrent didn't last long. In fact, it seemed to dissipate faster than it formed, about four months after they'd met. Harold had dropped around as usual to query something while casually massaging her trapezius muscle, only this time he asked her to stick around after work because he had something important to talk to her about. Austin had heard this, but he didn't comment, so Ellie followed his lead and refrained, even though she was electrified with excitement that she couldn't share with anyone because Paige was off sick.

When the work day wound to a close, she made her way to Harold's corner office. Harold was at the window, his hair coiffed to perfection and his tight tan chinos accentuating his toned butt and legs.

"Harold?" she asked, hating the nervous tremor in her voice.

"Please, have a seat," Harold said, staring off into the smoggy horizon. "So, Eloise. I've been noticing your work ethic lately. You show signs of real promise. We have this new client, and I'd like to assign you — in a full-time capacity. Are you interested?"

"Yes, I'm definitely interested! Thank you!" Ellie blurted, unable to restrain her excitement like she'd rehearsed.

"There is one thing, though," Harold said, finally turning to face her with penetrating eye contact that made Ellie's heart skip a beat. "This new client is going to be quite demanding, which probably means some long hours. Maybe even a few weekends. Will you be up for that?"

"Yes, for sure. I promise I won't let you down, Harold."

He flashed her a dazzling smile. "That's what I hoped you'd say."

The next morning, Ellie shared the good news with Paige and Austin — both of them were already salaried employees — and Paige cheered and whooped, while Austin barely managed to squeak out the requisite "Congrats."

Later that day, he spoke to her through the partition. "You know what he's up to, don't you?"

"What are you talking about?" Ellie asked.

"Harold. He's not interested in your talent, Ellie. He wants to fuck you. I mean, come on."

She was completely taken aback, stung by his harsh words. "That's not true! I work hard here … I've been busting my butt for the last four months to get hired."

Austin snorted. "You said it, not me."

"You know what, you can go to hell!"

"It's not my fault if you're too dumb to see it. Don't say I didn't warn you."

For the next few weeks, Ellie barely spoke to Austin unless she absolutely needed his help with a computer issue or a software update. Occasionally she'd hear him mutter something sarcastic in the wake of a Harold back rub, but that was it. No more witty banter.

But any regret she had about the abrupt end to their friendship was short-lived. One day, Ellie arrived at work earlier than usual. From the hallway, she saw Austin sitting in her cubicle, looking through images on her computer. They were personal photos she'd recently uploaded from her new digital camera — her sister Evelyn laughing, Stacy West hoisting a beer, herself and Paige sitting on Laura's couch, their bare legs entwined like pretzels. A sick feeling of invasion crept into her chest.

She gasped loudly, and Austin turned, his face awash with guilt. He feverishly closed the window and babbled about needing to install something on her computer, throwing in a bunch of jargon to make it sound legitimate. But she knew better. He'd crossed a professional line.

That day, still stung by Austin's insinuation that she didn't deserve her new job, she casually mentioned the morning's incident to Mei Lien, the office gossip. By week's end, whisperings about the offence had spread to the far reaches of Buzz. Other sordid stories surfaced — that Austin had once snuck into the women's washroom and hidden in a stall, that he sometimes used the office dial-up to download porn — and when Harold finally caught wind of the rumours, "Austin Pervert," as he'd now been dubbed, was hauled into a closed-door meeting and fired shortly thereafter. The whole situation unravelled so quickly that Ellie wasn't sure if she should feel guilty for sparking the young man's downfall, or relieved that he was out of her life for good.

A few days after his firing, the answer became frighteningly clear. She received an email from an unknown sender. "Watch your back," it said, and attached was a photo of her leaning over her desk.

Taken from behind, it was not a flattering photo. The way her tight-fitting slacks clung to her hips, exposing the pink T-bar of her thong and unsightly bulges in the gap beneath her cardigan, was frankly grotesque. She knew she should report the threatening incident, but the thought of Harold seeing her love handles was too mortifying. Instead, she deleted the evidence and spent the better part of three months looking over her shoulder, casting sharp glances at strangers, and imagining Austin lurking in the shadows.

Then one day Austin Pert was in the news. It was reported that a woman had caught him riding the subway with a boot-mounted camera aimed up her skirt. In the ensuing search of his apartment, police discovered hours of illicit footage on his hard drive, as well as a video camera he'd embedded in his neighbour's wall. Turned out he'd been using all his curated material to populate some porn site he was developing for voyeur fetishists like himself, men who got off on images and videos taken without knowledge or consent. It was a big, salacious story that hijacked the local news for months. During that time, Ellie felt a mix of negative emotions. Mostly disgust at herself for having been marginally attracted to someone so incredibly messed up.

The last she'd read, Austin had been charged and held in custody to await his trial. Whether he'd been sent to prison or not, she'd never bothered to find out.

CHAPTER 8

As Ellie floated in and out of consciousness, her mind racing with morbid possibilities, she tried to calm herself the only way she knew how: by envisioning the angelic face of her nine-year-old daughter, Beth. Lively, sassy Beth, with her pale-blue eyes and perfect smattering of freckles. She'd been named after Ellie's athletic older sister, Bethany — the golden girl who'd won at life, then been robbed of everything in an instant.

Bethany had been a truly extraordinary human. Pretty like Laura, but masterful in her movement. A graceful creature with an uncanny knack for precision. But what made her so special, in Ellie's opinion, was her modesty. Bethany never flaunted her talents or overindulged in her victories. She always supported her teammates and sung the praises of her less-coordinated siblings, even when they failed.

"Just close your eyes and picture the ball going where you want it to go," she'd once coached Ellie on the morning of her first soccer tournament. "Picture it, see it through, and it will happen … just like that."

Ellie had closed her eyes and done what Bethany said: she imagined the ball cutting through the air in a perfect arc, piercing the makeshift target Bethany had set up using a hula hoop and some string. She opened her eyes to enact the shot, taking aim and striking the ball, then watched in horror as it didn't just miss the hula hoop target, but soared straight over the fence and bounced off the gleaming hood of the Denkworths' new station wagon.

"Don't worry, we'll try again," Bethany said, her sinewy legs leaping into action as she dashed off to retrieve the ball.

When she returned, she was even more committed to Ellie's seemingly hopeless cause than she'd been just seconds before. "Hey, that was some kick, so we know that you've got it in you," she said, beaming with confidence. "Now if we can just rein in the aim … Quiet the voice in your mind that says you can't. Because you can, Ellie. I know you can."

///////////////////

"Ellie, can you hear me?"

It was Jake's voice. *His* voice, whoever he was.

Ellie nodded. She couldn't hear any sounds coming from down on the floor. Not a single breath or twitch of movement.

Was her husband still down there? Was he swimming in blood from his chopped-off toe? She wondered where the toe had rolled off to. Was it under the bed? She'd read that if you put a severed digit on ice immediately, it could be reattached, as long as the nerves and tissue were intact. Was there still a chance for this outcome?

"Good, you're awake," Jake said. "You have two guesses left. I know you can do it this time. It would really tear me up if you couldn't remember my name after I spent nearly half my life thinking about you … about *us* …"

"Nearly half your life …" Ellie said meekly. "So are you saying you were around twenty-five or thirty when I knew you?"

"Ha, nice try. I wasn't being quite so literal."

"This is sick! What you're doing is sick! I'm not play-ing your game anymore," she said, defiance in her voice.

Jake swaggered back and smiled down at her, his white teeth perfectly aligned. "I'm not asking you to play, I'm telling you to. If you don't co-operate, it's three strikes."

Ellie swallowed hard. "Is Neil okay? I can't hear him."

"He's just having a little nap. He'll live. He's a real looker, isn't he? I suppose that huge schnozz sort of suits him. He wouldn't fare too well in the joint, though, not with that face. I should know. My own new and improved mug didn't do me any favours in there. But I did it for you."

"You went to prison?"

Jake leaned closer, his eyes betraying his offence. "Yes, I did. You'd know that if you'd ever bothered to check up on me."

Ellie stared up at him, trying to think of an answer that wouldn't set off his rage.

Jake's eyes were fixed on hers expectantly. He stared at her mouth. Reached out and pulled away a few wisps of hair that had gotten stuck between her dry lips, tucked them behind her ear. Ellie's breath hitched, her body tightened as his fingers traced their way over her jaw, down the length of her neck, to her breast.

"I've been trying to be a gentleman and give you your space," he said. "But seeing you under that shower, dripping wet, bathed in moonlight, well, I guess it got me excited. Showed me everything I've been missing all these years."

The blood in Ellie's ears hammered. "Listen, I don't usually do that sort of thing. I was —"

"Oh, I know what you're going to say — that your sexy little show out there was meant for his eyes only. It was his desire feeding you, not mine. But it sure didn't look that way, not from where I was standing, in the woods with all the other hungry beasts."

"You fucking pervert! You don't know me — stop pretending you do. You're just some sick, perverted nobody!"

Jake's smile faded and rage snapped into his eyes. "You've always taunted me and teased me, so close but out of reach with your short skirts and long hair." He gave her breast a squeeze. "But I'm the one with the power here, don't you see?"

Ellie bristled under his touch, as his words replayed in her mind. *Short skirts and long hair …*

That described her style throughout most of her life, except for the five years after she'd given birth to Beth. During that period, she'd favoured yoga pants and had levelled off her long mane into a practical, low-maintenance "mom bob." Also, Jake had said previously that he didn't really know Neil, so he must have crossed her path before Neil entered her life in the spring of 2004. She must have encountered Jake in her mid to late twenties. Her foray into office life.

Could he be Austin Pert, her old Buzz colleague, the pioneer of internet porn who'd been charged with crimes against dozens of women? Could Austin have escalated his criminal activity to kidnapping? *And murder?* Ellie thought of the real Palmers, the old retired couple she'd never met, and briefly wondered how he'd killed them. She hoped it had been quick and painless, but considering the twisted game he was forcing them to play, she doubted it.

"Tick-tock, Ellie, tick-tock. Look into my eyes and tell me my name."

///////////////////

Neil had recovered from shock some time ago and was silently listening to his wife and that psycho fuck bantering back and forth on the bed. He'd been able to piece together that the man wasn't the real Jake Palmer, but an imposter. Someone from Ellie's past who she used to know but couldn't remember. Someone who'd been in prison.

If Neil couldn't break free of his restraints in the next few minutes and clobber the son of a bitch over the head with the chair, then he was about to lose a finger. But at that moment as he lay there dazed, watching the blood trickle out of his left foot, a daring escape didn't seem possible.

He tried to wiggle his wrists and ankles loose, but the cable ties were so tight that any minor movement just made the thick plastic sink deeper into his skin. He felt a sob escaping the depths of his stomach and forced it back down. It was better to keep pretending he was out cold.

Jake had his back to Neil. He pushed up his sleeves, and Neil caught a glimpse of a strange marking on his forearm. It was a series of black letters inked in a hard-to-decipher cursive, two words, both beginning with the letter B. Under the words were numbers. Years, by the looks of it: *1948–2004*. He strained to make out the words. *Brenda Brown*, or something close to it.

"Does it matter who you are? You're just some filthy creep, like all the other filthy creeps who end up in prison," Ellie was saying, trying to delay the inevitable, and Neil wanted so badly to get free so he could hold her and protect her.

"You're hurting my feelings, Ellie," Jake's voice said. "You don't want to do that."

Neil felt sick. The way Jake called his wife "Ellie" and spoke to her in such an intimate, familiar way, the fact that he'd watched Ellie shower that night, lurking in the woods, made rage bubble inside of him.

Neil had been the one who'd persuaded her to do it, after all. He'd wheedled her against her better judgment, coaxed her to get naked and dance around for him like some hired stripper. Oh, how badly he wanted to reverse time and erase the past, especially that damn night he'd spent at the Marriott San Francisco with Mia.

He started thrashing and wailing, bawling and howling around the wet gag that filled his mouth, his tactical decision to stay quiet forgotten. But none of his efforts amounted to anything, for he had been rendered useless.

///////////////////

"Well, look who woke up just in time for the next phase of our little game?" Jake taunted, as though this were some harmless college initiation. "Your wife is about to make her second guess. She's going to say my name, and then you get to keep the rest of your fingers and toes. Isn't that right, Ellie?"

The sound of her husband keening away like a dying animal and the knowledge that he must be in excruciating pain dissolved all the anger and defiance in Ellie. She started to tremble all over, as the gravity of the situation hit her with the abrupt force of a sucker punch. In that moment, she realized it was hopeless. They wouldn't make it out of this stuffy little room alive.

"Who am I, Ellie?" Jake said, gazing down at her with cryptic eyes. Eyes that may have belonged to the young man who'd occupied the cubicle next to hers, so many years ago. Eyes that craved candid, private images of others …

Ellie fought to stay calm. Knew her thirty minutes were up. She took a deep breath. Then another. "You're Austin Pert. We worked together at Buzz. You got fired for breaking into my computer. And you blame me for it. You blame me for losing your job. That's why you're doing this … to get back at me."

Jake sat quietly for a moment, staring into Ellie's grief-stricken eyes. Then he reached for her hair, separating the still-damp clumps and tucking them neatly behind her ears. "Wrong," he whispered. "Now I think I'll take the ring finger."

CHAPTER 9

As much as Ellie loved her sister, living with Laura hadn't been easy. Often, she'd stagger home in the middle of the night with some flashy, intoxicated sleazeball hanging off her. It was both disturbing and pitiful, a sad indication of her low self-esteem.

The men were all the same — photographers, movie producers, restaurateurs — all equal parts married, lecherous and full of themselves. What killed Ellie, even at twenty-four, was the way they all used the perks of their chosen professions to gain power over Laura, whether it was pull in Hollywood or the ability to secure a reservation at the latest hot spot. They dangled their carrots in front of Laura's wide, drug-glazed eyes in hopes that she'd take off her blouse — which she always did.

Even worse than those random late-night shags was Laura's proclivity for midweek benders. She'd announce on a whim that Glenn, Richard, Margot, and Alix would be dropping by for a few drinks, but they wouldn't be too disruptive or stay very long — neither claim was ever true. For Ellie, the TV could never drown out the noise of the rowdy five-pack as they snorted blow and cackled about the latest fashion industry faux pas. Even after she'd snuck off to bed and turned on the ceiling fan full blast, their obnoxious banter still cut through. Laura haphazardly fighting off Richard's wandering hands, or someone falling out of a chair. In the wee hours, like clockwork, Richard would creep into Ellie's room, slither up next to her, reeking of cigarettes and cologne. He'd whisper about how "irresistible" he found her, try to feel under the covers, beneath her pajama top.

Ellie despised Richard. Thought he was the lowest form of scum. After she kicked him out of her bedroom, he'd usually slink over to Laura's room, where she'd be too inebriated to fight him off. On more than a few occasions, Ellie had been forced to untangle him from her unconscious sister, drag him out by the ear, and dump him on the couch. Hell, he was lucky she never phoned security.

What saddened her most, though — even more than seeing her older sister slipping into such a vulnerable, destructive condition — was the reason Laura did it, why she opened herself up to that degenerate world of predators. It was because she missed Bethany. Because Bethany had perished so tragically, enduring three years of suffering before finally giving in to the inevitable. Three years imprisoned in her own skin, while Laura was blessed with *everything*.

Ellie knew with unfaltering certainty that all of Laura's issues in life — her penchant for nightly

inebriation and rolls in the hay with random assholes —
stemmed from desperately trying to blunt the pain that
had never loosened its grip on her heart.

//////////////////

In the late spring of 2000, Laura received a hand-
delivered invitation to the grand opening of a new club
called Andromeda. Ellie had read about the new club in
NOW magazine and immediately hated the sound of it.
So when the big night came and Laura's wingman unex-
pectedly fell through, Ellie silently fumed about having
to go as her sister's plus-one.

When Ellie emerged from her room sporting the
lame outfit she'd put together, Laura cringed and opened
up her own far superior wardrobe, a closet thick with
beautiful things. Expensive, skimpy things Ellie had
only ever seen in the glossy pages of magazines, or worn
by her statuesque sister. She caressed the silky tops and
the lacy slip dresses, feeling like a kid in a candy store,
ten years old again. Then they'd cracked open a bottle
of Prosecco and spent the better part of two hours playing dress-up, reminiscing about life during the good old
days. About summer in the suburbs. About jelly shoes
and middle school dances. About Bethany before the
accident.

Bethany. The girl with the strawberry-blond braids
and stunning megawatt smile. Bethany, who could kick
a ball better than any boy and who put up with Laura's
mood swings like a saint. As Ellie and Laura reminisced

about the sister they'd both adored equally, the world around them became brighter. No men, no illusions of grandeur. Just each other, a bottle of cheap bubbly, and the shared memory of an innocent time before their precious sister had been stolen.

"Do you still miss her?" Ellie asked.

"Every day," Laura said. "I miss her every day."

///////////////////////

Back in those days, Andromeda was the place to see and be seen. Ellie didn't care so much about being seen, but it turned out she loved to dance, loved to let loose and pretend no one was watching.

As Ellie's twenty-fourth year unfolded into her twenty-fifth, Andromeda became her Friday night go-to, where she and Paige would sweat out their toxins, have a few drinks, and shake off the stresses of Buzz. In the beginning, getting in meant braving a line-up that circled the block, shivering in heels among the cigarette-smoking masses. But in due time they learned that draping an arm around bouncer Trevor's shoulder, nuzzling his neck, and giggling in his ear granted pretty girls like them special access to the side door.

Those had been stormy days for Ellie. She hadn't loved herself much back then; there was an emptiness inside that she couldn't fill. Dancing with her eyes closed to block out her unsatisfying reality was the only thing that brought her any solace. It gave her a few hours of escape from her mounting disenchantment.

She wasn't exactly promiscuous, but the scene at the club did lend itself to close contact with the male gender: probing hands, wandering lips, the occasional altercation with an SDG (Standard Drunk Guys, she and Paige called them). And there was that one regrettable time she'd gone home with a complete stranger, waking up in his filthy sheets with no memory of how she'd gotten there.

Where Laura was unfazed by her reckless abandon, Ellie hated herself for it. For Laura, it was a side effect of losing Bethany, a way to numb her perpetual pain. For Ellie, it all stemmed from an incident that happened six months into her new job at Buzz, back when she'd been working tirelessly to make an impression on the boss and prove to him — but mostly to herself — that she really did deserve her paycheque, despite what Austin Pervert had said.

In short order, she'd risen in the ranks to become Harold's go-to, the trusty subordinate he could count on for anything. And though some of her tasks felt beneath her, like reorganizing the office supplies cabinet or cleaning the coffee mugs left in the sink, she lived in anticipation of him dropping by her desk and whispering, "I've got an important job for you."

One day, he'd asked her to stay late to help him finish a presentation, "a real doozy with an urgent deadline," he'd said. Ellie was delighted to be working alongside the boss, just the two of them in his stately corner office. She was delighted that he trusted her with such a consequential task. But as the afternoon became evening and the rest of the Buzz staff trickled off home, Ellie sensed a change in Harold. A distinct lessening of all that urgency.

Then, after she'd aligned all the headers and printed the document for one final proofread, he leaned over her. "Oh, Eloise, you smell so good." He pressed himself into her back, began rubbing her shoulders with an intensity that penetrated deep into her bones.

She knew she mustn't allow it, knew she had to stop him before his hands crept beneath her baby-blue cashmere sweater, before her bra came off and he groped her breasts. But she could barely summon her voice. Could barely find the strength to gently dissuade his advances. And then he took it even further, running his fingers under her skirt, slipping them inside her new Victoria's Secret black-lace panties.

It was just what that lout, Austin, had predicted. *You shouldn't let him do that,* he'd warned. *He shouldn't be touching you like that.*

And boy, did she wish she'd listened. Because the voice in her head screaming for him to stop was no match for the longing cries from her labia, and soon the presentation was splashed all over the floor with Ellie in its place, her legs splayed open on that big oak desk, her head knocking against a homemade *Super Dad* mug.

After that, everything at Buzz changed. Harold stopped swinging by her cubicle each day, stopped flirting with her in the elevator and praising her impeccable work. In less than twenty-four hours, she'd fallen out of his favour. His coldness crept inside her. She felt rejected, alone.

Worthless.

There was a new girl, too — Sasha. Pretty, bright, eager to please. Although Ellie worked tirelessly to regain his affection, Harold barely acknowledged her. If their paths did happen to cross, he'd politely ask her some benign question about a pending work matter while glancing at his watch, then he'd hurry off, his fingers snapping and loafers clipping in tandem.

He never summoned her for an important task again.

///////////////////////

As Ellie lay tied to the bed, disjointed memories from her Buzz days swirling in her mind, the dismal feeling of that bleak period began to fill her with panic, gripping her by the neck and prompting an onslaught of tears.

Then, out of her grief came a face. One she hadn't thought about in a very long time. It was the face of Paige's ex-boyfriend, Troy — or Man-Child, as she'd dubbed him.

Man-Child was a jealous boor with latent violent tendencies. Though he'd never hit Paige, the possibility was always there, always lurking like the unseen hazard on a dark, winding road. Ellie had suspected that Troy had a touch of fetal alcohol syndrome, and also, that he was trying to nudge her out of Paige's life. It was as though underneath the strained silence between them lay an equally silent truth: Troy didn't deserve Paige. Paige was way too good for him.

On one occasion Ellie had tried to broach the subject, making some casual remark about his fondness for "getting wrecked." But Paige had nipped the conversation in the bud. She could be upbeat and stoic to a fault, always skirting around the serious stuff in favour of keeping it light. Ellie wouldn't go so far as to call her friend naive, but there was a certain innocence to her that worried Ellie. Worried her, and made her feel fiercely protective.

Then one night, Man-Child had a meltdown of epic proportions. She and Paige were enjoying themselves at Andromeda, freely imbibing the gratis gin and tonics offered by the bartender, when Ellie detected Troy's smouldering presence on the fringes. She saw him watching Paige while he guzzled rye and gingers, doubtless judging her for being too provocative, too drunk. She'd tried to warn her, but Paige brushed it off with typical dismissiveness. "Troy's just being Troy," she said.

Ellie should have persisted, should have kept a better watch over the brewing situation. Because her hunch turned out to be correct. Troy flew at Paige, grabbing her by the arm and dragging her off the dance floor. In the process, someone got pushed over and several drinks went flying. Trevor had to break it up, engaging in a pathetic showdown against sloppy, bungling Troy, who gnashed his teeth and swung inept punches that bounced off Trevor's muscles like rubber.

After that, Paige was in tears, the closest to unhinged that Ellie had ever seen her. Ellie insisted on taking her home in a cab and standing guard all night in case Man-Child came to finish his quarrel. Paige lived in a basement studio in a rundown building on the east side of town. Ellie had only slept there twice, and on both occasions, she'd barely managed a wink. The way the radiators clanked and the neighbours' music and heated lovemaking thumped through the walls, it felt like a brothel or a fraternity. But Paige needed her, and Ellie had a bad feeling that Troy might show up and do something he'd regret.

Sure enough, when Paige was fast asleep and Ellie was just dozing off, she heard the sound of knuckles on glass. Loud, guttural sobs mixed with slurred apologies. For a while she lay still and tried to ignore it, but when the pounding grew louder and the snivelling more urgent, she got up, unlatched the window, and politely told him to go away. Troy didn't take kindly to Ellie being there. Her presence only increased his determination to get in. Which he did, by ramming himself into the window and tumbling onto the floor.

"Ellie, how about you head home now ... give us some privacy," he said, staggering to his feet, his bloodshot eyes searching for Paige. She was hidden from view, a comatose wedge beneath her pink daisy comforter.

"No, Troy. I'm not going anywhere. You need to leave," Ellie replied firmly.

Troy snickered at that, his nostrils flaring grotesquely. He might be attractive, she supposed, if he ever smiled. But Man-Child never smiled. He was the type of miserable-guy character who believed the whole world was out to get him, and him alone.

"Are you worried I'll hurt her, Ellie? Is that it? I'm not going to hurt her. I love her." As he spoke, his pasty lips parted enough for her to see his nicotine-stained teeth for the first time since they'd met.

"If you love her, then leave," Ellie said.

"I'll leave when I'm good and ready," he snarled. And then, for the first time, she saw lust creeping into his eyes. Troy stepped forward and took her chin in his hand, his features so slack, so inebriated, that a shiver moved through her spine. "What do you say we get to know each other … talk a little … I think Paige would appreciate that … us getting to know each other."

"Don't touch me," Ellie hissed, swiping at his hand. Given his severe level of intoxication and the fact that he wasn't sound of mind to begin with, Ellie had meant to tread lightly. Mollify and defuse. But she couldn't seem to control herself, not with all those cocktails still coursing through her own veins. "Get the hell out of here and never come back or I will call the police, do you hear me?"

That got Troy angry, and he lunged for her again, but Ellie was two steps ahead, scrambling to grab Paige's flip phone from the bedside table. When she finally got it open, she randomly stabbed at buttons just to prove she was serious.

"Fuck you," Troy said. Then he bent down and scooped up one of Paige's red pumps, squeezing it hard before lobbing it across the room to shatter the only lamp in the tiny basement apartment.

For a moment it was pitch dark, and Ellie's heart raced as she prepared for what might happen next. But after the resounding clatter had settled, and Ellie's eyes adjusted to the meagre light coming through the window, and the silence grew unbearable, Troy did what he was told. He stormed out the door, staggered down the hall, and never came back.

CHAPTER 10

"Neil!" Ellie wailed. "Neil! Can you hear me?"

He made some anguished cries — whether involuntarily or by way of answer, Ellie didn't know.

She couldn't see him. She could only imagine the gruesome scene unfolding at the foot of the bed — a fountain of blood spouting from his hand, splattering the floor and walls. He was still tied to the chair, so he'd be unable to tend to it. One finger and one toe. *How much blood could he lose?*

As if hearing her thoughts, Jake said, "Damn, what a mess." He was standing over Neil, looking down at him with a blank expression. "You know, seeing you flop around like that, I'm grateful to the old couple for investing in such high-quality furniture. An Ikea chair would have snapped in pieces by now."

He turned to leave, but slipped and fell. He landed flat on his back. After a pause, he sat up. "Jesus, that's a lot of blood ... and now it's all over me." He got to his feet and Ellie saw with horror that his hands and clothes were indeed coated in Neil's blood.

"I'd better go clean myself up," he said. "But don't get any funny ideas, Ellie. Remember the rules."

Then he left the room, slamming the door behind him.

"Neil!" Ellie cried out between heaving sobs. "Listen to me. We need to escape. We need to do something. He's going to kill us! He killed the Palmers and he's not going to stop —"

Neil started to violently slam himself around. Over his muffled cries, she could hear the chair striking the base of the wall. Then a wooden crack. She gasped, held still, and listened. The thrashing ceased.

"Neil," she whispered. "Did you —"

Just then, the door flew open, and Jake stepped into the room wearing a pair of dark-green coveralls. They were skin-tight and a few inches too short, no doubt having belonged to the real Jake Palmer. As he traipsed toward Neil, Ellie noticed he was holding a balled-up towel and a roll of duct tape. Her heart seized.

"Now don't go thinking I like you, Neil, but all that blood is beginning to put a damper on my mood. And since you're an integral part of our little game here, I'm going to have to do something about that. Can't have you bleeding to death — not yet, at least." He laughed and squatted down, out of Ellie's sight.

A moment later, she heard the duct tape unspooling as he wrapped Neil's hand, then a ripping sound as he tore off the tape.

"There, that should do it."

Ellie breathed, relieved that he hadn't noticed anything amiss with the chair. But now she worried that the extra padding might impede Neil from getting a handle on that loose chair leg. If she could draw Jake over to her, it would give Neil the space to finish what he'd started.

"Why are you doing this?" she demanded. "How long have you been planning this sick game of revenge?"

Jake took the bait. He approached the bed and smiled down at her almost tenderly. "I'm afraid I can't tell you that without giving away my identity. But I suppose I can tell you that it wasn't really planned, per se. It was mostly spontaneous after I happened to see you driving by with that *dick*. After that the plan just came together on its own. Payback for him … and for us, the reunion of two kindred souls."

"Kindred souls? Are you crazy? I don't know who the hell you are! Doesn't that tell you anything?"

"If you sift deep enough through those precious memories of yours, you'll eventually find your way to me. Then you'll see how all of this, all that I've become, is for you. How Neil was never supposed to end up with you — *I* was. Now," he clapped his hands and grinned at her, "it seems we've reached the final stage of our game. You've got one last chance to tell me my name. Get it right, or … I think you know what I'm taking next."

Ellie closed her eyes, unable to look at him. She was so terrified — one more wrong name, and Neil was dead.

Was it Troy? Paige's brooding ex-boyfriend who'd stormed off, humiliated, all those years ago? *No*, she decided. Man-Child had just been a big baby with a temper.

What about that guy from the dance club? The random hook-up that had left her so shaken, so disgusted with herself? Snatches of blurry detail came back. A dusting of pale shoulder hair. A nice full chest. He'd been sort of a babe, now that she thought about it. And funny, too, with a contagious, easy laugh that rippled through his taut body. Eyes that crinkled when he smiled. That was all she remembered, probably because there'd been nothing else to him. No sizzle, no substance. *No threat.* He hadn't been a latent sadist sizing her up as future prey, just a cute SDG looking to get laid. A warm, hard body who had successfully enticed her into a set of sheets that hadn't been washed in months.

Ellie combed through her memory for possible suspects, her own cast of unlikable characters whose intentions she'd wanted no part of. The flirty cop who'd let her off with a warning and his phone number. The cable guy who'd lingered too long, shared too much. Richard the coke-snorting predator. Harold the lecherous supervisor …

Men, men, men, she thought venomously. She was beginning to question whether any of them had integrity — her own cheating husband included. Even putting aside this MJ, Neil had always admitted to having a checkered past. Said he'd made some mistakes in his youth, done some stupid things he regretted. But he'd never gone into detail about what those stupid things were, and now Ellie resented not knowing.

Had he ever broken the law? Assaulted someone? Made enemies, like the man torturing them now?

Clearly Jake had it in for Neil. The question was, why? Did he simply hate Neil for marrying her, or did he know something else about her husband that she didn't?

No, that's a stretch. She was just paranoid. An emotional basketcase from all the trauma. She needed to keep calm and remember Neil for who he was, the man she fell in love with and married.

Neil had been the full package, not just another SDG. Smart, funny, attractive, and, most of all, good. Good like her father, who'd suffered so much pain. A kind, caring man who'd made her feel intensely loved and valued, despite all he'd been through.

Ellie suddenly felt a surge of angst — how would *she* be remembered after she was gone? Had she made her parents proud, like Bethany did? Certainly, she'd let down a few people along the way. That intern, Sasha, for starters. Ellie regretted having had such unwarranted disdain for that girl, whose only fault was being pretty and young. But ever since Sasha had joined the Buzz team, Harold had treated Ellie with chilly indifference, and her world had become tinged with grey, her disposition rancorous, like Laura's.

At age twenty-five Ellie learned a harsh lesson, that girls like her were a dime a dozen. It was as though there was a factory somewhere that just spit them out. Mass-produced young beauties to keep the HHs of the world amused. And the realization sickened her. Furthermore, she was disgusted at herself for having been so stupid, fooling herself that Harold believed in her more than he'd desired her.

She hated herself for caring so much, too — for feeling shunned and rejected. Harold was the asshole, after all, not her. That was what Paige had said. He was the asshole for cheating on his wife with someone half his age. He had taken advantage of his authority, Paige had aptly pointed out. He had clouded her better judgment. As much as Ellie had been a willing participant in that brief carnal encounter, it had left her feeling icky and regretful.

Empty.

//////////////////////

It was the night of Buzz's Christmas party. A select group of clients and staff had been invited to come nibble on catered sandwiches and raise a toast to another profitable year. Afterward, with the dregs of a spiced rum cocktail in her hand, Ellie had slipped back to her desk to finish some work. She couldn't face the weekend with untended business on her mind.

The office was calm and quiet, just the way she liked it. But not for long. Shortly into her work, Ellie heard distinct noises emanating from the kitchen. Giggling, tittering. A man's low whisper. A chill swept through her as the hard truth smacked her in the face. Harold was right now replacing her with a tastier flavour.

Compelled to catch HH and Sasha in the act, Ellie crept toward the kitchen, her heart beating up in her throat. As she got closer, she could hear the heated smack of kisses, the honeyed moan elicited by a man's fingers touching a girl's wet privates. For a moment Ellie paused and reconsidered.

She herself had been guilty of the same indecency just a few months earlier, and she could only imagine the horror of being caught by a fellow staff member.

But screw it, she decided. Harold's closed office was one thing, the communal kitchen was another.

She rounded the corner and couldn't believe her eyes when she saw Harold with not Sasha, but *Paige*. Paige, with her bare buttocks pressed against the counter where they made their morning bagels. Paige, with her head thrown back and her belly taut as Harold peeled off her pink silk thong. Ellie retreated before either of them saw her — and as she fled back to her cubicle, all her faith fled, too — in friendship, humanity, and her own self-worth.

All of it was fizzling and dying like the flame of a candle at the end of its wick. Something ignited in its place. Anger.

That night, unable to get Paige's hurtful betrayal out of her mind, Ellie did something she had never done before. She dressed in one of Laura's sexiest clubbing outfits and headed to Andromeda by herself. She wanted to dance. Needed to dance, to feel the eyes of unknown men on her, wanting her from a distance. As she closed her eyes and moved to the beat, she felt the throbbing of the bass deep inside her, touching her in places that no man had ever touched her before. She became aroused by her own energy. Fed by the energy of strangers. So many eyes on her, flickering among the bright lasers that flashed on her nimble body. Eyes belonging to faces she didn't know or care to know.

She became a stranger even to herself.

CHAPTER 11

The bedroom smelled rank, rife with the stench of body odour and blood that emphasized the urgency of Ellie's task. But as the pungent air filled her nostrils and the sickness churned inside her, Ellie flashed back to a night, not a man. The night of her twenty-sixth birthday. It was the first and only time she'd ever taken the drug known today as MDMA.

She'd been feeling so low. The bartender, who offered it to her, pointed out that the drug was called Ecstasy for a reason; one little pill would help her shed her pain, tap into her inner rhythm, and make her smile like the Cheshire cat. "It'll cure whatever ails you." When he put it that way, she couldn't resist. He also assured her that he'd look out for her if anyone got too close or bothered her.

But no one did bother her that crazy, hazy, stupid-fun night. In fact, she had the time of her life dancing with some enchanting, long-limbed, blue-eyed boy. A perfect stranger who, it turned out, was the perfect companion for her happy little experiment. He was a wiry young creature with boundless energy — hot, vital, explosive — though none of it was aimed at her. He wasn't attracted to her sexually, he explained. He liked her aura and just wanted to dance. Ellie liked what he said about her aura. It made her feel special and lifted her weakened spirits.

And dance they did.

Then, as they were cooling off with some water, she regaled him with her tale of betrayal at the hands of HH and her backstabbing best friend, Paige. The nameless boy turned to her and said something she would never forget. "The relationships in your life at this moment are precisely the ones you need … in this moment. There is a hidden meaning behind all events, and it serves your own evolution." He gazed at her, holding back a single globular tear. "Deepak Chopra taught me that. Beautiful Girl, you need to trust me. Trust him. The time has come for you to choose the path of enlightenment. Find the spiritual light and let it guide you. Only then will you stop being a prisoner of your past and start being a pioneer of tomorrow."

With that, he kissed her on the lips and swanned off into the strobes. Ellie never saw him again.

//////////////////////

Continuing to work at Buzz was hard on Ellie. She hated it there, hated who she'd become. She and Paige had yet to reconcile — which in a small office took considerable effort. Often it meant waiting for the next elevator or hiking up six flights of stairs. But after three months of not speaking, Ellie was beginning to soften. Deep down, she knew Paige hadn't intended to hurt her; she'd simply been seduced in the same dumb manner Ellie had.

Furthermore, Ellie had noticed the way Harold had begun to treat Paige — the chilly avoidance, the terse interactions, the evasion of eye contact. Even from a distance, Ellie could see the shame and regret in her friend's eyes. Paige must have been blinded by the possibility of a real grown-up love on the heels of dipshit Troy.

When Paige didn't show up for work one day, nor the day after that, Ellie became deeply concerned about her friend's well-being and decided it was time to bury the hatchet. Harold wasn't worth any more tears, any more lonely nights of regretting, questioning, suffering in solitary confinement. Ellie had made it through the long, dark tunnel of regret and emerged into the open air. Now she needed to take Paige's hand and drag her out into the sunshine with her.

She arrived at her best friend's door, a bottle of wine and a congealing cheese pizza in hand. But her knocks elicited no response. She could see light shining under the crack of the door, could faintly hear sitcom dialogue with its pervasive accompanying laugh track, but her subsequent knocks went unanswered.

Ellie dug out her cellphone and tried Paige's number, only to hear it ringing through the wall. A pang of worry shot through her. Suddenly, she feared the worst — that Troy had come back, caught wind of her tryst with Harold, and had flown into a jealous rage.

Panicked, she pounded harder, calling out Paige's name and even kicking at the door with her feet. Still nothing.

She fought back tears, picturing Paige lying on the floor, bleeding to death — or worse, already dead. With all her weight, Ellie slammed her body against the door, her fists still madly banging. Finally, beyond the door, she heard feet shuffling over, the unlocking of the latch. Then, the door opened and Paige appeared, rumpled and red-eyed in baggy pajamas. Her ever-present earphones blocking out the world.

At the sight of each other, Ellie and Paige burst into tears and embraced with the intensity of twins who'd been separated at birth. That night they made a pact to find new jobs and leave Buzz behind them. Escape that soul-sucking establishment before it caused irrevocable damage to their already injured spirits. They were not factory-made office girls — consumable, disposable, replaceable — and they would never again allow anyone to treat them that way.

It was a new dawn, a new day. Good things were on the horizon, Ellie could feel it in the marrow of her bones. She left Paige's, hopped in a cab, and went home feeling as though she was at the precipice of something new, the beginning of a chapter that she would write for herself.

Back at the condo, Ellie sprang inside and called Laura's name, intending to share her new plans with her beleaguered sister. But all her positive feeling was zapped away in an instant. There was Laura passed out on the floor … unconscious, but alive.

Ellie filled a glass with water and splashed it on Laura's face. It was enough to rouse her, thank goodness, but Ellie knew that wouldn't always be the case. Laura, with her model looks now fading, was on a downward spiral. One day she'd die of a drug overdose or some alcohol-related mishap — falling off the balcony, or stumbling on her stilettos into moving traffic.

Their parents had no idea what life had become for their two city-dwelling daughters, whom they saw only every other Sunday. In the years since Bethany's death, they'd placed all their faith in the Lord, entrusting Him to chaperone and protect their remaining offspring. Ellie didn't blame them for it. In fact, she was glad they'd found a way to cope, to persevere despite their insurmountable grief.

Ellie wrestled Laura into bed, already deflated of her newfound joy. She was too tired from all the drama to work on her resume. Then there was the added pressure of what the following day entailed. To her regret, they'd made a commitment with their sister Evelyn, the eager-to-please daughter who'd gone ahead and organized a group gift for their parents' upcoming anniversary. It was some Groupon deal for 60 percent off a one-hour glam session at a "professional" studio. Ellie imagined a shady basement lair with bad lighting and tacky backdrops. Worse, now Laura would be recovering from this bender … and that poor photographer wouldn't know what hit him.

//////////////////

The photographer, it turned out, was Abeer Singh, a tall East Indian man who was slender as a leaf and had an abundance of rich, dark hair.

"Ladies, there must be some mistake. You must be looking for the modelling agency down the hall," he teased, unaware that he was in the company of one of the world's top models.

Ellie and Evelyn found him charming at once; his infectious spirit put them at ease in front of the lens. But Laura refused to crack a smile. She was accustomed to being photographed by visionaries of the industry, had appeared in the pages of *Vogue* and strutted down the runways of Paris — now here she was, being asked to smile into the lens of some Groupon-using hack. It was as though the world had flipped upside down. Ellie was mortified and wanted to throttle her sister.

But Abeer was undaunted. He was like a zoologist who'd just stumbled upon a rare, exotic bird and was employing the precise skills needed to develop trust. He picked up on Laura's corrosive temper and gently reined it in, artfully equating her beauty to the likes of Kate Moss. Fed by the compliments and the genuine attention, Laura eventually started to thaw — and then she started to perform.

Ellie and Evelyn had never seen their sister in the zone before. She was striking A-game poses for Abeer's camera as the two of them struggled to keep up. And the resulting portrait of the three of them turned out to be rather sweet, a true representation of their varied looks and personalities. But best of all,

the photo session was a gift that would keep giving —
for all of them.

///////////////////////

Ellie was the first to notice the changes in Laura that
began about a month after their photo shoot with Abeer.
The tip-off was catching the night owl up before 8:00
a.m. donning a pair of black Lycra cycling shorts.

"What are you doing in those?" Ellie had yawned,
helping herself to some coffee.

"Oh, just going for a bike ride," Laura said, bounding around like an energetic pre-teen and smelling of
fresh-squeezed orange juice.

Ellie stared at her sister, dumbfounded. She'd never
seen Laura ride a bike in her life, let alone dressed the
part of a seasoned professional. But Laura paid no notice
to Ellie's confusion and skipped out the door.

Later that week, Ellie stumbled upon the missing
piece of the puzzle: Abeer's name doodled on a scrap of
paper. Seeing evidence of Laura's having a crush was an
anomaly in a lifetime of her being the one desired and
wooed by men and women alike. At first Ellie couldn't
even take it in. Still, she refrained from mentioning it. The
fact that Laura seemed to be morphing into someone else,
someone *likeable*, was a process she didn't want to rush.

"So," Ellie said a few days later, unable to contain her
curiosity any longer. "Been on any dates lately?"

Laura dropped her issue of *Women's Health* and
looked at Ellie curiously. "Why do you ask?"

"Let's see … because you're glowing. Because you haven't lost it in, like, three weeks. Because you have a creepy perpetual smile on your face, and you're reading an article about superfoods."

Ellie cocked an eyebrow and waited for her sister to deny it. But, to her surprise, Laura didn't refute a thing. Instead, she pulled up her knees, smiled brightly, and began to dish.

According to Laura, the unlikely romance had started about a week after their glam shoot. Abeer had contacted her about some charity art show he was organizing to raise funds for a local women's shelter. Laura, who had never been known as a philanthropist, had agreed to sit as his model — for free — and even to attend the event as a celebrity guest, two acts of generosity that had stunned even herself. Since then, she and Abeer had been virtually inseparable. She was rediscovering what sobriety (and daylight) had to offer and, most surprisingly, falling in love.

Though Ellie was shocked to hear this revelation — and a little dismayed that her sister had kept such a whopping secret all to herself — she was anything but skeptical. She'd met Abeer only the one time, but that was enough to see how different he was from the shady sleazeballs Laura usually chose.

And as the weeks unfolded, Laura began changing in other ways, too. She stopped wearing so much makeup and worrying about her aging complexion. She took up yoga and started cooking healthy meals for herself. She quit the nightly partying in favour of staying home with an Oprah's Book Club pick. Each of these changes alone were perhaps minor, but cumulatively, they meant everything ... because Laura was happy. And the more time she spent with Abeer, the happier she became. It was as though he'd come along at the just right moment and saved her from herself.

Ellie's own self-destructive tendencies hadn't reached the point of her needing to be saved, but her sister's transformation touched her deeply. She herself had already begun to turn the page of her own sorry tale by making some uplifting changes. For starters, she'd read Eckhart Tolle's *The Power of Now* and internalized some great morsels of spiritual wisdom.

But seeing Laura finally happy was like true enlightenment. It taught Ellie to forgive herself, to let go of the past and the things she couldn't undo. It taught her that everyone deserved love, and that perhaps anyone could find it. She wasn't on the hunt for Mr. Right, but now, with her faith in humanity restored, Mr. Wrong was the last guy in her sights — sights that felt true for the first time in her life.

CHAPTER 12

"Ellie, are you in there? It's time to finish our game," Jake said, the tip of his knife grazing her cheekbone. "Your time is up. I've been more than patient with you."

Ellie opened her eyes and looked directly at her captor. He *was* familiar. She definitely had met him before. Encountered his intensity. But his identity still eluded her. She had been brought to tears rehashing the unsavoury parts of her past, the experiences that had made her feel so poisoned, so polluted.

But now, with thoughts in mind of pure, decent Abeer and Laura, whose love was true from the start — she felt refreshed.

All fuelled up to dig in and finish this fucking game!

She thought back to the dance floor at Andromeda, to the three years she'd spent there shutting out the world, sweating out her persistent misery. There was something about that seamy place ...

She thought about the night she and Paige had gone out to celebrate the fact that they'd both started new jobs.

At the restaurant, they spotted Harold with his pretty porcelain wife. Harold had smiled at them woodenly and waved. But then the room had felt thick with tension, with his lecherous breath. To their great pleasure, Harold's complexion turned blotchy red as he hustled his clueless wife out the door, probably feigning some illness.

After that, Ellie had convinced Paige to go to Andromeda for one final hurrah. The place was no longer the hot spot it had once been; now it pulsed with cologne-drenched revellers who descended in droves from the suburbs. But Ellie wanted to dance, to get Harold's putrid stench off her.

And was she ever glad they went — for that was the night she met Neil. The moment she'd first laid eyes on him. She could still picture him in perfect detail. The hue of his hair, the protruding ridge of his nose. The way he fought to look interested in what some loquacious redhead was saying. He was sad, though, she could sense it. And uncomfortable, as though he didn't want to be there, talking to that girl.

Paige had noticed Ellie's unusual level of interest in the cute stranger at the bar and insisted that Ellie go over and speak to him. "Just march on over and introduce yourself," she'd said.

But Ellie had a better idea: she'd send him a beer. That would *really* get his attention. Acting on unprecedented impulse, she slipped through the crowd to the bartender, Colin or Cliff or something. "I'll take a Heineken please, but not for me ... it's for that guy over there," she said, pointing.

The bartender seemed perturbed. "That guy? Why? I already mixed him something. Just delivered it to him myself. And he hasn't even touched it yet. Do you know him?"

"No, never seen him before in my life. But he seems familiar. Does he come here often?"

"No, it's his first time. I never forget a face," the bartender said. He frowned and leaned in closer. "It's not like you to send drinks to people. What do you see in that guy?"

"I can't really explain it, I just feel like we might be … I don't know, kindred souls, or something. It's crazy, I know."

"Kindred souls?" The man's cheeks reddened and for a moment he looked shocked. Cross, even. "How's that possible? You don't even know the guy. And what about me? Haven't I always been here for you? Watched over you, kept you safe?"

Ellie turned and looked up at him, really looked at him for possibly the first time in their three-year acquaintance. She and Paige engaged with him often, but only to order up their drinks or thank him for the occasional freebie. He also dealt drugs to the music crowd, DJs and out-of-town acts who'd hit the club after hours. He was a plain-faced guy with a penetrating stare and a strong, muscular build. But there was something unsettling about him, something dark in his eyes. His intensity sort of creeped her out. Still, she didn't want to hurt the man's feelings.

"You're out of my league," she said, pulling out her change purse to pay for the beer.

"Try me," he said. His tone deepened, and he pressed his palms down on the bar and stared into her eyes with a chilling, unflinching gaze. It spooked her and she knew she needed to be very clear with her rejection.

"Aw, you're sweet, but I suppose you're just not my type."

"You're saying *he's* your type?"

"Not exactly," she said, smiling to ease the vibe. "Usually I like them tall, dark, and devastatingly handsome. Hot like George Clooney. If a man like George walked in here right now, he'd be getting this Heineken, not that skinny twerp."

The bartender's face brightened and his posture loosened a bit. "You're right, he's puny. If I send him this beer, do you promise me you won't waste your time with him?"

"Sure," Ellie said, shaking the man's hand like it was some sort of pledge. She couldn't tell if he was being serious or not, but played along anyway. She figured she'd let him down gently, then flee to the safety of the dance floor.

All she cared about was meeting that cute guy with the chestnut hair whose nose was too big for his face. She was tingling with curiosity, the desire to find out more about him. And when he eventually turned around with the cold Heineken she'd sent him, spotting her in the crowd and mouthing the word *thanks*, her entire future flashed before her eyes, and she knew in her heart that everything was going to be okay.

//////////////

"I know who you are. Yes, I know you," Ellie said, her throat so dry, so tight, she could barely squeak out the words. "I'm sorry it's taken this long to remember."

She was sure it was him, that bartender from Andromeda. Cliff. Or Colin? *No, not Colin.* It was something else. A single syllable. It began with a C, of that much she was certain.

The man's face softened, his deadened eyes filling with hope. Ellie was baffled and terrified all at once by the idea of some bartender she'd barely known, nor cared to know, spending the last fifteen years searching for her and imagining them together in some intimate way. How had he become so obsessed with her, and how had she never picked up on it back then?

Ellie shuddered. *None of that matters now*, she told herself. All that did matter was that she remembered him, and now she and Neil might actually get out of this. The man was delusional, that much was clear. Maybe, if she could convince him of whatever he wanted — that he had a shot with her, or that she loved him back — she might gain some control. There was a chance, at least …

"Thank you for finding me," she said. "I've thought about you often. It's just, with all the changes you've made … to your face … it threw me off and I didn't recognize you."

The man blinked back tears and gazed down at her with the longing eyes of a lover. "Of course. I knew it wouldn't be easy. But I also know that kindred spirits can see through such superficial changes right into each other's souls."

"Yes," Ellie said, her breath catching. "I like what you've done. You look good. But you're right, it's what's inside that matters."

"I agree," he said, stroking her cheek. His thumb was firm and coarse. "It's what connects us. It goes much deeper than skin, doesn't it?"

"Yes," Ellie said again.

He swivelled toward the foot of the bed, shot Neil a look of scorn, then turned back to her. "But I'm appalled at what you did, Ellie. You promised me you wouldn't waste your time. How could you? *Him*, of all people. I'm not sure I'll be able to forgive you for that."

"Listen to me," Ellie said. "Neil and I are over. I wanted to tell you that earlier, but things were so crazy. The thing is, Neil has found someone else ... and he's fallen in love with her. I just discovered it myself. So you see, your timing is perfect ... and I'm grateful you came along. Like it was always meant to be."

"Prove it," he said. "Prove it to me by saying my name. Just tell me my name and everything will be as it should."

She had to get it right. Neil's life was at stake. This was it, her final chance.

What was his fucking name?

She wanted to cry, to scream in frustration, but that would only expose her bluff. She needed to stay calm, to convince him she knew it. Knew him. And that she'd always loved him, ever since they'd first met in that dance club some fifteen years ago.

She strained to recall his name. At the foot of the bed, Neil was quietly sobbing, not struggling anymore, and this gave her a mental kick to try harder. He would die — they both would — if she didn't come through.

Behind her fluttering eyelids, she tried to paint a picture of Andromeda, the sights and sounds of that unsavoury place, that grim, unsettled time. She could see the bouncer, Trevor, with his ham-hock arms and his wide, toothy grin. She could hear his raspy voice as he called out to the bartender, just as he always did. "Hey, Clive, a round of tequilas … Hey, Clive, some champagne for the ladies … Clive, a chilled bottle of vodka over here …"

It was Clive.

His name was Clive.

"I'd never forget you … Clive," Ellie whispered, and the man shed a tear as though his name, uttered by her, was the greatest sound he'd ever heard.

CHAPTER 13

Clive Rutger Brown.

That was the name he'd been given by his mother, Brenda — or "Downtown Brenda Brown," as she'd once been known in the neighbourhood. Brenda had been Clive's sole caregiver from the morning she'd brought him home from the hospital, a red-faced, screaming poop machine with scrawny chicken legs and mangy black hair. So she said. Clive's mom never spoke of her only son in endearing terms, addressing him almost exclusively as "Twerp." She said he didn't deserve his real name because he was so weak, sad, and pathetic.

A boy who looked like a maggot.

Rutger had been her granddaddy's name, and he'd been a sturdy Dutchman with big muscles and waves of golden hair. Nothing like her ugly runt of a son, who would never grow into a *real* man. Never find a woman to love because he wasn't manly or deserving enough.

Still, despite her outward contempt, Clive knew that deep down, Brenda loved him. Knew his absent father was the real source of his mama's pain, her rage, her disapproval of everything Clive ever did. Clive had never met his dad, never laid eyes on him, not even in photographs, and he hoped he never would. Not if it meant hurting his mama. Not if it meant inciting her rage.

But that was the past, and he didn't like to dredge up those rotten memories anymore. He had been hell to raise, after all — a sulky, sickly thing and an embarrassment to the male gender. Which was why she had to go out every night and get wasted at the local bar. Even when he was as young as three, she'd lock him in his sealed-up room and escape to Dewy's for a few stiff drinks. Take the edge off so she would be less inclined to strike him. He'd needed a lot of punishing back then because he was always crying and soiling the place. If he'd been in his mother's shoes, he'd have surely kicked the shit out of him, too.

Then, when Clive was about seven, he figured out how to pick his way out of his room. He followed her to the special place that drew her nightly, creeping along behind her, hiding in the shadows as she toddled ahead in her spiky heels and tight pleather skirt. At the noisy bar on the corner, she ordered herself a double G and T with a twist of lemon, "just to take the edge off."

All those nights, he trailed her, and she was never once the wiser. Never saw his pallid face peering in from the darkness outside. She'd stay on her stool for that first round, then after her third or fourth G and T, she'd be up on her feet, swaying to the music. There must have been music playing, although Clive never heard any through the closed windows. Men would gather around her, chanting, "Brenda, Brenda, Brenda," urging her on. Men with dark circles under bloodshot eyes and pasty, stubbly faces. Ugly men who made him think of his own dad. Self-serving and pathetic. Men undeserving of her.

Fucking twerps.

///////////////////

"I knew you'd remember me, Ellie, I just knew it," Clive said, gazing into the eyes he'd been imagining for so many years. At last, he could see himself reflected in them — the powerful new man he'd become. "I'm going to get you out of here. But first, I have to kill Neil."

Ellie's eyes filled with panic, and her face contorted in a way he didn't like. "No, Clive, no!" she said, trying to rise up. Her wrists still bound, she fell back onto the bed. "Don't kill him, please! It's just … my babies, they need him. He and I, we're finished, like I said. But in order for me to be with you, to be free of my past, I need Neil alive … so he can take care of my babies. Don't you see? I couldn't be happy, not ever, Clive, unless you let him live."

Clive had actually forgotten about the kids, the boy and girl off at some sleepaway camp, and the very mention of them right now irritated him. He hadn't factored them into his plan — it was quite a big oversight, actually. He knew how important parents were to a kid, the mother especially. He'd loved his own mom desperately, and his heart ached with sadness just imagining his younger self without her. Clive's mother had often told him that orphanages were terrible, loveless places. No child, no matter how horrid, should have to go to such a place.

But really, did Ellie take him for an idiot? Whether or not Neil was in love with another woman, he'd be bound to come looking for them. Bound to call the police and get his revenge for the finger and toe he'd lost. Besides, Neil was supposed to die. Killing him had always been part of the plan. It had been Clive's driving purpose since the moment that had sparked it all.

"You're lying to me."

"No, I'm not lying, Clive. I swear to you, Neil wants out of this marriage, and so do I. Please, you have to trust me. Just leave him here, tied to the chair, and I will come with you. Then we'll be together — the way it should be, right? I mean, someone needs to stay with my kids ... I couldn't bear to know they were out there, uncared for. I couldn't be happy with you. Do you understand me, Clive? Do you?"

///////////////////////

Neil could barely stand what he was hearing. It was all he could do to contain his distress, his guilt over the fact that he'd cheated on the woman he wanted more than anything to protect. And the fact that she knew. Yet here she was, trying to protect *him*, using his infidelity as a means to save his life. It was the worst torture he'd ever endured. Worse than the blade severing his toe and his finger.

Who was this lunatic, Clive, and how did he know Ellie? Neil had never met him, he was damn certain of that. But then again, the way Clive looked at him with such intensity, hatred practically boring through Neil's skin, got him wondering if there was more to this bizarre reunion than Clive was letting on. Perhaps Neil had done something to trigger the man's revenge. But what? His adult life had been nothing but a blur of mundane duties at home and at work. He'd had no encounters with sketchy outsiders aside from the occasional oddball he'd meet at some industry event. He simply couldn't fathom Clive's motive, other than sheer psychotic delusion.

For some reason, he got the sense that Clive was someone Ellie had known from that dance club, Andromeda, where they'd met in 2004. He'd set foot in that place only once. Whoever Clive was, he clearly had a sick infatuation for Ellie, and now she was playing along, pretending she loved him back. This made Neil desperately afraid, as he knew it would likely lead to terrible consequences. Maybe even worse than their current situation, if that were possible. Neil had been quietly grinding away at the cable ties with the cracked edge of the chair leg. He had to get free, had to stab this psycho fucker through the heart before he laid another finger on Ellie.

"Okay," Clive said. "For your kids' sake, I'll grant your wish. Even though he deserves to die for what he did, for hurting you and destroying your family, I'm going to let him live. Your children shouldn't be sent to some filthy orphanage or foster home. That wouldn't be right."

"Thank you, Clive, thank you," Ellie gasped, her voice so hoarse and distorted by phlegm that Neil barely recognized it.

"Now, don't move," Clive instructed her. "I'm going to cut your restraints."

Neil heard Ellie suck in her breath, then the blade slicing through the cable ties one at a time — *pop, pop, pop, pop.* A wave of relief that she was finally free washed through him; she might actually get out of this room alive.

Suddenly, Clive appeared, standing over top of him. He was gripping the blood-streaked knife, and Neil saw untapped madness in his eyes — madness that he'd yet to unleash. Neil's hope turned to dread. With his own eyes, he tried to plead with Clive to let Ellie go, but the man looked away.

"Let's get out of here, Ellie. I've got everything planned, everything you need ..."

At that moment, Ellie's feet swung over the mattress, and for the first time since he'd left for the grocery store earlier that day, Neil and Ellie made eye contact. Still lying sideways in a pool of his own blood, Neil craned his neck and let out a series of muffled cries. He prayed that she understood what he was trying to tell her: that he loved her and was coming for her.

//////////////////////

Ellie emerged into a long, bright hallway. She figured at least three hours had passed since Clive had grabbed her, so it had to be around 8:00 or 9:00 p.m.

Taking her by the hand, Clive led her to the washroom, a spacious room with a skylight that she would have drooled over at another time. He nudged her inside.

"I've left some things in there for you — new clothes and hair dye. I'd like it cut shorter, too." He reached out and drew a line at the base of her neck, a few inches below her chin.

Ellie went into the washroom and locked the door. She sank to the floor and unleashed a flood of silent tears. *Everything will be okay*, she told herself. *Neil is alive.* She just needed to figure out a way for them to escape.

Somehow she would wrangle the knife away from Clive, stab him where it counted, then run like hell. As the saying went, "where there's a will, there's a way," and she damn well had the will.

Ellie looked up at the skylight, briefly considered the two-storey drop from the roof, and dismissed the idea. If she attempted to flee, Clive would kill Neil in retaliation. No, she needed to be patient. Pick the right moment. Gain his trust and wait for her best chance to grab the knife.

Wiping her tears away, she got to her feet. Next to the sink was a plastic bag and a pair of red slingback kitten heels, used. She dumped the contents of the bag out onto the antique vanity: cheap blue eyeshadow, hot-pink lipstick, a box of hair dye, and dull pair of scissors. Hanging from the shower curtain rod was a gaudy red top and a stretch-polyester miniskirt. Stereotypical hooker garb.

There was a rap on the door. "Get moving," Clive said.

Ellie raised her middle finger and thrust it at the door, then stood up and got to work chopping off and dyeing her hair. The name of the shade was Sandy Dusk, and according to the package, the process was as easy as one, two, three.

Midway through her transformation, there was another knock. "Everything okay in there?"

"Almost done," she said, amazed at how steady her voice sounded.

But then, as she started to remove her pajamas — she was naked beneath them — it occurred to her that there would be nothing between her and the skin-tight outfit he was forcing her to wear. Panic overwhelmed her. A horrific flash of things to come. The room began to weave as she fought to stay calm.

Inhaling and exhaling in slow deliberate breaths, she eventually managed to regain a modicum of control, just enough to struggle into the garments that gripped her every curve. But it was the makeup that altered her appearance the most profoundly, colours so garish she barely recognized her own reflection.

Repulsed by her appearance, and feeling a swell of hatred for this man claiming to be her soulmate, she picked up the scissors and slid them into the elastic waistband of her skirt, then hesitated. *No, no, too obvious.* The man was insane, but he wasn't stupid.

Clive was standing guard when she emerged. He grew starry-eyed at the sight of her. "There she is … there's my girl." He let out a long breath and reached to touch her hair, to caress a loose wet lock between his fingers. "You're here. You're really here."

Ellie didn't move or speak. Clive's intense emotional reaction to her transformation had caught her off guard. It made her realize something: that the scanty clothes, short hair, and brash makeup weren't just an arbitrary disguise. No, it was a deliberate attempt to make her look like someone — someone he had loved.

"You don't mind if I search you for those scissors, do you?"

"The scissors are right there," she said promptly, pointing to the sink.

"Good girl." Clive smiled. "Now, I hate to rush you, but we'd better get a move on before someone comes looking for the poor old Palmers. After you." He shoved her with the handle of his knife.

Ellie hobbled down the carpeted steps, her feet already aching in the tight shoes. The house was big, but not an open concept design like theirs, so she couldn't see anything beyond the hallway that led to the front door. At the entrance was a shaggy welcome mat embroidered with a loon, and next to it, a vintage brass umbrella rack. It looked heavy, with real skull-damaging potential, but she knew it would be too cumbersome to pick up and heave on the fly.

"Stop," Clive ordered, his fingers digging into the back of her neck. "Let me go first to make sure the coast is clear." With his free hand, he unlocked and yanked open the door. He quickly scanned the property before pulling her outside.

Ellie stumbled out into the humid air. The sun had all but set, and the sounds of lapping water and buzzing insects were briefly comforting as Clive hustled her toward the garage. The side door was flanked by a pair of sandbags. He pulled it open, turned on the light, and pushed her into the cool, musty room. Two vehicles were parked inside — a dark-blue vintage Jaguar and a black Mazda6.

Clive indicated the Mazda. "Get in and buckle up. I'll be right back. Don't get out of the car, or I'll have to kill you."

He switched off the light as he went out the door, and a moment later, she was alone in the darkness. Her own heavy panting reverberated around her. She took hold of the door latch, then paused. *Is this some sort of test? A trap?* She listened but she couldn't hear anything beyond her own breathing. When she was certain he was out of earshot, she creaked open the door to turn on the dome lights.

The room was damp, but clean. Immaculate, like the main house. Ellie took her chance, slipping out of the Mazda to creep back over to the side door. She turned the knob and gently pushed it. It didn't open — something was blocking it. Likely that pair of sandbags. She edged toward the base of the garage doors and tugged at the handles, but neither would budge. Her last resort was to find a heavy tool like a shovel or a tire iron that she could crack over his head. But there was nothing. Not even a goddamn garden hose.

She froze as heavy footsteps approached, dashing back to the Mazda and closing her door just as the automatic garage door slid open. Clive stomped in, sweating and puffing. Ellie was too wound up to try to ascertain why. Instead, she scrambled to fasten her seatbelt as he sparked the engine and they made off down the driveway onto the secluded country road.

Then, as they rounded the last corner of the tree-choked embankment, and the Palmers' grey house disappeared from sight, she asked in a quiet voice, "Where are you taking me, Clive?"

He didn't answer.

///////////////////

Neil was frantically thrashing in his chair when he heard the front door slam, followed by a flurry of footsteps retreating into silence. Desperate to stop Clive, he threw himself against the wall with all the force he could muster. Neil heard the sweet sound of triumph as the leg of the chair cracked and snapped off at its base. Finally, he was able to wrestle his hands free. He knew the left one wouldn't be pretty, but aesthetics didn't matter. He tore at the tape securing the blood-soaked towel in place and prepared to face the carnage.

Then Neil heard another sound: an automatic garage door opening. Frantically, he struggled to free himself, but he couldn't shed his bindings completely. With most of the chair still dragging behind him, he half crawled, half pulled himself over to the window, just as a shiny black sedan was leaving the driveway.

That was when he smelled it: gasoline. And smoke.

Reeling in pain, he somehow pulled himself over to the door and pressed his good hand to the lower panel. It was hot to the touch. Beyond it, he could hear the pop and sizzle of fire.

Cautiously, he reached up and opened the door. The hallway was a blazing inferno. The staircase was engulfed in flames. There was no escape.

PART TWO

SHOW ME YOU LOVE ME

CHAPTER 14

Over the past twenty-nine years, Bethany had never been so present in Ellie's head as she had been since Clive had taken her. Now those few cherished memories of her long-dead sister replayed themselves like videos stuck on repeat.

"Come on, Ellie, I know you can do it!" Bethany yelled. Her muscular thighs poked out from pale-pink gym shorts as she squatted next the hula hoop, smiling encouragingly at Ellie, who was unconvinced. "Believe in yourself, see it through, and then make it so."

Ellie took a shaky breath and closed her eyes. Once she felt calm and centred, she reopened them, hauled back her foot, and readied herself to take the shot. But visions of failure infected her brain, upending her confidence and making her hesitate for a third time.

Noting Ellie's reluctance, Bethany sighed and jogged over. She never went anywhere at a leisurely pace — it was either half or full throttle. "Listen to me," she said, looking Ellie square in the eye. "Quit thinking about missing the shot and start thinking about *making* it. Come on, now, believe in yourself. Winning is a head game, and right now you're losing it. Just focus and remember what I told you: control the outcome or the outcome will control you ..."

//////////////////////

Clive's meaty paw came down on Ellie's bare thigh, snapping her to attention as the car flew down the dark two-lane road. Of course, she knew he'd only get more adventurous, let those festering impulses free to wander. But she also knew she needed to stay calm. Maintain awareness. Watch and listen. *Control the outcome ...*

As long as she played her part well, convinced Clive that she was whatever he wanted her to be — his soulmate, his fantasy, his prostitute (judging by the gaudy way he'd dressed her) — he'd relax, loosen the reins. The car would need gas eventually. He'd have to get out to refuel. And when he did, he'd have to leave the chef's knife behind in the car with her, wouldn't he?

Or perhaps he'd opt to take her into the kiosk with him, at which point she could signal to the clerk that she needed help, and they would alert the police. However the night unfolded, she'd find a way out. This much, she believed.

But then, as they drove farther and Clive became quieter, Ellie's feeling of hopelessness crept back. She began to wonder how Clive had reached this level of delusion, how he'd leapt from petty drug dealing to severing digits and murdering senior citizens all in the span of twelve years. He'd been a bartender at a thriving downtown club once, which meant that he'd been stable enough to hold down a job. When had he turned so violent?

Since leaving Maplewood, something about Clive's demeanour had changed. His breathing grew heavier, and he seemed disengaged. All the posturing and taunting, the disturbing professions of love, had ceased. Now he was driving as if on autopilot. His eyes were fixed straight ahead, but mentally, he was elsewhere.

Ellie found this quiet version of her captor more distressing than the swaggering loudmouth he'd been at the Palmers', but she had to break the silence and speak to him. Dig for whatever information she could get. There was something more to this fucked-up story than he was letting on. This didn't feel like a cut-and-dried case of infatuation — or at least that's what her instincts told her. Was it possible Clive's motivation was rooted in something else? Something deeper than his lust?

"So, what have you been up to all these years?" she asked, her voice thin, shaky.

But Clive didn't seem to hear the question. He stared at the road ahead as though he were the only one in the car.

"You said you were in prison. That must have been awful," she persisted, this time stealing a glance at his profile. It was the first time she'd dared to look at him since they'd peeled out of the garage. But even her gaze was ineffectual; Clive remained oblivious.

She noticed something on his arm, a tattoo of some kind. Words, possibly a name written in curvy black ink. Beneath it, a series of numbers. Dates, maybe.

"Well, I'm sorry about what happened to you," she said. "If you want to talk about it, I'm a good listener."

Finally Clive turned to her with acutely threatening eyes. "That's a part of my life I don't talk about. Never bring it up again, do you hear me?"

Ellie nodded, turned back to the road. Its ghost-white surface unfolded into the stark curtain of darkness. She wondered how she was going to get a hold of that knife.

//////////////////

When Neil came to, dizzy and nauseated, he was lying flat on his back under impossibly bright lights. Everything hurt, yet he couldn't distinguish single injuries through the haze of sheer pain. His brain felt swollen, like it was pressing against the sides of his skull. His thoughts were confused and disjointed. Then it all came flooding back like a nightmare.

"Neil, is it?" a woman's voice said. Crisp, loud, forceful. "I'm Detective Flora Fitzgerald of the Ontario Police Department."

"My wife, Eloise," Neil said, wincing. "He's taken her."

"Who's taken her?"

He struggled to sit up, but could only manage with difficulty to prop himself up on his elbows. He was in a hospital room. The detective was a tiny birdlike woman with tufts of brown hair framing her long, angular face. She looked like someone's meek aunt, or an insurance auditor. Not what he'd expected from the strong projection of her voice.

"His name is Clive. He took her ... from our cottage," Neil wheezed. "He tied her to the bed, tied me to a chair. Said he knew her ... from the past."

"Do you know this man?"

"No. He made us play a sick sort of game. He wanted to make her say his name ... but she couldn't remember him. He'd had surgery, I think ... changed his face. Said that if she guessed wrong, he'd cut off one of my fingers or toes."

"I take it she answered wrong a couple of times," Fitzgerald said.

Neil was in no mood for her facetious remarks. He desperately wanted to get up and start searching for his wife himself, but he was wrapped virtually head to toe in gauze, and he could tell that any sudden movement he made would cause the bitter contents of his stomach to project out onto the floor. It felt like he'd broken a few ribs in his fall from the window, too.

"Look, the man is a psychopath. I only know that his name was Clive. I don't know where he's taken her, but we need to find her. She is in grave danger. He's delusional. He wants her to be, you know, in love with him. She's playing along so he won't kill her."

"We're doing what we can, sir. In the meantime I need you to stay calm. First, give me a description of your wife and this Clive fellow. Then go back and tell me everything, from the moment you first laid eyes on him to the moment you called 911. Can you do that for me?"

Fitzgerald did sound helpful now, even empathetic.

"Yes," Neil said, leaning back gingerly and closing his eyes to curtail the nausea. "I can do that."

Over the course of the next hour, he relayed everything he could remember, in painstaking detail, about the man Clive. He began his account with Ellie's encounter with "Jake" in the woods, when, believing he was the neighbour, she'd politely invited him for dinner. Neil described him as mild-mannered and friendly, about fifty, good-looking, with a striking resemblance to George Clooney. In retrospect, he'd been the antithesis of the neighbour they'd been warned about. Neil's throat constricted with regret that he hadn't caught on to the deception as it was happening.

His voice cracked as he tried to carry on, his mind flooded by visions of Ellie being forced to do terrible things. He thought about the pained sense of betrayal his wife must have been feeling right before Clive had abducted her. He was overwhelmed by guilt and shame. All he wanted to do was to get up and run.

To find Ellie.

Flora Fitzgerald waited in silence for Neil to compose himself. She was usually pretty good with this sort of thing, taking victim statements. But this man's statement was a tough one to follow — and to swallow. Things like what he was describing just didn't happen in her quiet, picture-perfect jurisdiction. No, here there would be the occasional drowning, seasonal coyote sightings, and the odd missing lapdog, but never a double homicide by a suspect bearing a striking resemblance to a celebrity twice named Sexiest Man Alive by *People* magazine. More than once, she'd actively resisted the urge to shake her head.

"So, you think this Clive may have known your wife from her mid to late twenties, maybe from that dance club you mentioned, Andromeda?"

She scribbled down the name of the club in her notepad, then added, *staff list 2000 to 2005?*

"That would be my best guess," Neil said, glancing at the door.

He looked agitated, and Flora wondered if he could use a hit of sedative. Given his intense pain, it was unlikely he'd be able to flee in his condition, but she got the sense that Neil Patterson wanted to be anywhere but here. "And he also told you he'd been in prison. Did he indicate when, or for what?"

"No," he replied, cringing as he rearranged himself on the bed. "But it was after the last time Ellie saw him … which would have been around 2004, I guess. He also mentioned something about his new and improved mug attracting unwanted attention in prison, so it must have been soon after he'd had his surgery."

"Hmm. A convicted criminal." Flora made note of this detail. "And what about you, your marriage? How are things between you and Ellie?"

"Great … fine," Neil said. "I mean, we've been

married nearly ten years. Don't all marriages have their ups and downs?"

Flora peered at him. She tapped her ballpoint pen and said, "Never been married myself, but that's the impression I get."

Neil didn't respond. The pallor of his face suggested that he was swept up in a powerful wave of nausea or pain.

Figuring she'd probably questioned him long enough for now, Flora got to her feet. "You've given me two great leads here. I want you to get some rest while I head back to the station and do some digging. I'll check in with you in a few hours."

"But there are police out there looking for them now, right? They're searching the roads and highways for that black car I saw?"

"Of course, we're doing everything we can," she said. "We've also notified Camp Metawe of the situation. Your kids are safe. They're out-tripping on some island at the moment, but you can rest assured, they're protected."

Neil thanked her. She strode toward the door and paused to glance back at him.

"Don't worry, Mr. Patterson, we'll find your wife."

CHAPTER 15

Neil and Ellie had been dating for nearly two weeks when she'd invited him to her sister's wedding. He'd been so nervous to meet her family, particularly the imperious bride, but seeing the groom at the altar had lessened that anxiousness. Rather, it was a *mandap*, a structure of pillars draped in lilies and other ceremonial florals. Beneath it, Abeer had radiated pure calm.

In the twelve years since, Neil had grown steadily fonder of his one and only brother-in-law. They related well. Shared a dry sense of humour, a nerdy fascination with electronics, and a trust. That was why Abeer was the person Neil called the second Fitzgerald's footsteps petered off down the corridor.

Abeer was silent as Neil apprised him of the situation over the phone — that Ellie had been kidnapped, that he was in hospital, and that the police were actively pursuing the perpetrator. There was no need to ask if he would make the two-hour drive up to Maplewood; he could hear Abeer in furious motion already, racing about to collect his wallet, his keys. Neil asked him to head to the cottage first to feed Hamish and let him out, then to swing back to the hospital in Maplewood with Neil's cellphone and a change of clothes. He also tasked Abeer with the most difficult job of all: informing Laura and her parents of what had happened.

After he'd finished the call, Neil looked at the time. It was 10:48 p.m. Abeer wouldn't be there for at least three hours. The wait would feel like an eternity — and Ellie didn't have an eternity. Neil untangled himself from the various restraints securing him to his bed and attempted to stand up for the first time since he'd been tortured. He had a number of injuries, but at least he hadn't shattered his femurs dropping from the second floor.

He limped over to the door, pain sweeping through him, cracked it open, and peered out at the long, brightly lit corridor. It was quiet but for the small blips emitted by unseen monitoring machines. *Where is everyone?*

Sure, it was Sunday night in a small community hospital, but still, the lack of personnel was alarming. Then Neil noticed that the nurse's station was empty. His eyes lit up. The computer was calling out to him. It would take some effort to get to, but that didn't matter. Neil just wanted to get on the internet, if only for a minute, so he could jump-start his research on this Clive freak. Someone would know something — he was certain of that. Clive had a history of violence, and at some point his history had intersected with Ellie's. With the right keyword search, Neil might uncover some nugget of information. He knew it wasn't his job to do the uncovering, but every neuron in his being was screaming at him to take action.

Ellie needed him. He'd already let her down once. He'd never do that again.

//////////////////

They'd been avoiding major highways, sticking to back roads, driving in and out of sleepy towns that each bore an uncanny resemblance to the one before it. Ellie wished desperately that she were caught in a dream. An awful recurring nightmare. Unfortunately, she knew better. All this was really happening — she was wide awake and in a living hell.

She closed her eyes and wondered where Neil was at that very moment. Had he escaped that chair and phoned the police? If so, then the police would be honing in on her whereabouts right now. She just needed to hang on and stay in character.

For the most part, she'd been watching the road since the start, scanning for landmarks and familiar sights, people she might make eye contact with. But so far she hadn't seen anything in the dark, rambling countryside. Not a single soul.

They reached a town that felt strangely familiar and it took Ellie a moment to figure out why. Then she remembered. She and Neil had just driven through it a few days earlier, after dropping the kids off at summer camp.

It was the small town of Rockdale, Ontario.

Clive was beginning to twitch and grunt, showing signs of mounting agitation as they coasted past the quaint brick buildings of Main Street. Storefronts were set well back from sidewalks trimmed with flowerpots and cast-iron street lamps. Mom-and-pop shops were ensconced under pretty awnings, and there was not a single recognizable chain store. As they reached the far end of town, things got noticeably seedier. That was when Clive turned to her and mumbled, "Almost there."

Ellie felt sick, knowing the drive was coming to an end. If only there were someone she could lock eyes with, anyone at all. But there was no one around. Just them. Theirs was the sole vehicle meandering through a town that looked uninhabited. Clive took a sharp corner onto an unmarked side road, then another left into an alleyway. At the end of the alley stood a ramshackle garage, its bent metal door jammed permanently open. He eased the car inside and switched off the engine.

"Stay where you are. I'll come get you out," he said.

Ellie couldn't have disobeyed him even if she'd wanted to. Her legs had gone numb. In fact, she couldn't feel anything from the neck down. As long as they were in the car, strapped into their respective seats, she was mostly safe from his hands, his desire. But once they got out and were concealed from the rest of the world, there was no telling what he'd do.

She watched, her heart racing, as Clive came around the front of the car and unlatched her door. He put his hand out, and Ellie had no choice but to accept it. He yanked her to her feet. She forgot about the kitten heels and stumbled into him. Triggered by the sudden contact, his body seemed to tighten into a myriad of tiny knots, and Ellie shivered.

She stepped away, found her balance. Fought to contain her tears. She could smell rot and mildew, garbage and paint thinner. The combination of awful odours almost made her retch.

Then Clive looked at her and said something that sickened her even more. "Baby … we're home."

///////////////////////

Neil and Ellie had been newlyweds when they purchased their first home together, a narrow brick townhouse in one of Toronto's less reputable neighbourhoods.

A shoebox with potential.

And lucky for Ellie, Neil was handy, as good with a wrench as he was with a processor. By day, a computer technician at a large engineering firm. By night, a carpenter, plumber, painter, interior designer. Anything she needed him to be, all bundled into one dashing package.

One night she had found him stretched out under the kitchen sink, fiddling with the drainpipe. The muscles of his bare abdomen rippled in a way that quickened her pulse.

"I thought plumbers were supposed to be flabby and hairy," she said, admiring his physique. "You're going to give me warped fantasies, buddy."

"If plumbers are your thing, I'll play along." Neil flashed her his legendary grin, his teeth clamped together in perfect symmetry. Then he rolled over onto his hands and knees to reveal an exposed ass crack.

"Oh, baby, look at that crack," Ellie purred, joining him on the floor. The ceramic tiles were cold and hard, but she didn't care. She couldn't wait to get naked, to peel off all her clothes and feel Neil's hands all over her body, his tongue tracing over her neck, her breasts, between her parted legs. She couldn't wait for him to thrust inside her, to slam her against those cold, hard tiles and make her explode with blinding pleasure.

They could never have guessed that nearly nine and a half months later, baby Bethany would be born almost in that exact spot.

Ellie's labour had come on so quickly in the middle of the night that there wasn't time to get to the hospital. She'd awoken in splitting pain, her swollen body wrenching apart from within. Lying down was impossible. The only position she could tolerate was standing up, gripping Neil's shoulders, with her head pushed against his chest as she moaned along with the escalating surges of agony. Her daughter's head crowned, revealing a mass of dark, gooey hair.

Neil had somehow extracted himself from her death grip just long enough to call an ambulance. His voice was steady. *Too steady*, she remembered thinking, angered all of a sudden that he and all his kind were spared such ravaging pain. But by the time the paramedics arrived, he'd already done most of the delivery himself. She'd never forget his pale face, the tears of joy he'd cried when baby Bethany — known thereafter as Beth — was swaddled in his arms. Her head a little misshapen, but healthy. That had been the most traumatic, painful hour of Ellie's life, and it could easily have ended with her hemorrhaging to death. In fact, she believed wholeheartedly that if Neil hadn't been there to help her through that extraordinary labour, she wouldn't have survived.

She still remembered that little house in full sensory detail: the scented candles they'd kept stored in the pine hutch, the texture of the Moroccan carpet in the front hall, the warm glow cast by her grandmother's antique stained-glass lamp, the feeling of Neil's arm around her as they lay entwined on the couch, listening to their sleeping daughter's breaths ...

//////////////////////

"So, what do you think?" Clive asked. "Needs some fixing up, I know, but it'll be fine for now."

He was dragging her up a crumbling walkway to a rundown bungalow with boarded windows and a weed-infested lawn.

"Looks nice," she lied, her eyes stinging and her throat so parched it hurt. This was the point of no return, being locked up in some filthy hellhole with Clive. Her new home, as he'd put it. She knew that once she walked over that threshold, she'd be trapped. Trapped and at his disposal, and then her nightmare would only worsen.

No, she couldn't let him take her inside. She had to think of a way out. To manipulate him somehow …

As Clive was rummaging for his key, Ellie wracked her brain for any stall tactic that might divert them from going inside. He'd shown a touch of gallantry in the garage just a moment ago, so Ellie decided to appeal to his chivalrous side.

"Hey, is there a bar around here? I'd really like a drink. You know, to take the edge off."

/////////////////////

To take the edge off.

Ellie's words drilled deep into Clive's mind, delivering a sweet reminder of the past. A flash of his mother's painted face, the scent of her gin-tinged breath. Yes, he knew women needed to do that from time to time — *take the edge off* — yet something nagged at him. Something told him to proceed with caution.

The idea of going to Dewy's did excite him. It would give him the chance to show off his new woman, make them see that he wasn't just some pathetic twerp, some loser. But he wasn't sure that he could trust her. Not yet. Not without the constant threat of the knife. What if she screamed or tried to run? Did she fully understand that they were reunited now, kindred spirits, together forever?

Clive hadn't been down to that old bar in ages, not since his early twenties. Back then, no one had shown him any respect. Always whispering his mother's name — "Brenda, Brenda, Brenda" — when all he wanted was a cold pint and some peace and quiet. That asshole of a bartender, Dewy's son, Randy, was the worst. "Hi, Clive, how's your mother?" he'd ask innocently, then cough "tramp" behind his hand like Clive wasn't smart enough to pick up on it.

Of course, all the old regulars would chuckle at his expense. But if they only knew what Clive had seen with his own eyes. Randy bending his mom over a broken table in the storeroom. Randy grunting and slapping her behind as he rode her like some filthy pig. Some worthless whore. He would have done something to stop it, would have ripped the man off her and beat the living shit out of him, had he not locked eyes with his mom and seen her desire, her silent calling out for more.

"I'd like to take you for a drink, but how can I be sure you're not going to try anything stupid?" he asked Ellie, holding up the knife so she could see it. "I mean, just a few hours ago you were trying to save Neil. You were hardly being co-operative."

"I promise, I'll do everything you say. I'm just feeling a little tense, that's all," she said. "All I want is a drink to calm myself. I think it'll help … help me make this night a little more special for us."

Clive smiled at that. He took her chin in his hand and said, "Okay, I'll trust you. But just to be sure we're on the same page here, remember … if you do or say anything to make me doubt you, I will hurt you in ways you never even thought possible. I don't want to, but I will."

"I won't let you down, Clive. I'm yours now, remember?"

Then she kissed him, a soft girlish kiss on the lips. The dark behind his eyelids lit up with colours so bright, it was as though the whole universe had exploded around him.

CHAPTER 16

Neil was halfway to the empty computer station when he heard a deluge of voices coming from down the hall. Cameras clicking. Shouted questions. A faint description of someone's injuries. It was a press conference being held somewhere on this floor. He strained to listen but didn't move any closer, knowing that if he were spotted, he'd be sent back to bed.

Then, rising sharply out of the commotion, came his name ... Ellie's name, and the Palmers ... and it occurred to him all at once that the press conference was about *them*. Of course — a retired couple had been murdered on their lavish country estate. A woman had been kidnapped, a house set on fire. The man who was the only witness to it all had been butchered and hospitalized.

This was big stuff.

He retreated to his room full of worry. Things were about to change; he was about to be the centrepiece of a media frenzy that he wanted nothing to do with. He thought about Detective Fitzgerald, the way she'd inquired about their marriage. Jotted her notes. Probed and pried. Judged.

Suddenly Neil felt trapped. Anxious about Mia and the text messages she'd sent. Mad at himself for holding back what might have been pertinent information. His mind raced as the severity of the situation sunk in. The intimate details of their lives, his past mistakes, conjecture about what really happened — the world was going to devour it all like some ratings-driven soap opera.

On impulse, Neil hobbled to the closet, stripped off his hospital gown, and struggled back into his smoky, blood-splattered clothes. He needed to get outside, to escape the reporters, the doctors, the detectives. Find a quiet place to hole up and think. Figure out how he was going to track down this Clive motherfucker and kill him.

////////////////////

Flora took a sip of hot coffee, then spat it all over her desk. It was scalding, and her mouth burned. She hated when that happened — she wouldn't be able to taste right for days.

It was getting late, almost 11:00 p.m., and this Patterson woman was missing, allegedly held captive by some highly disturbed individual. By the husband's estimation, they'd left the Palmer house in a newish black sedan sometime before 9:00 p.m., but her officers had yet to spot a vehicle like it carrying passengers that matched their descriptions.

In the meantime, all they had to go on was his first name —presumably Clive, but who really knew? Beyond that, it seemed he'd either worked at or frequented the Toronto night club Andromeda in the early 2000s. According to her research, the club shut down in 2005. It had been a hotbed of illegal activity, but ultimately it was a Fire Code violation that forced its closure.

The former owner, a guy by the name of Andrew Muir, had since relocated to Miami and opened a new spot called Club Vibe. She'd managed to dig up a listing for this Muir guy and left him a message asking that he call her back, but so far the man had yet to comply.

Flora blew on her coffee as she considered everything she knew about Patterson. There was something fishy about his behaviour, and she wondered whether he'd been honest with her. It was unusual for her gut response to be so conflicted. The reality was that most cases involving a husband and wife ended up with one of them in handcuffs. But something told her this guy was innocent. Aside from the fact that he'd been bound and tortured, Neil Patterson oozed sincerity and genuine despair.

Yet still, his story bothered her: a vicious psychopath had murdered a pair of helpless seniors, assaulted and threatened a husband and wife, butchered the husband, kidnapped the wife, then set fire to the house so he could vanish with his captive and live happily ever after. Of course, a scenario that was easier to believe was that Neil had killed his wife in cold blood, chopped off his own digits, and lit that fire himself. Maybe the Palmers had witnessed his unchecked temper, so they had needed to be dealt with, too. However, his injuries had looked bad. *Too bad to be self-inflicted*, she thought.

It would be a while before the charred remains of the house were fully scoured and analyzed, before the forensics report came in. Until then, they'd have to go on Neil's word.

"Hey, Murray!" she bellowed at the young officer who'd been first on the scene. "Did we get a trace on those fingerprints yet?"

As luck would have it, they'd been able to lift a clean set of prints from the garage door handle.

"Not yet," Officer Murray said. "Gimme ten minutes."

"Sure," she muttered.

It was also lucky that Neil had had a picture of his wife in his wallet. Flora had retrieved it from his pants pocket in his hospital room. Now she looked at the image of the grinning mother of two. Though she hadn't handled many cases like this one before, she did know that every second mattered.

////////////////////

The scene at the small community hospital was not at all what Abeer had expected. It was as though he'd stumbled onto the set of a Hollywood movie. There were camera crews camped outside, reporters milling about, all of them staring at their cellphone screens.

As he entered the parking lot, the herd perked up. But their heads went down again; apparently his brown skin didn't betray his familial connection to the victims. He parked in a free stall without anyone noticing. The sight of the media circus was jarring, made him grateful he'd left Laura at Neil and Ellie's cottage to tend to the dog. She'd been close to hysterical on the car ride up. Encountering this swarm of badgering reporters surely would have pushed her over the edge.

Abeer turned off the engine, opened the door, and was about to step outside when his eye caught a figure emerging from the shadows.

"Don't move, I'm getting in."

It was Neil, his voice raw and frantic.

Abeer stared at Neil, stunned. He knew his brother-in-law had been badly roughed up, but the man in front of him looked like a character from a postapocalyptic zombie film. There was a black-orange lump the size of a clementine on his head, and his shirt was coated in soot and dried blood. A splint and a swath of dressing covered his left hand, a similar set-up on his foot. And those were just the visible injuries. Abeer suspected that beneath all the external wounds were psychological ones that hadn't yet been addressed.

"What are you doing out here? Why aren't you in bed?"

Neil crouched down next to Abeer. "Listen to me," he said, wild-eyed, "that man is going to hurt Ellie, I'm sure of it. I've got to find her. The police ... I get the feeling they think I did this, that I started that fire and made Clive up. They're going to waste time and resources investigating me. So we need to look for her ourselves. I haven't been arrested, so they have no right to detain me."

Abeer sighed. He was deeply concerned for Ellie, but interfering with the law seemed like a bad decision. "I understand, brother, but think about it this way. If you vanish from the hospital in the middle of the night, it might convince them that you're involved. There'll be an outright manhunt for you."

"I know the risk," Neil said. "But Ellie needs me. Imagine if some lunatic drove off with Laura. And you knew he was going to hurt her ... likely even kill her."

Abeer considered Laura and all she'd been through before they met — Bethany's death, years of drug abuse and reckless debauchery, the downward spiral of self-destruction she'd barely survived. The death of yet another sibling would surely cause a relapse.

"Fine, get in. Where do you want to go? Back to the cottage?"

"No. Just drive, I'll think of something."

Abeer nodded reluctantly, sparked up the engine, and tried his best to dismiss the nagging thought that they were making a terrible mistake.

///////////////////

Ten minutes to the second after Murray had promised it, Flora was staring at her primary suspect's mug shot. She had to admit, the man did look uncannily similar to Clooney, so Neil hadn't been lying about that, at least.

According to his police record, Clive Berringer was a fifty-year-old Caucasian male who'd been convicted of high-level drug trafficking in late 2004 while employed as a bartender at Andromeda. He'd been sentenced to twelve years in prison and was released this past May. Then, strangely, all traces of the man ended there. No address, no phone listing, no employment record. No credit info. It was as though Clive Berringer had ceased to exist the moment he'd stepped out of prison a free man.

Flora felt deflated. She'd gone from red hot to tepid in less time than it had taken for her damn coffee to cool. She reached for her mug and gulped some down, ignoring its objectionable flavour with some effort.

Her cellphone rattled and she jumped to answer it. Hopefully it was that Muir guy calling her back from Miami.

"Detective Fitzgerald," she said.

"Hi, this is Ms. Berningham from Maplewood Memorial Hospital. I'm calling to notify you that the patient Neil Patterson … well, he's gone."

"He checked out?"

"No, not exactly. He just up and left the hospital without telling anyone. Must have gone out the back way."

"Well, fuck a duck," Flora said.

Clive held Ellie's hand as they strode down Main Street toward his mom's old haunt, Dewy's. He felt scared, but also excited, his mind in two places at once. But that was normal for him. Sometimes he had flashbacks that felt so real, so vivid, he wasn't sure if he was in the past or the present.

For instance, at that moment he could see his mother toddling ahead in her high-heeled shoes, her tight skirt stretched over her curvaceous ass. He could smell her perfume mixed with a hint of her shampoo. She stopped. Rummaged through her purse. Pulled out a cigarette and lit it under the yellow glow of the street lamp. Then she carried on walking, inhaling and releasing the smoke in a slow, seductive trickle. The legs of her shadow stretched twice their true length in the dusk.

Clive knew Ellie couldn't see what he saw — that these visits were meant solely for him. He desperately wanted to catch up with his mother, but Ellie was walking funny, like her shoes didn't fit. Anyway, they'd all be at Dewy's in just a few minutes. They'd have a drink so Ellie could take the edge off. And he'd show the others what a man he'd become.

////////////////////

Randy was getting ready to close up shop when he heard the jingle of the bell that alerted him, gratingly, to every departure and arrival. A *late* arrival, which was unusual for a Sunday night in Rockdale. Dewy's was the only watering hole this side of town, but still, not too many ventured out past eleven anymore, not like the good old days.

He finished putting away the clean glasses, then he turned to face the newcomers, a hulking beefcake packed into coveralls and a scantily clad woman in heels. The sight of the woman startled him. She reminded him of someone he used to know. The sandy hair, the skimpy outfit. Downtown Brenda Brown was her nickname.

Back in the seventies and eighties, she used to come in almost nightly to get her drink on. She was quite a scrumptious little package, at least in the early years, Randy recalled. But everyone knew she was nasty to the core, like her insides were rotten. Had a kid she kept locked up at home, and of course that kid grew up to be a freak, too. She'd called him "Twerp," even when he'd grown old enough to drink. From time to time he'd appear out of nowhere, order a pint of beer, find a quiet spot in the corner, and never utter a peep to a soul. He'd just sit there, staring off into space like some dim-witted fool. If his mother happened to be at the bar, too, she'd belittle him, smack him around, and eventually send him scurrying home.

Randy shuddered, thinking about the time he'd fucked Brenda in the storeroom. She'd been dancing all provocatively, teasing him with her bounteous cleavage, until he finally gave in and gave her what she wanted. He'd always regretted it, though.

"Can I help you?" Randy asked, glancing down at the woman's physique. He was sixty-eight and old enough to be her dad. But what did she expect, coming in dressed like some tramp?

The man in coveralls was visibly pumped-up and high-strung, the type Randy knew better than to mess with. With an expression that was almost sinister, he said, "My girl here will have a gin and tonic with a twist of lemon. I'll have a beer … make it a Heineken."

CHAPTER 17

As Abeer turned on to the highway, leaving Maplewood Memorial behind them, Neil began recounting everything that had happened since Saturday. Abeer listened in horrified silence as Neil described Clive's game. Occasionally he jotted down a note on a scrap of paper, knowing that reminders would come in handy later. He was running on adrenalin, but soon the pain would take over and his brain would be fried; the more organized he was now, the better. He just needed a starting point, and he sensed that starting point was Andromeda. Either that, or prison, but he had no way to rustle up information about past inmates. So he'd start with Andromeda.

Neil put down the pen and picked up his phone, using his good hand to open the Google app. He typed, *Andromeda Toronto Clive*, and was pleasantly surprised when his search unearthed a few archived articles about a knife incident back in 2003.

"A knife fight at the downtown Toronto dance club Andromeda has left one man seriously injured and another in police custody," the first source cited. "According to eyewitnesses, the victim was stabbed after an argument escalated into a violent brawl just before midnight."

He scrolled through the other articles, but the name Clive didn't come up. Then he found something that piqued his interest: a feature-length piece about the club's demise in 2005 and the Fire Code infractions that had led to its closure. The club's owner was identified as Andrew Muir and the head of security as Trevor Glover.

He typed *Trevor Glover* into the search engine and watched as a slew of Facebook and LinkedIn results came up. The first Trevor Glover was a sixty-eight-year-old chartered accountant from England. The second, a recent Harvard graduate with distinction. After that came a string of wholesome-looking dads and a couple of grinning salesmen in suits, but no one who fit the bill of security guard. He almost gave up. Then, at long last, he came upon the Facebook profile of a freakishly large bearded man in his late forties covered in grim-looking tattoos.

"This guy," Neil said, showing Abeer his phone. "He used to work at Andromeda. He was the bouncer. I think I remember him."

"Any contact info?" Abeer asked, returning his gaze to the road.

"No. I'll message him. It's worth a shot."

Neil fired off a note in Facebook Messenger.

> Looking for a guy named Clive who
> used to frequent Andromeda. Maybe

an employee? It's an emergency.
Please get back to me as soon
as possible.

He signed off with his name and phone number, then hit send. Next, he'd switch his efforts to finding Andrew Muir.

"Hey Neil, do you have any direction in mind here besides just sort of driving in circles?" Abeer said, stifling a yawn.

Neil considered their route, trying to convince himself that what they were doing wasn't hopeless. His cellphone rang. *That was quick*, he thought, expecting it to be Glover. But it wasn't the bouncer. It was Detective Fitzgerald, and her sharp tone indicated that she wasn't very happy.

"Hello, Neil. Imagine my surprise when the hospital called to tell me you'd disappeared," she said. "In your rough condition, I find it very disconcerting."

"My wife has been kidnapped by a psychotic killer, Detective. Lying in a hospital bed didn't strike me as a valuable use of my time."

"It's not your job to find her. It's mine."

"I know that, but —"

"No buts, Mr. Patterson. I need you to go back to your cottage and get some rest. If you remember anything important, call me. But that's it. You're not to do anything else, do you understand me? Because if you don't comply, you will be arrested for interfering in a police matter. Do I make myself clear?"

"Yes, very. Have you had any luck yet? Do you know his name, at least? Where he's from? Anything?"

He heard her suck in her breath and release it slowly. "As a matter of fact, yes. I have his full name and criminal record in front of me as we speak. But I'm not at liberty to share that information. Go home, Neil, do you hear me? Go home and get some rest."

She disconnected abruptly.

///////////////////

Clive took a noisy swig from his Heineken and glanced around at the bar. Not much had changed at old Dewy's over the last couple of decades. Same tatty bar stools, same tired decor. Even Randy looked unchanged for the most part, just more bloated and with considerably less hair. It pleased Clive deep in his bones that the asshole didn't recognize him, that his new face and the new persona he'd worked so tirelessly to perfect disguised him from this old acquaintance.

"How's your G and T?" he asked Ellie, who was perched beside him, ignoring her drink. "Not the way you like it?"

She promptly reached for the glass and took a sip, then set it back on the bar. She looked stiff and anxious, which was not how Clive wanted her. And the way Randy kept busy with his back to them was getting under his skin. He'd wanted to show off his lady. Show the prick what a man he'd become. But so far Randy had been too occupied to notice.

Clive swigged his beer. Let the cold brew trickle down his throat. "Drink up, we're leaving," he told Ellie. That was when he noticed something that made his blood boil. Ellie was staring at Randy with such focused intensity that Clive figured she was either making eyes at him or shooting him some kind of a signal. "What the fuck are you doing?" he breathed in her ear.

Ellie looked up. She seemed surprised that she'd upset him. She pointed past Randy at the booze bottles lined up against the far ledge. "I was just wondering what brand of gin he used. Tastes all right, but not nearly as good as the ones you used to make me."

Clive grunted. "Well, doesn't matter. We're going home." He lifted his beer, draining it in a series of noisy gulps.

"What's the rush? Can't we stick around for one more, Clive? Pretty please?"

He shifted on his stool, scratched his cheek. Then he felt something warm on his leg. Ellie's hand, squeezing his thigh. The uncoerced contact and the hint of desire in her eyes turned Clive on. He decided to give her what she wanted. Keep her happy.

"I suppose you can have one more drink. Randy, another G and T for my lady here."

///////////////////

Randy had been tidying up, wishing his new patrons would fuck off home, when the big man addressed him by name. He wasn't wearing a name tag or anything — never did — so the fact that the stranger knew his name was off-putting. "Do I know you, friend?" he asked.

"What, you don't remember me?"

Randy approached the man, leaned on the bar, and scanned his handsome features. "Lots of folks come through these doors, buddy, but I rarely forget a face. Nope, never seen you before in my life."

"What about a piece of ass? Do you ever forget a piece of ass?"

The crass comment shocked Randy, and he imagined the woman must have been offended, too. Although she appeared to be strung out on cocaine, so maybe she hadn't noticed. She was pushing forty, by the looks of it — too young to be any acquaintance of his. The resemblance to Brenda sure was uncanny, though. "Excuse me?" he asked.

The stranger thrummed his fingers on the bar impatiently. "I said, do you ever forget a piece of ass?"

Randy remained silent. He wasn't going to play along, let some hopped-up meathead toy with him when all he wanted was to close up shop and get home.

"Babe, do me a favour. Stand up and show this man your ass, will you?"

Randy watched, stunned, as the woman reluctantly obeyed, rising from her stool and turning around to show him her rear end. For a moment he thought she was going to bolt for the door, but maybe he was just projecting his own reaction.

"Look, I don't know what you're suggesting here," he finally said with his hands raised, "but I've never seen either of you before in my life."

"So she doesn't remind you of anyone, Randy?"

"Well, that's a different question. She looks like any number of women I've seen in here over the years." He picked up a bar towel and started to wring it. He could feel sweat forming on his forehead.

"I think you can do better than that. You can think of *one person* in particular."

Randy didn't want any trouble, and his veteran instincts were alerting him of just that. This guy was heating up; he had tightened his grip on the woman's arm, as though she were his hostage or his personal possession. Now Randy was starting to worry about her well-being — as well as his own.

"Yeah, I suppose there's someone in particular I'm reminded of."

"What's her name then, this woman you're thinking of?"

"I don't know. Betty or something." For some reason, Randy didn't want to come out and say it.

"Betty?"

"No, not Betty. Started with a B, I'm pretty sure. Maybe it was Brenda."

As the name left his tongue, he saw the man's face light up like a child who'd just won a swimming ribbon. And though he bore no resemblance to anyone he'd ever met in real life, Randy had a funny feeling he knew the man. Brenda's boy — that freaky kid, Clive — suddenly flashed into his mind. But Clive rarely spoke, never made eye contact, whereas this guy oozed hostility and arrogance.

"Very good, Randy," the man said, clapping his hands hard. "You know, I think she would have been touched to know that you remembered her, that you didn't just fuck her and forget about her like all the others. You see, she died some twelve years ago. Guess you were too busy to make the funeral."

"Is that right? I didn't know she'd died," Randy said, feeling his throat dry up. He needed to defuse the situation, keep things civil until they were safely outside. "That's a real shame. Well, my condolences to you, sir. Anyway, I've got to close up now, so you two best finish up and be on your way."

That's when he saw it, a look of distress radiating from the young woman's eyes. He couldn't have missed it if he'd tried. He had to phone the police — or better yet, sound the alarm. He'd installed a panic button a year ago and since then, full of buyer's remorse, had bitched about how nothing that happened in Rockdale was bad enough to warrant such an expensive system.

His hands were trembling. He cleared his throat. "Let me just cash you out now."

Then he turned. Just as he reached for the panic button, something came smashing down on his head. He fell to the ground and saw what it was: a steel bar stool.

Again and again it pierced his scalp, cracked his skull, bludgeoned his brain, until all he could see was the colour red. The red halogen welcome sign blinking over the entrance. The warm trickle of blood dripping into his eyes.

Neil found a number for Andrew Muir at his new venture in Miami, Club Vibe. It was Sunday night, so the club was probably closed, but Neil would call and leave a message anyway — ideally one that conveyed urgency without alarming Muir into silence.

He dialed the number.

"Club Vibe," a young woman purred. "How can I help you?"

Surprised to have gotten through, Neil felt his nerves kick in. He tried to deepen his voice and said, "May I speak to Mr. Muir?"

"One moment, please," she replied.

Neil shot Abeer a thumbs-up.

After a pause, she was back. "I'm sorry, what exactly is this in regards to?"

Neil stumbled over his words, feigned a cough, and started again. "There's been a crime up here in Canada — a woman is missing — and Mr. Muir may have important information about the suspect involved in her disappearance."

He could hear two muffled voices conferring on the matter; the young woman had likely pressed her hand over the phone. He pictured them in some inconspicuous back office, shrouded in smoke. Muir at a desk counting out piles of cold, hard cash. A generous line of cocaine laid out in front of him. Heavy bass pulsing through the walls.

"Hello, this is Muir," a man finally said.

"Hi, uh, thanks for taking my call."

"Detective Fitzgerald, right? I got a few messages to call you back. It's been busy, what can I say? Anyway, the guy you're after, Clive Berringer, he was an employee of mine at Andromeda … a bartender. A real weirdo, come to think of it. Quiet, mostly kept to himself. Turns out he was into some shady side work … drug dealing," he said, his tone suggesting such nonsense was beneath him. "But you'll note that although he was convicted for it, I myself was cleared of all drug-trafficking charges. That's all I know. Trust me, we don't keep in touch."

"I see," Neil said. "Do you happen to know where he lives these days? Any information that could help us find him?"

"Like I said, we don't keep in touch. Truth is, I paid Clive under the table. Never got any credentials from him — no social insurance number or anything like that. When we first opened, he used to come in from time to time as a customer. Loved watching the ladies dance. Then, I guess sometime in the year after we opened, one of my bartenders was rude to a very important guest — there was an altercation, so I had to turf him on the spot. Clive happened to be there and asked if he could take on the job. It was a busy night, so I gave him a shot. He wasn't bad, knew his way around a bar. And it turned out he was very punctual, never missed a shift. But like I told the cops back then, I knew nothing about the drugs stuff. That was his business, not mine." Muir went quiet for a moment, and Neil imagined he was snorting that thick line of blow. Then he cleared his throat. "Come to think of it, I did always sort of question his identity. The name Berringer, it didn't quite fit."

"What do you mean, didn't fit?"

"It just felt wrong. I always call people by their last names — it's my thing. Anyway, this guy Clive, he never turned his head when I called him Berringer. Only ever answered to his first name. Then at some point he got all that surgery done, took some time off to recover. Came back to work a transformed man. But the new face didn't seem to get him anywhere, sadly for him. Later that same year, he was busted."

Neil's mind swirled with questions. If Berringer wasn't Clive's real last name, then who were the police chasing? How would they find him? And why had he changed his face, his identity?

"You still there?" Muir asked.

"Yeah … just making some notes," Neil said. "Listen, if there's anything else you can tell me, anything that might help us find this guy, I'd really appreciate it. A woman's life is at stake, an innocent mother of two. God knows what he'll do to her if we don't catch him soon."

"Nah, can't think of anything else. Good luck to you."

The line went dead.

CHAPTER 18

Ellie was thirteen the year her sister finally succumbed to her injuries. Bethany Anne Blakely had miraculously lasted three years with a severe brain and spinal cord injury. Three wasted years in a persistent vegetative state.

During those years, the sisters went to visit her every Sunday, while their parents went daily. It was hard to see their sister like that. She was not quite Bethany anymore, but a strange waxen rendering, still and colourless, withering away in a germ-free, climate-controlled room that smelled of urine and disinfectant. Just a bag of fluids and bones hooked up to machines that blipped and chirped, doing all the work for her. She bore only a slight resemblance to their sister, the girl who'd once had it all. Who'd won at everything, then been stripped of everything. Everything they knew and loved about her had gone. Fled into the ether.

One dismal afternoon in what was to be Bethany's final week of life, Ellie went by herself to visit her sister at the far-flung care facility. It was the first time she'd ever travelled unaccompanied to the outskirts of town by transit. She'd been feeling annoyed at her family, Laura in particular, and oh, how she'd wanted to vent. Let it all out. The only person she could think of who would listen without judgment was Bethany.

"I hate her. I really mean it this time," Ellie had complained from the armchair next to Bethany's bed. "The way she acts so superior to the rest of us, like none of us matters but her. She is such a bitch, you know? A full-fledged raging bitch, worse than ever. She has Mom and Dad wrapped around her finger — they treat her like a princess. As if she's the only one of us who has any problems. It's just not fair, Beth. When Laura's in a bad mood, which is practically every minute of every day, we all have to walk around her on eggshells. Like if anyone crosses her, she'll turn into that demon girl from *The Exorcist*, her head will spin around, spew vomit, and pop off."

That was when Ellie saw it — the smile. The corners of her sister's chapped lips pulled upward. It was fleeting, and if she'd blinked, she would have missed it. But she hadn't missed it.

Ellie's heart did flips. Bethany was still in there, still a real person. Her functioning brain was trapped in an impermeable shell, sealed off from the physical world. But Ellie had penetrated that shell. And if she could do it, then surely a world-class team of specialists could figure out a way to draw her out permanently.

Bursting with hope, she jumped up and dashed out of the room, almost knocking over a gangly young man in the hallway. Their shoulders clipped and Ellie shouted a hasty apology, glancing back. But the stranger just shrugged, seemingly unbothered, and stalked off down the hall.

Back at home that night, Ellie's elation didn't last long. It took Laura all of five seconds to crush all her hope. "PVS patients have no perception and no ability to react to external stimuli, you loser," she scoffed, rolling her eyes. "Haven't you heard anything the doctors have been telling us for the past three years? Bethany is brain dead. Her movements are involuntary. She's a vegetable. Stop looking for miracles and grow up!"

But Ellie couldn't stop looking for the positive. Her innate optimism was a blessing and a curse. So much so that when her parents came into her bedroom a few days later to tell her that Bethany had slipped away in the night, Ellie smiled — though she'd meant no disrespect. She smiled because her sister had finally been released to a better place. A big, bright, heavenly place, like a clear summer sky or a frozen lake. A boundless place where she could run, float, fly, and pirouette to her heart's content. Where no one could ever hurt her again, and she could live as she was meant to.

/////////////////////

When Ellie came to, she was no longer at the bar with Clive, but curled up on a child-size mattress in a bedroom no bigger than a storage pantry. Snippets of memory started to form. Clive repeatedly smashing the bartender's head with his stool. Her own blood-curdling scream as she flung herself onto Clive's broad back. Blood spurting from the man's open skull like soda from a shaken can. Clive smacking her across the jaw with such force that she'd been propelled headfirst into the bar, where total blackness had enveloped her.

There was a reading lamp on the nightstand next to her, and Ellie reached for the chain and tugged it on. Intense pain shot through her head and jaw as cold, blue light flickered from the fizzling bulb. She scanned herself. She was still clothed and in one piece. None of her own blood stains — just Randy's.

How had Clive managed to get her unconscious self back from that bar? Surely someone had witnessed something, heard her intense screams, which had left her hoarse. The police would be combing the crime scene now, collecting fingerprints and witness statements. In a small town like Rockdale, a dead body in a public place wouldn't go unnoticed for very long.

Ellie sat up with a measured effort that sent everything around her into a tailspin. She rubbed her eyes and saw the frame of a window covered in plywood. Not a trace of natural light made it through the nailed planks. Across from the window was a door. She dragged herself up off the mattress and crept toward it, careful not to make a sound.

She pressed her ear to the wood. Outside, nothing stirred.

After a few moments, she decided it was safe to try the handle. She twisted it once, waited. Jiggled it again, then pushed vigorously and determined there was a padlock or a bolt securing it on the other side. She took her chance and thrust her whole body's weight against the door. But it barely budged. She knew escape would only be possible if Clive released the bolt — which meant she'd have to get wily.

Looking down, she noticed scratches on the lower panel of the door.

Fingernails?

Breathlessly, she crouched down and ran her fingers along the flaking paint. There were dozens of scratches, maybe hundreds. And as she stared at them with mounting fear, it dawned on her what they meant. Others had been locked in that very same room. Others, just like her, trapped and awaiting their terrible fate.

Suddenly all her strength, all her resolve, fizzled out. The notion that she could exert some sort of power over Clive, outwit or deceive him with some phony allegiance of love, seemed absurd. *Laughable.*

No, she had no power, no control, no advantage over Clive. She wasn't his proclaimed soulmate, the only woman he'd ever captured out of a twisted, lifelong obsession. She was just one victim in a long string of them.

Another hopeless soul, waiting to be snuffed out.

Somewhere in the back of his mind, Clive could hear banging. He was in the kitchen, stooped over in a chair. Eyes glazed over, lids partially closed. But his mind was far from sedate. Rather, it was actively engaged in a time and place that made his pulse race, his breath grow shallow. He was seeing things no little boy should see. Hearing things no little boy should hear — not even bad boys, like him, who were rotten to the core.

Worthless little maggots. Useless wastes of space.

"You're lucky I don't hit you so hard over the head that your bloody brains ooze out your ears like strawberry jam, Twerp!" his mother roared in his mind. "Now get in that room and don't make a sound or you'll stay in there all week!"

Clive hated being left alone in that room, hated himself for making his mama punish him like that. But he needed to be punished for being so foul, so pathetic and stupid. Why couldn't he listen, be a good boy?

Soon she wouldn't love him at all, and he'd be sent to an orphanage. A miserable place where only the worst little boys were sent. Boys who were the bottom of the barrel, boys who didn't deserve their mothers' love. Boys who were fucking worthless, like him.

Clive blinked. Refocused his eyes on the door in front of him. Then, he lifted his hand and slapped his own face.

/////////////////////

Ellie threw herself onto the dirty mattress and cried. She could feel the hysteria building inside her, but also knew she couldn't unleash it. Her only hope of escape was to stay in control. But it was so difficult. Here she was, a grown woman of forty. A sister, a daughter, a mother of two. A wife. Stolen, plucked from her peaceful existence by a man she barely knew.

Wife … she shuddered, thinking of those text messages from MJ, the two little words that had changed everything, making her doubt her marriage, her love. Was MJ somebody's wife? Or some young vixen, single and free? Free to flaunt her youthful charms and revel in a superficial existence without any thought or care for anyone but herself.

Free as she herself had been in her twenties.

Free and miserable.

A home wrecker.

Ellie pulled up her knees and cried as she considered her own mistakes. Was this her punishment for that time in Harold's office? Karma for those misspent years having empty flings and passing judgment? Had she failed Neil, thus sending him into the arms of another? Had her lack of affection been the catalyst that tore them apart?

Certainly in the beginning she had been a good wife, always in tune with his wants and needs. But lately she'd been so hard on Neil, so brittle, resenting him for his freedom to come and go while she struggled to be everything for everyone. A cleaning lady, a taxi driver, a cook, a caregiver … she was exhausted. She hadn't envisioned herself staying home with the kids while her husband earned the bacon. She'd always imagined that she would be successful in her own right. Even worse was that she'd tried and failed. Her small publishing company had been unable to survive in the digital era. How had she not seen that coming?

She felt sick just thinking about the air of chilly indifference she'd been giving off ever since her company had folded — as though all that she had was a bore and a displeasure. Not enough. Now she would give anything to have it again. Now here she was swathed in some sleazy outfit, locked in the home of a killer. Without hope. Without a future. Without her precious family. Doomed to die in the foulest of ways. Worse than Bethany, even, who'd spent three years trapped in her own putrefying skin before she died, because the man who had taken her intended to harm her. Intended to make her suffer. A man who had possibly spent fifteen years of his life fantasizing about capturing her, and others like her, as some warped revenge for a lifetime of being dissed by the opposite sex.

Ellie cried out for Bethany, the spirit she hoped was watching over her, feeding her strength. Guiding her to safety. Then she held her breath, held in her sobs.

She could hear movement outside the door. A chair sliding.

Footsteps.

He was coming for her.

Neil felt a surge of hope as they pulled in to the parking lot of a dingy all-night diner. He knew he was walking a thin line with the law — and that he'd inadvertently drawn Abeer into his web of risky activity. But the conversation he'd had with Andrew Muir had given him the courage to go on. He was on the right track.

Abeer hopped out of the car and glanced back at Neil. "Can I get you something?"

Neil shook his head, having barely heard the question. He was preoccupied with Clive Berringer, wondering who he was, where he'd come from, and most of all, where he'd disappeared to.

Muir had said that the last name didn't fit, that Berringer was made up, and Neil was beginning to suspect the same. The internet turned up nothing of use. But at least the search was in motion; he'd made contact with someone who had actually known that piece of shit. That meant there were others out there — like tattoo boy, Trevor Glover. Maybe the bouncer knew more than the boss. Maybe he'd had a work friendship with Clive.

Neil was about to check his Facebook app to see if Glover had replied to his message, when a text came in from Mia.

> Trying not to take your silence personally.
> Should I be worried?

Neil grimaced. Her unwelcome intrusion, her brazen neediness at a time like this, filled him with anger. He'd have to call her and be frank with her that it was over. It had simply been a diversion. A mistake. The fact that Ellie was out there not only alone and terrified, but also likely doubting his love, tore him apart.

Of course, none of this was Mia's fault. They'd met at the conference's welcome reception, shared a few laughs. The way Mia flirted with him, with her hoisted-up breasts and her glistening mane of hair, had made him feel so desirable. It had been a long time since he'd felt that way. Then, as the flirting escalated, and Neil realized that she was inviting him back to her room for sex, he became so blinded by his libido that he was able to convince his drunken self that one slip-up in ten years of marriage wasn't so bad — Ellie would forgive him.

The second it was over, he knew it had been a mistake, and he'd felt miserable and guilty ever since. Still, he'd kept in touch with Mia via text (another mistake). He wasn't sure why, since he had no intention of a reunion. Perhaps it was simply that Mia filled a void. Fed his ego. But Ellie was the one he loved. His one and only, and now he needed to prove that by finding her, bringing her home.

He opened his Facebook app and stared down at Glover's ham-hock arms covered in fire-breathing skulls, red-eyed doll's heads, and other doomsday imagery. The sight of the tattoos jarred a memory, something he had completely forgotten about. Clive had a tattoo of a woman's name. Neil closed his eyes and tried to recall black lettering he'd glimpsed on their captor's bicep. Both names began with the letter B. Not B as in Berringer … no, it was B as in Brown. *Brenda Brown.*

Just as the name came to him, Abeer swung open the door. He was carrying two large coffees and a pair of prewrapped sandwiches.

"Abeer, I just remembered something. Clive has a tattoo of the name Brenda Brown on his arm. I'll do a search. Maybe it'll lead us to Clive. She must have been someone important to him. His wife or maybe his mother." *Or his first victim*, an unwelcome voice in his head added.

"That's great. Why don't you call up that detective and tell her? Get the police on it, while we head home and you get some sleep," Abeer said. "I know you're distraught. You've been through a terrible ordeal. But we can't lose sight of what's right. We're not gun-toting vigilantes, here. We're just two normal guys. Law-abiding citizens. We need to let the police do their jobs."

Neil appreciated the voice of reason, but he wasn't giving in without a fight. "Waiting by the phone isn't going to help Ellie. Anyway, Laura's manning that post."

"I just spoke to Laura, speaking of. She says a police officer just swung by to check that you'd gotten home from the hospital okay. She thought something must have happened to us on the way back, and we might be in danger. The point is, they know you're not at home and they're not going to be very forgiving. You were told to stay out of it, Neil. Honestly, you're acting crazy, and it's just not like you."

Neil closed his eyes and fought back tears as he prepared to bare his soul about Mia. Abeer was the most upstanding, level-headed person he knew. If anyone could help Neil weather the emotional storm, it was him. But before Neil could begin, his cellphone rang. He cursed when he saw who the caller was.

"Hello, Detective," he said grimly.

"Hello, Neil. Not tucked in your bed like you're supposed to be?" Fitzgerald, in contrast, sounded pleasant. Chipper, even.

"I'm at a diner having a coffee and a sandwich with my brother-in-law, Abeer. I'm not breaking the law by feeding myself, am I?"

"No, you're breaking the law by calling up a witness and pretending to be part of this investigation. I spoke to Muir. He said he'd already spoken to the police and had nothing more to say. Imagine my surprise."

"Hey, he jumped to that conclusion. I never claimed to be with the police."

"I don't know what you think you're doing, Patterson, but whatever it is, it's not helping matters. It's just going to cause your wife more harm. Do you hear me?"

"Okay, I do have some information that may be of help," Neil said. "I don't think Clive's last name is Berringer. He must have changed it at some point before going to prison, so there's likely a whole history to this guy we don't know anything about. Also, he had a tattoo on his arm — a woman's name, Brenda Brown. I'd forgotten about it until now. There were two years under that. Years of birth and death, I'm guessing."

"Do you remember what the years were?"

"I think the second one was 2004, but the first one, I don't remember."

"That's very helpful. Now listen to me, Neil. I want this guy in custody as much as you do. But it's time for you to go home. I'm not asking, I'm telling. If you disobey me again, I will have you arrested. So finish your meal and go get some sleep. Toodle-oo!"

Neil put down the phone. His adrenalin and his hopefulness were rapidly draining.

CHAPTER 19

Clive was in Grade 5 the first time anyone had taken notice of him — real notice, in the form of genuine concern for his well-being. Mr. Berringer, Clive's teacher, was new to the school, having recently uprooted his family from Toronto in search of a "cleaner" life. The whole class had snickered when he'd put it like that, because apparently Mr. Berringer hadn't experienced a windy day in Rockdale yet. On such days, the wind carried over the stink from the local garbage dump — hence the town's nickname, "Rottendale."

During the first few weeks of fall, Mr. Berringer had kept his distance. Like all the other teachers, he was dazzled by the good kids. The athletic, smart, popular ones. Kids with clean hair and all the right answers. Kids who shone with potential. Clive knew he didn't fit that mould; he was frail and sickly, with sunken eyes and sallow skin. On top of that, he was dumb as a stump and useless at just about everything. But as much as he tried to go unnoticed, to sneak in late and never utter a peep,

Mr. Berringer began to pay attention to him. He'd stand over Clive's shoulder a lot. Call on him to answer, even when it was clear he hadn't heard the question. Clive hated it most when Mr. Berringer asked to see his work. Clive's handwriting was so atrocious, he couldn't even read it himself.

All he wanted was to be invisible.

Then one day Mr. Berringer followed him home from school. He'd been so discreet about it that Clive hadn't noticed him lurking behind. Usually Clive spent the thirteen-minute trek pretending he was a Viking or a Roman gladiator. Mr. Berringer probably thought that was stupid.

After Clive had gone inside and shut the door, he heard three gentle knocks behind him. His mom wasn't home, and he knew she'd be irate if he let someone in without her permission. Besides, it might be a bully — or worse, a whole gang of them. His mom always said he'd be a target for bullies, easy prey because he was so dopey looking, so pathetic and useless. He decided to stay hidden and not make a peep until whoever it was gave up and went away. But after a few more persistent knocks, he heard a man's voice say, "Please, son, I know you're in there. It's Mr. Berringer, your teacher."

His heart pounded as he considered what to do. He couldn't pretend that he wasn't there, because his teacher had obviously seen him go in. He couldn't escape out a window or the door up front, because those had all been nailed shut. Finally, with no alternative that he could think of, he released the lock and nudged back the door just enough to see a sliver of his teacher's face. One crystal-blue eye peering down at him.

"Hi, Clive," Mr. Berringer said. "I just happened to look out my window at school and saw you walking along by yourself. I wanted to ask you something. Would you like to join the cross-country team?"

Clive looked at his feet, felt a lump form in his throat. No one had ever asked him to be part of a team before. "No, thank you, I'm not a very good runner," he murmured into his hand.

"Oh, I doubt that. And anyway, a little training can do wonders for promising young athletes like you. Is your mother or father at home? I'd like to ask them myself, if that's okay."

Mr. Berringer smiled and reached for the door handle. Clive panicked and snapped it closed. "No! No one's home," he said through the door.

"Well, can I come in and talk to you for a sec?"

"I'm not allowed to talk to strangers."

"But I'm not a stranger, Clive. I'm your teacher, and I just want to make sure that you're safe. Maybe we could talk about what happened to your neck there, how you got those bruises. You can trust me."

Clive reached up and touched his neck, then he locked and bolted the door. To avoid facing Mr. Berringer the next day, he skipped school. He also skipped school the day after that. On the third day, someone new came knocking — a lady from Children's Aid. Her name was Miranda, and she was fat as a heifer, with bushy orange hair and an oily pink nose. She smiled incessantly, a saccharine smile that made Clive nauseous. Then she made him angry, forcing him to go with her, to pack up his few belongings and leave his home and his mother behind.

Clive was promptly sent to live with foster parents in a small, plain town forty minutes from Rockdale. He only got to see Brenda occasionally, which upset him greatly, and Miranda was always present when he did. Always squeezed in between them, clasping her sausage fingers and breathing loudly through her pert little nose.

Brenda looked at him differently during those visits. It wasn't disdain so much as disinterest, like she didn't feel anything toward Clive anymore.

No rage, no venom, no scorn.

No love.

And Clive never forgave Mr. Berringer for that.

///////////////////

"Ellie, I know you're awake," Clive said, hovering over her near-naked body.

She was curled up on his childhood bed, her bare legs tucked in so close to her chin she could have kissed her own knees. Clive took notice of how the sparkly red fabric of the top clung to the side of her breast. But she looked frightened, and he didn't like that. He wanted to see desire in her eyes, some heat. Furthermore, he was still mad that she'd tried to send a signal to that rat bartender, Randy. She'd deliberately crossed a line.

"Now listen to me," he said, his eyes close and threatening. "Maybe you don't realize who you're dealing with here. I'm not some pathetic loser you can manipulate. I am not who you think I am, not anymore. I've changed ... I've transitioned. I've become the man I was always meant to be, the man *she* wanted me to be."

"Who?" Ellie asked.

But Clive didn't answer her. He was swept away into that alternate headspace, the one that combined the past and the present so that he couldn't tell them apart. He liked it there, sometimes — liked being a small boy in his big man's body.

But leaving the present to be with his mama meant leaving Ellie alone.

And he didn't like that ...

///////////////////

Ellie was beginning to suspect that Clive suffered from a severe mental disorder, perhaps dissociative identity disorder. So far she'd encountered three distinct states of personality: the posturing lug, the deprived child, and the one before her now ... Mr. Unreachable.

"Clive, are you in there? I asked who you meant by *she*."

Then — snap — just like that, he was back. Back, and angry.

"Don't you ever fucking mention her to me again, do you hear me?"

She nodded, closed her eyes tight. Clive was unbearably close, his sour breath in her face. His breathing accelerated. She sensed he was sexually excited, and it was all she could do to refrain from screaming.

Clive moved away and let out a sigh. There was a long moment of silence. "It's okay. Just don't let it happen again."

Ellie nodded, opened her eyes.

"Now, then" — he took her hand — "let's put the past behind us. Get on with our new lives. I want us to be happy. Don't you?"

She nodded again.

"Good. With Neil gone that shouldn't be a problem."

Ellie's breath hitched. She looked at Clive in confusion. "What do you mean, gone?"

He smiled, squeezed her hand. "I know, I know. I said I wouldn't do it. But Neil had to die, that was always the plan. And you should be grateful that I delivered on my promise to make him suffer for what he did."

Ellie was speechless, her head throbbing intensely. Had she heard right? *Is he lying?*

"I asked you to spare his life," she choked out. "People make mistakes, people cheat on their spouses all the time, but that doesn't mean —"

"Shut up and listen to me," he hissed, snatching her hair at the roots and twisting her head to face him. "I deserve your gratitude, do you hear me? Neil is gone, and now you are free. Everyone he hurt is free. *He* caused you pain. And you were never supposed to be with him in the first place. That was just a mistake, a misunderstanding. You were always supposed to be with me. And you promised me …"

Clive was still speaking, his lips moving and parting, but nothing he said made any sense. Ellie was frozen in disbelief. Too shaken to even breathe.

No, he has to be lying, she told herself. He was punishing her for trying to communicate with Randy at the bar. There was no way Neil was dead. A world without him was impossible. She refused to believe it was true.

"Clive, I don't feel so good, I just …"

He yanked her to her knees, jostled her to her feet, and dragged her over to the door. "Go take a shower, clean Randy's filthy blood off you. Makes me sick just looking at you."

He pushed her out into the kitchen. Ellie knew she needed to heed her surroundings, familiarize herself with the house's layout, but she was too shattered by what he'd just told her to think straight.

She managed to steal a few glances around her — at the wooden table and two flimsy chairs, at the thick curtains drawn in front of the only window not boarded up, at the mustard-coloured linoleum tiles with peeling edges that bore witness to a dismal, unsanitary existence. She felt like she'd stepped back in time into someone else's miserable, soulless past.

"There's a towel in there and some new clothes," Clive said, shoving her hard into a tiny bathroom. "Don't be long. I've got a new game in mind."

Ellie closed and locked the door, then gripped the teal pedestal sink to keep from falling. She thought back to her brief stint in the Palmers' garage, the way Clive had gone off, then returned moments later sweating and panting. Had she smelled smoke on his clothes? Had he gone back and set fire to the house?

It was possible, but not a reality she was prepared to accept. Not now. Not when she needed to stay in control. Besides, Clive didn't know that Neil had broken the chair leg and been seconds from breaking free. *Of course he escaped*, she told herself. Neil was alive and the police were hot on her trail. It was the only version of the story Ellie would allow herself to believe.

Wiping her tears, she looked in the mirror and took in her startling reflection. She was a stranger. A pale, frightened waif with brassy, chin-length hair and sky-blue eyeshadow smudged around her eyes. There was blood splattered on her left cheek, smears of blood on her hands. She turned away, too disturbed to face her own broken likeness.

She glanced at the toilet and realized she desperately needed to pee. As she was relieving herself, she looked up at the boarded window and imagined the world beyond it that would just be waking up. She tried to pull strength from the thought of the everyday goings-on around her: ordinary families still in pajamas. Coffee brewing. Parents nagging their kids to get a move on. Her own little darlings were out there running free, storming down some rugged forest path with canoe paddles in hand, new friends and summer adventures calling out to them.

Ellie felt a surge of gratitude that both her babies were safe, as yet unaware of her predicament or of the torture Neil had endured.

Neil … who was also safe. *Safely recovering at the hospital.*

She stepped out of her clothes and into the teal bathtub. The tiles were trimmed with mildew. Black rot and orange stains showed where water had dripped incessantly for decades. She turned on the shower and waited a few minutes before stepping into the steaming-hot torrent. Then, quietly, she cried out Neil's name.

CHAPTER 20

"Umm, Detective?" Officer Murray said. He was just a big kid, really. Scrawny, oily, always tripping over his size thirteen feet. "I think you're going to want to hear this."

"Hear what?" Flora asked, leaning back wearily to face him. She had been up all night. Now that she was fifty-five, all-nighters took a significant toll, both mentally and physically.

Murray, by comparison, was anything but weary. The excitement of working such a high-profile case had pumped him full of vim and vigour. "A man was killed last night, beaten to death with a metal bar stool at a place called Dewy's over in Rockdale."

"Yikes. That's pretty violent for Rockdale. Any other reason I should care?"

"Yeah, the fingerprints. They were able to lift some off one of the legs of the stool. It's still too early to say definitively, but it looks like a match for Clive Berringer. There are also indications that a woman was there."

"Well, fuck a duck," Flora said. "I suppose we'd best get our asses to Rockdale."

"That's not all. Seems our grieving husband has a curious past."

"Oh, yeah? How so?"

"Well, he wasn't born Neil Patterson, but Adam Neil Hughes. His parents changed his name officially in 1986, right before they uprooted the family from their fancy home in Uxbridge and relocated to Winnipeg. Patterson was the mother's maiden name. She died of cancer three years ago, but the dad, Peter Hughes, is still living out there. He's a retired lawyer."

"That is curious. Let's get him on the phone and see what the name change was all about. A lawyer, eh? What kind?"

"Criminal."

///////////////////

A few miles shy of the cottage, Neil suddenly began pouring out his soul, confessing to having cheated on Ellie while he was at a conference. Abeer was shocked and saddened, for more reasons than he could count. Laura's inevitable outrage swirled in his mind. For the first time in his life, Abeer wanted to swat Neil upside the head for being such a jackass.

He swallowed the urge, however. "I can't tell you whether what you did was forgivable, or if it means the end of your marriage. That's for you and Ellie to decide. But I can tell you this — I'll be there for you, no matter what happens. Tonight, tomorrow, and ten years down the line. I love you, man. We'll get through this."

Neil wiped his eyes. "Thanks, buddy. I really hate myself right now. Maybe I deserve this," he said, raising his bandaged hand and staring at the gap where his ring finger used to be. "At least that fucker chopped off the right one."

"Nobody deserves something like that," Abeer said. Then, after a pause, "Do the police know yet?"

"Know what?"

"About your affair."

"No, I never mentioned it."

"Given the circumstances, don't you think you should disclose it? I mean, you're at the centre of a police investigation. It might be important. A lead, you know?"

"A lead? Hardly," Neil said curtly, turning away. "Mia has nothing to do with this. Clive came for Ellie."

Abeer let it go for a moment. "We've both seen our share of crime movies. Something tells me the police are going to find it relevant that Ellie discovered you'd had an affair right before all hell broke loose. The timing is pretty curious. And what do you know about this Mia woman, anyway? I'm just saying that if Ellie already knows, what's the harm in telling the police?"

"The harm is that they'll start looking at me and Mia, wasting valuable time and resources down a dead end."

Abeer nodded, kept his eyes on the road. "Just think about it, okay? They might find out anyway, and the longer you wait, the worse it'll look. "

Neil picked up his cellphone and tuned him out. He was running on no sleep and barely any food. Abeer worried his friend was on the cusp of losing his mind. Surely, he'd land himself in jail if he didn't rein in his reckless behaviour.

"I'm going to search for an obituary. Brenda Brown ... obituary ... 2004," Neil said as he punched in the words.

"That's a long time ago," Abeer said.

"You never know."

A moment later, Neil lurched forward. "I found it!"

"Really?"

"It's a death announcement from the Presbyterian Church in a town called Rockdale. Here, I'll read it: 'It is with deep sadness that we inform you of the death of Brenda Marie Brown, a lifelong native here in Rockdale. A small memorial service was held on November 18, 2004. Brenda was survived by her only son, Clive.'" He looked up suddenly. "Hang on, I know that town. Ellie and I just drove through it a few days ago. Holy shit, it all makes sense now! I'll bet that was where he saw us ... he recognized Ellie and followed us to the cottage. Turn around," he said to Abeer. "We've got to go to Rockdale. It's just two hours from here, maybe less. I think this is the missing piece we've been looking for."

Abeer had been overcome with relief when, less than an hour ago, Neil had finally agreed to pack it in, head back to the cottage for some food and rest. Hearing his friend's new directive made his skin bristle. "No, Neil, I can't do this anymore," he said. "I need to get you home. I mean, look at you. You need pain relief, sleep. I'm sorry, friend, but I have to put my foot down this time."

Neil turned to him with supressed anger in his eyes. "Abeer, we are going to Rockdale. Ellie needs me, and I won't stop until I find her. Are you in or are you out?"

There was an edge to his voice, one Abeer had never heard before. Clearly, there would be no debating this. Neil was in dire straits and committed to finding his wife, no matter what the bitter consequences. The fact that he was still somehow going, in spite of his plethora of injuries, filled Abeer with both sadness and admiration. Yes, they were meddling in police matters, defying direct orders from the OPP. But Ellie, his wife's sister, was in danger, and he'd never forgive himself if she came to harm and it turned out Neil's hunch had been correct.

Abeer sighed, pulled over onto the dirt shoulder, then spun the car back the way they'd come. It was going to be a long day.

///////////////////////

Clive sat at the kitchen table listening to the distant trickle of water. He felt anxious, perturbed, although he wasn't entirely sure why. He'd succeeded in his plan, after all. Fulfilled his lifelong mission. Disposed of Neil and taken back the woman who was meant to be his.

His woman to touch, love, and protect. His woman, who was about to show him how much she loved him back. That was the next step, the new game. Her chance to prove that it had all been worth it. A moment that would make his mama proud.

Clive didn't know much about women, never mind how they showed their love for a man. Everything he'd ever learned about the opposite sex came from observing Brenda. He knew they liked to dance, to feel desired, wanted. That part was going to be easy; nothing thrilled him more than gazing upon the supple body of a female. He also knew that true, deep love often was exhibited in fits of rage. So far, Ellie hadn't shown any of that heat, that fury, the unquenchable carnal longing.

From the moment she'd caught his eye, young and naive, bursting with foolish hope, he'd known she would suffer at life's cruel hand. She was cursed, just like him. Clive had been astute enough to recognize this even though her wounds were superficial, unlike his. That first time he'd seen her at Andromeda, the strobes lighting her curves, her breasts rising and falling as her limber neck arched and rolled, he'd been unable to look away. He was fixated, infatuated, and over time she became his pretty little secret. His fresh-faced, in-the-flesh muse. Long before he ever spoke to her, he'd fed her with his desire. Nurtured her from afar by projecting his lust into her, knowing that one day she'd reciprocate. She'd give it all back — her body, her mind, her soul.

And now here she was, right where he wanted her. His own kindred spirit, contained within his walls, just as he'd always dreamed. But so far, nothing was going the way it should. Brenda had always exuded that sense of desire, whether at home or down at Dewy's. She'd been a woman with a rare insatiable appetite. A ravenous creature misunderstood by the world, misjudged by all but him.

He recalled coming back to live with Brenda after his fifteenth birthday, after Children's Aid had deemed her fit to care for him again. He'd arrived to a smiling, genial version of his mother, a fridge stocked with food. His foster parents, Sam and Shelley Pickers, had been reluctant to leave him, but he'd insisted. Sam and Shelley were the most self-righteous pair of do-gooders he'd ever met, folksy crusaders for good, wholesome values. Throughout their five-year guardianship, he had resisted their attempts to brainwash him into believing his mother was evil. He barely spoke, despite their painstaking efforts to draw him out, their unremitting need to turn him against his own flesh and blood. Through it all, he had remained her devoted son.

Then, in the weeks and months after his homecoming, Brenda began to change some more. She was no longer the fiery-tempered force of nature she'd once been. Clive's presence didn't incite in her that hateful rage, that unpredictable torrent of love that he once had.

This bothered him, of course. It disturbed him that she'd become so tepid, so bland and sluggish. The way she'd shuffle through the house with a blank stare, forgetting where she was going. She wore the same ugly pajamas that smelled of filth, loose-fitting flannels that hung off her scraggy body like rags. And she rarely ventured outside, only doing so in moments of pure desperation, when her medicine needed replenishing.

Clive didn't know much about his mother's illness, aside from the fact that it demanded silence, being left alone, and that it sometimes made her wail out loud and break things. Other times, she went so quiet that he'd wondered if she'd snuck off and left him for good.

One day, Brenda forgot to lock her bedroom door. She'd also left it slightly ajar, just enough for Clive to see her lolled back on the bed, her eyes fixed on the ceiling, one skeletal leg poking out from under her stained bedsheets.

The sight scared him. Burned itself into his adolescent mind. The toenails, once beautifully painted, were now gnarled and grey, the once silken hair now limp with grease and so sparse that patches of her scalp were visible. What had become of his mama?

Clive's curiosity got the better of him; he crept into the forbidden room, gazed down at her altered features. It was the first time he'd ever been so near to her, so blissfully close that he could have kissed her. He liked being there beside her, surrounded by all her things. The lacy, provocative things she'd once worn to tempt men's eyes. He took some of them — just a small sampling. A few precious keepsakes to stash in his own room, under his mattress. Pretty things that smelled of sex and smoke. Tawdry, private reminders of her.

Then he found something awful, something vile and upsetting. Next to her half-conscious body, tangled in the bedsheets, was a small, clear pipe, the kind drug addicts used to inhale crystal meth. At first he felt betrayed. Angry at her for allowing some filthy drug to rob her of everything she'd once been, for turning her into exactly what she'd always despised about him.

A useless slab of meat. A pitiful waste of space.

He was so angry his immediate impulse was to smother her, to annihilate this thing that had taken the place of his beautiful mama. She would have respected him for it, he reasoned. She'd have wanted him to put her out of her misery. Like the broken little bird whose neck he'd once snapped after he found it lying maimed in the alleyway.

But he couldn't do it. Instead, he grabbed her bony shoulders and rattled her awake, knowing that the old Brenda would have beaten him unconscious for touching her like that. "Mama, it's me!" he wailed through tears. "Look at me, I'm in your room. I'm not allowed to be in your room."

Gradually, the murk lifted from Brenda's rheumy eyes, and Clive's heart raced with anticipation. Then she smiled — not a warm, motherly smile, but a dark, malevolent one. A black-toothed grin that got under his skin and made his neck hairs stand on end. He was glad to see that devilish side of her again.

"You," she growled. "I knew I gave birth to you for a reason, you pathetic maggot! You sorry excuse for a boy! Now you listen to me, Twerp. I gave you life, and now you owe me. Do you hear me?"

"Yes, Mama," Clive said. "What do you need?"

At half past ten on Monday morning, Flora and Murray pulled in to Rockdale, drawn to the swarm of police activity. It didn't take long for the local police chief to bring them up to speed. Dewy's pub was your typical small-town watering hole. The victim, Randy Miller, had been the original owner's sixty-eight-year-old son. A lifer here in Rockdale — until Clive Berringer stormed in late on Sunday night and bludgeoned him to death.

But what had prompted the deadly assault? Flora went over the many possible triggers. For starters, had the suspect come in alone, or with the Patterson woman in tow? The logical assumption would have been that he'd come in solo for a post-kidnapping nightcap. But on the contrary, the evidence seemed to suggest that there'd been a female with him: the half-finished gin and tonic, the lipstick on the rim of the glass, the two skewed stools.

And yet, this made no sense. Why would a kidnapper bring his prisoner to a public space? And why Dewy's, of all places? Had it merely been a random pit stop, a chance to use the facilities before they barrelled on through town? Flora highly doubted it. The smashing in of the victim's skull suggested that Clive had known Randy Miller. Known him, and hated him.

The unlucky waitress who'd made the grisly discovery was a woman called Brandy. "So you came in at roughly eight o'clock this morning, unlocked the door, and saw Mr. Miller's body — where, exactly?" Flora asked.

"Over there," the young woman said, pointing to the open end of the bar. "He was covered in blood. I knew he was dead the moment I saw him. It was the sickest thing I've ever seen. His head was all folded in on itself. I could see his brains," she sobbed into a handful of tissues.

"That must have been awful," Flora said, patting her fleshy arm. "I just need a few more details from you, then you can head off home. Have you worked here very long, Brandy?"

"Two years," she sniffed.

"And in all that time, did you ever come across any customers who went by the name Clive?"

Brandy blew her nose and shrugged. "Not that I'm aware of, but I don't know them all on a first-name basis."

"Of course. How about someone who was particularly handsome, say, George Clooney handsome? Ever see a hunk like that in here?"

The young woman looked at Flora sideways like she'd lost her marbles. "This is Rockdale, ma'am. No one here looks like George Clooney. I'd sure as shit remember if they did."

Flora nodded and handed Brandy her card. "If you think of anything else that might help us, give me a holler." She stood up. "Seems our man Berringer has a knack for vanishing into thin air."

"Did you say Berringer?" Brandy asked.

"Yeah, that's right. Ring any bells?"

"Well, the name Berringer is familiar. Not Clive, though. Mr. Berringer was a teacher at the Rockdale Elementary School. We all loved him to death when we were kids. He was the nicest teacher ever. Now his daughter Lily cares for him — he's got some kind of dementia. They live on the other side of town in a big yellow house with a wraparound porch. You can't miss it. It's the prettiest place you've ever seen, right out of a fairy tale."

"Thanks, Brandy, you've been really helpful."

Brandy smiled meekly and ventured one last nervous glance at the blood-soaked floor. "Sure am glad I'm not the one who has to clean that up," she muttered, hurrying away.

///////////////////

Ellie emerged from the bathroom, her body spilling out of yet another clingy outfit. Same tawdry style, slightly different nuance. Her head pulsed so fiercely from its collision with the bar that she wondered if she might pass out. Hoped she would, even. At least then she wouldn't have to face whatever horror was coming next.

Clive was sitting at the kitchen table with his hands clasped in front of him. She could feel his eyes on her breasts, her erect nipples, which she knew were visible through the sheer fabric of the shirt. He didn't smile or speak, just openly stared. Ellie froze in her tracks. Her instincts told her to keep well away. But then, something did draw her over to the table.

Next to a tall glass of milk was a perfectly square sandwich on a plate. Her eyes locked on the meagre offering, and an audible growl escaped from her stomach. It

had been about twenty-four hours since she'd had anything to eat. Twenty-four hours since poached eggs on
toast with Neil.

"Go on," Clive said, motioning for her to sit down.
"It's peanut butter."

Ellie obliged, shuffling over to the other chair. She
took a seat, picked up the sandwich and gave it a sniff.
It looked and smelled okay — but could she trust him?
Of course, she told herself. After all, Clive had made it
perfectly clear that his fantasy didn't involve her being
unconscious. On the contrary, he seemed to want her
very much awake and in the moment, an active participant in whatever ungodly game he had planned next.

As Clive stared at her, Ellie forced herself to choke
down a few hurried bites to fuel herself up for forthcom-
ing battle. The door to the outside world was directly
behind her, likely locked with a series of deadbolts, but
that wouldn't be enough to stop her. Not this time. She
just needed to figure out a way to knock Clive unconscious. Stab him with a knife — if it came down to it.

"So, this is where you grew up?" she asked, chewing.
Stalling.

Clive rubbed his face and leaned back. "Yup. This is
my happy childhood home."

Ellie couldn't tell if he was being sarcastic or not.
It certainly seemed unlikely that he had any pleasant
memories from this dark, filthy abode. What healthy
attachments could one form within these crumbling,
water-stained walls? The house felt like the set of a horror movie or a snuff film, with its boarded windows

and worn, dirty sofa. If Clive had really grown up here, that might explain a lot about the warped person he'd become. He was mentally ill for a reason. She suspected he'd been born into misery, the victim of a callous, abusive upbringing.

"Do you have any brothers or sisters?" she probed, glancing around the cramped space. Searching for something heavy, solid.

Clive didn't respond for a moment, his irritation visibly mounting. He rubbed his face again. Muttered, "No, it was just me and my mom. No siblings … no dad."

His answer surprised Ellie. She'd assumed Clive's aggression issues were the result of a violent father — one who'd seriously messed with his developing mind. She still wanted to know more, to uncover his weaknesses, but all signs indicated that he was not in the mood for sharing. Unable to resist, she asked one last question. "Is your mother still around?"

At that, Clive erupted, slamming his fists on the table with an explosion of force that threatened to split it in two. "Now you listen to me," he raged, his voice deep and threatening. "I don't want to talk about myself, or my mom, or anything else, for that matter. Understood?"

Ellie nodded.

"Good." He leaned back. "Finish up. It's time for our next game."

She stared at him, terrified.

"Don't worry. No one's losing any toes," he said. "In fact, this game is all about pleasure. It'll take us back to that special time and place when we were just getting to know each other … remember? Back when I'd watch you dance, and you'd pretend you didn't see me watching …" His voice trailed off, his focus drifting away with it. "You liked that, didn't you, knowing I was out there, protecting you from afar."

Ellie was baffled by what Clive was saying, and stricken by how quickly he could retreat into some other dimension, his eyes sinking back in his skull as if he'd fallen into a trance. She wondered if she might lose him completely. If his spell was deep enough, she could steal away to the door, disengage the locks before he snapped back to reality. But then, just like that, his focus returned, and the crazy grin reappeared on his face.

"So," he continued, as if he hadn't been away, "the rules are simple. You dance, and I watch. You make me feel that heat, that desire, and I reward you in the manner you deserve. Any questions?"

She had no questions, because she had no breath. She felt like it had been knocked right out of her and been replaced by the colossal sob that was rising in her throat, threatening to escape.

He wanted her to dance …

Yet somehow, she followed his command. Rose to her feet and clumsily found her footing through the haze of disbelief that was clouding her mind. Tried to fulfill his strange request by letting her spirit take flight and flee, so she could command her body to do what he wanted. This would be one of the most bizarre, demoralizing moments of her life.

She just hoped it wouldn't be her last.

CHAPTER 21

"Jesus, looks like something bad happened here," Abeer said, prompting Neil to lift his burning eyes from his phone. He was still searching for anything he could find on Brenda Brown.

Seeing the hive of police activity, his chest filled with panic. Did all this — the caution tape, the police barricade, the active crime scene — have something to do with Ellie?

"I need you to go find out what happened. I'd do it myself, but they might be looking for me."

Abeer pulled into a vacant parking spot and unbuckled his seatbelt. He turned to Neil and patted his shoulder. "It's going to be okay, I promise. I'll be right back."

Neil nodded but didn't respond. Couldn't. His fear had gotten the better of him, crowding his mind with gruesome images of his wife's corpse lying on some beer-slopped barroom floor. He knew this wasn't a coincidence. This investigation was tied somehow to them. All he could do was wait and see.

///////////////

Abeer loped over toward the sectioned-off storefronts, where a handful of police officers were talking in front of a barricaded pub. He approached them casually. One of the officers, a young man who must have been taller than six and a half feet, made immediate, stern eye contact.

"This area is off limits, sir. You'll have to cross over and continue on the other side."

"Actually, I was just driving past … saw the commotion and wondered what happened," Abeer replied, feigning detachment.

"Are you from Rockdale?"

"No, sir, just passing through town. I'm a photographer."

"Oh, so you're with the media. Well, there's nothing official to report just yet. A man was killed, but that's all I'm at liberty to tell you. There'll be an official statement likely within the hour."

He felt a rush of relief upon hearing that the deceased was a man, but he knew Neil wouldn't be satisfied with that vague bit of information. He'd want to know if the killing had been connected to them, whether the dead man was Clive or some random bystander. And if it had been connected, where was Ellie now?

"Kind of unusual for a small town … a man dying at a bar, I mean. Can't imagine it happens all that often." Two of the officers exchanged glances but didn't say anything. Abeer pressed on. "It's just that I heard there was a murder a few towns over, and that a woman is still missing. Wondered if this incident was somehow connected."

The young officer cleared his throat. "We're still waiting for more information on that, sir. As I told you, we'll be making a statement within the hour. Move it along now, understood?"

Abeer nodded and obliged him by beetling off back to his car. The towering young rookie's shifty eyes had given him all the answers he needed. The crimes were somehow connected, he was sure of it.

///////////////////

Flora stepped out of Dewy's and approached Murray on the sidewalk. She liked using him as a sounding board, a blank face to listen and nod along as she rambled through her disjointed thoughts and theories.

"It seems our suspect was here last night, and like you said, someone was with him. Maybe it was the Patterson woman, but I have a hard time believing he'd be stupid enough to bring his victim to a public space," she went on. "Then again, we're dealing with a deviant mind here, so I suppose standard logic doesn't apply. Anyhoo, if he was stupid enough to do that, maybe it explains the assault on poor Randy Miller, the owner of the joint. Maybe Randy stepped in and tried to help her. But then ..." She paused for a moment to think. "Clive likely knew the bartender, which means this wasn't just a chance encounter. The way he went to town on the poor man's skull suggests some pent-up hatred. Don't you think?"

Murray had been nodding along in agreement at everything his superior said. "Maybe he brought her in there to show her off. You said she was pretty, right? Maybe he wanted to be seen with her. Show the old bar-flies what he'd caught."

Flora blinked up at him, feeling a *whoosh* of sudden clarity. If there'd been a stepstool on hand, she would have kissed Murray right on those juicy young lips. What he said made perfect sense. It put Clive's motive and behaviour in a far more logical order. He was out to prove something, to gain acknowledgment for his transformation. He'd already had an expensive facelift and undergone some sort of physical metamorphosis with his body. Maybe the woman was his cherry on top. The sweet proof he needed to show the world that he'd risen above his wretched, dejected past.

And where would a person on such a mission go? They'd go home, of course. Back to where it all began — the teasing, the taunting, the abuse. She'd bet that Rockdale was Clive's hometown, and he'd come back in a blaze of delusional glory.

"Come along," Flora said, storming off toward the cruiser. "There's someone we need to go talk to."

"Oh, yeah, who's that?"

"Berringer, Clive's namesake. Apparently, he lives on the other side of town."

///////////////////

While Abeer was gone, Neil tried to imagine his life without Ellie, his kids' lives without her. But it was impossible. Impossible to untangle her from everything they'd become, everything they had yet to become. Every memory, every anticipated milestone was rooted in her. Ellie was like the sun at the centre of their solar system; her light and energy sustained them.

Unlike his own mother, who was quiet about her love and offered it in calculated, measured amounts like a reward to be earned, Ellie gave her love generously. Not a day went by that their children didn't hear the words "I love you" or genuinely feel enfolded in it. He, on the other hand, had felt the chill of her love's gradual retreat. But that had only been recently, for the last eighteen months or so. And then, *boom*, just like that, it had returned, her love the same intoxicating remedy to all dreary things it used to be.

His heart ached as he recalled their first years together, how carefree and wildly in love they'd been. Not until Michael came screaming into the world, a colicky preemie with a bad bout of jaundice, did things start to become tumultuous. Ellie hadn't seemed herself those days. She'd been so tired, her hormones surging. And meanwhile Bethany had been such a handful at two and a half. But Neil had only recently been catapulted into a new executive position, leaving Ellie to cope on her own day in, day out. Besides his empty fling with Mia and the few stupid stunts he'd pulled in his youth, that was Neil's greatest regret: seeing his wife's weary face each night when he came home from work, hearing the desperate edge in her voice, knowing that she was at the end of her tether, close to an emotional breakdown, yet doing nothing.

"Neil," Abeer said, swinging open the door, his brown eyes bright with hope. "It wasn't Ellie — it was a man. They wouldn't tell me who, but she's alive, bro, Ellie's alive!"

/////////////////////

Ellie stood up and closed her eyes, searching for strength, hoping for a miracle. *You dance*, he'd said. It seemed like an impossible feat. How was she supposed to suppress everything inside her — her terror, her anguish over Neil, if what Clive had said was true — and put on a sensual performance? Not only that, but a performance good enough to somehow arouse Clive into such a thorough state of oblivion that he wouldn't notice her sashaying over to the counter and fishing a large chef's knife out of the drawer.

Suddenly she was struck by the absurdity of it all, the sheer folly of her new predicament. Did this imbecile really expect her to deliver an X-rated striptease like some seasoned erotic dancer, right here in his rotten little kitchen without music? And, was he really so delusional that he actually thought she'd want him to reward her for it?

"Clive," she said, "I'm just not feeling it. It's not you, it's the room. The silence. Maybe if we had some music ..."

"I'm sure if you concentrate hard enough, you can imagine some music. Go on." He leaned back and clasped his hands behind his head, his eyes already hungry.

Ellie tried to remember the seductive beats that used to drive her onto the dance floor back at Andromeda — it was mostly techno and electronica back then — but for some reason nothing was coming to her. In fact, the only song she could think of was an old Rolling Stones tune, "Beast of Burden." Something about the title and the repeat request to be put out of misery seemed relevant to her situation, and given that it was the only musical current she could summon, Ellie closed her eyes and went with it.

She began to arch her neck, stretch her spine, and sway her hips as the familiar lyrics floated to the fore of her mind, supplanting at least some of the fear and chaos. Soon it felt oddly comforting, and she wasn't sure why. Then a hazy memory came to her and she fought hard to explore it in full.

It was a moment years ago, back when it had been just the two of them. They were sitting at their kitchen table. Neil's sleeves were rolled up because he'd just finished installing their new gas stove. Each of them was sipping a cold bottle of beer. Behind them, a song on the radio prompted Neil to get up and crank the volume. It was "Beast of Burden," and boy did he ever like it. It got him dancing in a way Ellie had never seen — bold and shameless, as if no one else was in the room. No one hooting and howling at his ungainly moves.

Despite her screams of laughter, she'd loved it. Ate it up. Urged him on. Loved the way his ass looked in his faded Levis. Told him to rip off his shirt — which he did, before pulling her into his arms. She could smell his sweat, feel his bare chest and the heady thump of his heart. Then the two of them had danced together, unabashed. Two distinct forms meshing into one. *Kindred souls …*

Ellie relished that memory, letting it flood her senses and pulse through her veins. Oh, how she wanted to be back in that time, that place. Safe and unhindered, contained in a fortress of Neil's potent love. And as she delivered the most seductive moves she could muster for Clive, the memory of Neil became an invisible force field, protecting her and giving her strength. Reminding her of who she was, where she came from, and most of all, where she would return.

/////////////////////

Abeer and Neil left Main Street and veered down a random side road. They knew they had come to the right place, even if they weren't entirely sure the murdered man had anything to do with Ellie.

"So, what now?" Abeer asked, hoping Neil would have some sort of plan.

But his brother-in-law shrugged. "I suppose we could hit up that church, the one that posted the death announcement. It was a long time ago, but there's a chance someone might still remember her."

"Sounds good," Abeer nodded. He glanced over at Neil and was dismayed to see that he was deathly pale. He'd come down from his wild-eyed, adrenalin-fuelled state in a matter of minutes as soon as he'd learned that

Ellie wasn't the one lying dead in that bar. Now he was pallid and shrunken, his eyes red and swollen. "Here, give me your phone. I'll look up the address. You take a rest."

Neil handed over his phone without dispute, leaned back, and closed his eyes.

The image on the lock screen was a winter shot of Ellie and the kids wearing colourful toques and matching smiles. Abeer couldn't look at it. He quickly fumbled his way into Neil's Waze app and used it to search for Rockdale Presbyterian Church. "Got it," he said. "We'll be there in less than four minutes."

But Neil didn't answer. Abeer looked over and saw he'd already drifted off into a fitful sleep.

///////////////////////

The small church was a picture-perfect, crisp-white building surrounded by trimmed grass and round hedges. There was a sign by the entrance that read, *As sinners, we are only saved by God's grace through faith in the Lord Jesus Christ's life, death, and resurrection.* Abeer felt a strange flutter in his heart, a hesitation in his limbs as he made his way up the stone footpath, as though someone were about to lurch out of the shrubbery and wrestle him off the holy grounds. But he ignored the feeling and carried on.

He pulled open the heavy arched door and stepped inside the church. It was astonishingly beautiful. He took a moment to appreciate the cathedral ceiling, the rows of pews, the exposed wooden beams, and the musty smell of bibles. Churches were not a familiar space for Abeer, but, surprisingly, he felt calm and centred as his photographer's eye wandered, feasting on the light gleaming through the stained-glass window and glancing off the pulpit in ethereal streaks.

To the side of the pulpit, he spotted a little room with its door slightly ajar and a light on inside. A bald, bespectacled man was installed at a desk, poring over some loose pages. His sermon, probably, Abeer thought as he approached the office and rapped on the door.

"Hello, sir ... or Father, is it? I'm very sorry to disturb you," he said, his nervous energy building up again. "I'm hoping you can help me find someone, a woman. Actually, she's dead ... but I think she may have attended your church."

"Does this woman have a name?" the man asked, peering up over his glasses. He was plump, with bright, rosy cheeks and a kind, steady gaze that put Abeer at ease.

"She does. Brenda Brown. You posted a death announcement about her twelve or thirteen years ago."

"Ah," the pastor said. "So, you're looking for a deceased woman from the last decade who may have attended my church. Now, that's a first."

Abeer chuckled and said, "Actually, it's just her address I'm looking for. I think her son might be living there now."

He felt tongue-tied all of a sudden, unsure of how much information he should impart, or whether he should refer to Clive by name. The truth was, he didn't know if he was breaking the law or not. He had no idea whether he could be charged with police interference or being a public nuisance. At the end of the day, he figured he could just plead ignorance, which wouldn't be a stretch from the truth.

The pastor cocked his head, tapped his fingers. "Hmmm, Brenda Brown. The name does sound familiar. But I'm fairly certain she wasn't a member of our parish. What did you say the son's name was?"

"I didn't, but it's Clive. He'd be in his midfifties today."

"Clive … oh, yes." He narrowed his eyes and nudged his wire-rimmed glasses higher up on his nose. "Brenda was a troubled soul. A single mom and a hard drinker. Developed some other substance abuse problems along the way, I'm fairly certain. Her boy, Clive — well, he bore the brunt of her wrath, sadly. No, they didn't come to church. But they lived quite close, over on the east end, in one of those condemned houses off Main and Wellington. No clue which. Can I ask why you're looking for him, young man?"

"Um, well …" Abeer began hesitantly, "he's committed a crime, and we're just trying to locate him before he commits another, a worse one."

"I see," the pastor said. "So you're with the police?"

"Not exactly. Just doing a little behind-the-scenes legwork … in co-operation with the police," Abeer lied, feeling as though a lightning bolt might shoot down and strike him dead on the spot.

"Well, good luck to you, then. My prayers are with you, my son," he said, turning back to his notes.

//////////////////////

After hearing the heavy front door thud to a close in the distance, the pastor picked up the phone to call the local sheriff. He harboured no ill will toward the young Indian man — in fact, he'd quite liked him. It was for that reason that his seasoned instinct told him to intervene. He felt that the young man's life was in danger. He could feel it pulsing in his bones like the arthritis that flared before each coming storm. Something was brewing, and he knew without a shadow of a doubt that Clive Brown was at the centre of it.

CHAPTER 22

Clive's eyes were wide open, his erection substantial, but he was no longer seeing Ellie. No longer swept up in the sultry performance she was delivering just for him. For Clive's mind was elsewhere: adrift in the past.

Suddenly he was at Dewy's, a small child of seven, peering in from the leaf-coated sidewalk. The sky was a dark mass of low-hanging clouds. It was cold, and he was alone, shivering. On his feet were nothing but a pair of filthy socks. But no amount of discomfort could pull him away from that spot, not even the trembling fear inside him that if she caught him, she'd hurt him. Punish him for disobeying, for following her to her special place.

Inside, the men catcalled and taunted, "Brenda, Brenda, Brenda," feeding his mother their brutish lust. She spun around provocatively, loving the attention, shaking her breasts, her ass, unbuttoning her blouse as the room erupted in cheers.

Then, *snap*, Clive was transported again. Another time, another place. Now he was much older, on one of his secret missions to the city. Brenda had entrusted him with an all-important job: sourcing and obtaining her medicine. It had begun as a game to win her love. Her long-sought-for approval. She'd send him out and time his return. Praise him when he earned it. Yell, thrash him, and withhold her love when he came home empty-handed. Which had been often, in the beginning.

But he took the game seriously, got faster and more adept. Without him, without her medicine, she would die, and he would never forgive himself. He couldn't imagine life without his mother, not even now that he was a young adult. Other than her, he had nothing. No one. He feared the thought of having to soldier on without her. More than anything, he craved a woman's touch, a woman's tenderness, but he knew deep down that Brenda was the only woman who would ever love him, touch him. He knew this because she'd always told him so. That he was ugly and worthless, a pathetic waste of space. That no woman in her right mind would ever stoop to love a foul little beast like him.

At the thought of this, Clive felt vindicated. For he did have someone to love and who'd love him back … Ellie. Then, as Brenda evaporated like a spectre before his eyes and Ellie's full-bodied presence returned, he smiled — but only for a moment. That smile was snatched away by the tiniest sound, a squeak. And that's when Clive saw that Ellie was at the counter, trying to pull open a drawer.

"What the fuck do you think you're doing!" he roared, charging at her and grabbing her by the arm.

She looked scared and guilty, and Clive didn't like that. Then she did something he did like. She kissed him, thrusting her tongue deep into his open mouth. Just as he'd always imagined.

//////////////////////

Flora and Murray entered the lush, green countryside, leaving the small northern town behind them. They were looking for a yellow house with a white wrap-around porch. Something out of a fairy tale, according to the waitress, Brandy.

"Any word back from Neil's dad?" Flora asked.

Murray nodded. "Peter Hughes, what an arrogant son of a bitch. Got all huffy and entitled when I asked about his relocation to Winnipeg back in the eighties. Said Neil had been going through a rebellious phase — failing at school, stealing booze, and such. Essentially, he just chalked it up to a reset. Said he wanted his son to start over in a new place where his old delinquent friends wouldn't find him. Didn't want them interfering with his son's chances of getting into a good school. He sounded legit. Then when I told him about the situation here, he was truly horrified. Hasn't heard from Neil yet. They're not in regular contact."

Flora bit her thumbnail. She felt dubious. "Why the name change, then? Were they running from something?"

Murray shrugged. "Doesn't appear that way. No evidence of any arrests or criminal behaviour. Hughes started up a law firm out there and retired about four years ago, right after his wife got sick."

"Cancer, right?"

"Yup."

Flora wasn't a parent herself, but it seemed excessive to uproot your family, move across country, and change your son's name just to keep him on the straight and narrow. She was just about to verbalize this when a pale-yellow speck came into view, then grew into a sprawling homestead in a rolling meadow. "There it is," she said, pointing Murray toward the long tree-lined driveway. It was truly breathtaking. Something out of a fairy tale, indeed.

They hopped out of the car and sauntered up to the porch, Flora's stride double that of her long-legged subordinate's. She tapped a brass knocker and a woman, fiftyish, promptly let them in. Judging by her mussed apron and the pleasant aroma wafting from the house, she was in the midst of baking something Flora imagined was a strawberry-rhubarb pie.

"Everything okay, officers?" the woman asked, wiping flour off her hands.

"Everything's fine, ma'am. Sorry to drop in on you like this," Flora said. "Are you Lily Berringer, by chance?"

"Used to be. I'm Lily Peters now."

"Well, Mrs. Peters, there was an incident last night at that bar over on Main Street, Dewy's. You know the place?"

"Yes … I mean, I know the place, but I've never been in there. Why? What happened?"

"The owner, Randy Miller, was beaten to death with a bar stool. There's a good chance the man we're after was a local here in Rockdale. We think maybe your father taught him in elementary school."

"My father taught Grade Five for thirty-four years at the only school in town," she said. "So, if your suspect grew up here, then yes, I'm sure Dad knew him. The thing is, Dad isn't very well these days. I'm not sure he'll be much use to you in his condition."

"Mind if we give it the old college try?" Flora asked, smiling.

"Sure, come on in. He's in the sunroom. Can I get you some coffee or tea?"

"No, thanks, ma'am," Murray said. "We'll just be a moment. We appreciate your co-operation."

Flora always got a kick out of the way the young officer's voice dropped an entire octave whenever he was trying to impress upon someone that he was a *real* cop on duty. She could picture him as a kid rehearsing in the mirror, pulling out his toy pistol and perfecting his cop expression.

Lily led them into a large breezy solarium adorned with wicker furniture and sheer white drapes that billowed in front of the wide-open windows. In one of the chairs sat a frail-looking senior in a green cardigan, staring off at the horizon. Flora could tell from his frame and his features that Mr. Berringer had once been tall and strapping. A Paul Newman type. She crouched beside him, but her close proximity evoked no reaction.

Not a single involuntary twitch.

"Hello, sir," she tried anyway. "I'm Detective Fitzgerald. I'm sorry to disturb you on such a fine day, but I just wanted to ask you a few questions about one of your old students. A boy by the name of Clive. He goes by Clive Berringer now. He would have been in your class some forty years ago. He was likely an oddball kid … quiet, reclusive. Maybe gave off signs that he was abused or neglected."

Mr. Berringer continued staring off into space. Flora realized it was pointless — there was no use wasting her breath hassling the poor old soul any further. Digging back forty years would be a tall ask for anyone. She straightened up and saw that Lily was pursing her lips as though straining to recall something.

"That name, Clive … and the way you described him," she said. "Now, I can't be completely sure it was the same person, but the year I was in Grade Five, there was a kid named Clive. He came from a poor family, abusive, likely. I remember him because Dad followed him home one day and was very concerned. He had to report his findings to Children's Aid. We had just moved up here that fall. If I remember correctly, the boy was sent to live with a foster family out of town, so we never saw him again."

"Do you happen to remember his last name?"

"No, but I can assure you it wasn't Berringer."

Flora nodded. "Apparently he has a tattoo of the name Brenda Brown on his arm. We're thinking that could be his mother."

"Possibly. I'm sure Children's Aid could dig through their records and get what you need. Let's see, that would have been the fall of 1976. If memory serves, they lived in that pocket of condemned houses over on the east side. That's not very far from Dewy's, actually."

"Thank you, that's very helpful," Flora said. "And if your dad has a moment of lucidity, we'd appreciate any information you might be able to extract from him."

Lily frowned. "I wouldn't count on Dad remembering much, or being able to communicate his thoughts, even if he could."

"Is it Alzheimer's?"

"No, Dad had a stroke about sixteen years ago. Fell off a ladder while he was cleaning the gutters."

"Oh, I'm sorry to hear that."

"I don't know, personally, I have my doubts about whether that's what really happened." She glanced at her father and leaned in. "My dad was fit as a fiddle, never missed a morning run. After all his tests and scans, the doctors couldn't determine whether the brain hemorrhage caused the fall or the other way around. Some strange things had been happening, you see. A stalker had been harassing Dad not too long before that. Sent a few threatening letters."

"A stalker?" Flora perked up. "Was it a man or a woman?"

"Neither, it was a kid. Or at least that's what the poor handwriting and the misspelled words suggested. The language was very childlike."

"You say this was sixteen years ago?"

Lily nodded. "The police chalked it up to a prank. Everyone in Rockdale loved Dad. No one disliked him, especially not his students. Eventually, when the letters stopped, we just moved on and forgot about it. Until the accident. That was when I started wondering if there was a connection. If someone had *made* him fall."

Murray and Flora exchanged glances, then they both looked down at the old-timer. Sixteen years ago Clive would have been in his midthirties. A grown man. "What sort of threats were in those letters?" Flora asked.

Lily bit her lip and looked embarrassed. "Oh, gibberish mostly, crayon scratches with the odd expletive thrown in. Things like, 'You will die for what you did, you meanie. You are just a loser. I hate you.' Nothing more than that, really."

Flora furrowed her brow and nodded. She could see why the police had brushed it off as just a childish prank. "Well, thank you for your time, ma'am. You've been extremely helpful."

As they left the Berringer home, Flora turned to Murray. "Let's hit up that section of homes on the east side of town while we try to get someone from Children's Aid on the line." She paused. "Ask them to search for a Clive Brown."

////////////////////

"Hey buddy," Abeer said, urging Neil awake. "I think I just got something useful from the pastor."

Neil's eyes flashed open. He was drenched in sweat. He looked around himself manically as his grim reality congealed around him. The fragments of a memory from the depths of his mind filled his throat like bile. He must have been dreaming. The dream had been about something wretched he'd done, something that had catalyzed this living hell. Not his affair with Mia. No, something else, something worse …

"So, get this," Abeer continued. "It turns out Brenda Brown was Clive's mom, like you thought. She was a single mother, and they used to live in one of those rundown bungalows we drove by earlier, just off Main and Wellington. He didn't know the exact address, but I thought we could do another drive-by now." He turned on the engine. "You should call up that detective and tell her what you found. I mean, it's not like we're going to go door to door or stake out the joint ourselves."

He laughed nervously.

"Yeah, I'll call her soon," Neil said, rubbing his irritated eyes and clearing the mucus from his throat.

They turned the corner and made their way back toward Wellington Street in silence. When they were nearly there, Neil sat up and looked hopefully at Abeer. "Actually," he said, "that's not such a bad idea."

"What?"

"Going door to door, like a canvasser. You could pretend you're collecting for a charity or petitioning against a new garbage dump or something. Anything to get you up on the doorstep and peering into the windows."

"Wait — me?"

"Well it can't be me, can it? Besides, it'll be safe. Clive isn't going to be opening his door. Just good, decent people with nothing to hide."

Abeer scanned the dingy houses — each one looked like a crack den — and raised an eyebrow. "There's got to be at least eighteen houses in this one block alone. It'll take all day," he pointed out. "Why not let the police do it?"

"It won't take all day — a minute per house, max. Most of them look deserted, anyway. And if the police show up, it'll scare him off. If we can identify the right house, then we can call in the cops."

"So, what's the story going to be, then?" Abeer asked, shaking his head in a way that indicated he was reluctantly on board.

"Say you're with Statistics Canada, polling the neighbourhood to see how many people live in each house. Just keep it short and sweet. Do you have a clipboard or reading glasses handy? The dorkier you look, the better."

They rummaged around in the back seat and found a few props. Then Abeer took a deep breath and got into character.

CHAPTER 23

Clive was feeling discombobulated, a little woozy. He'd never kissed a woman with so much passion before. In fact, he'd only ever been with two women in his life. The first time was with some anonymous skank who'd wanted free dope. She'd dropped her sweatpants on command, let him fuck her from behind, right up against his mom's shitbox Malibu in some filthy back alley where he used to make pickups. It had been worth it, though, to feel a woman's skin. To get up inside her.

The second occasion had been much more satisfying. It was shortly after he'd altered his face, when women were beginning to take notice of him. Even so, it was unusual for him to be pursued so aggressively, especially by a sophisticated lady in high boots and a luxurious suede coat. She'd trailed him in the grocery store and struck up a conversation about the exorbitant price of berries. Introduced herself as Tricia. He liked the way her name sounded, the way it tasted, lingering in his mouth like those hard candies that left your tongue all red.

Tricia was a recent divorcee, lived in a fancy condominium just around the corner from the Hasty Mart. She told him she had a daughter, but the girl was off someplace with her dad. At the checkout, she said he reminded of her George Clooney, which of course came as no surprise. After all, he'd paid a bundle for that precise look. Then, when they were out on the sidewalk, about to part ways, she leaned over and whispered into his ear, "It's always been my fantasy to be fucked by George Clooney."

Clive couldn't believe what he'd just heard, and hell, who was he to stand in the way of her fantasy? On the elevator ride up to her place, she told him she wasn't wearing any panties and invited him to see for himself. So he got down on his knees, hiked up her skirt, and found himself gazing at the most beautiful thing he'd ever seen — the smooth, hairless genitals of a female. Not a second later, he was feasting on her sweet spot, attacking it ravenously as she squealed and moaned in pleasure. They'd practically destroyed her apartment as he tossed her around like a blow-up doll ... which, he assumed, was why she'd been so angry afterward. The smashed lamp, the busted coffee table, et cetera. But, hell, she'd started it. What had she wanted from him, a damage refund?

But Ellie, sweet Ellie, with her pretty pink pout and bright angel eyes — he didn't want to scare her, didn't want her to recoil from his too-eager advances. He wanted her to *want* him, to open herself up to him. To spread her legs and beg for it, like Tricia had.

"Slow down, Clive," she said, gently pushing him away. "You're moving too fast."

"Do I have to?" he replied, panting.

"Yes," she said. Her cheeks were flushed the prettiest rosy-red he'd ever seen. "You're just being so aggressive … you're scaring me a little."

"Well, what can I do to make you more comfortable?" he whispered. Then he leaned in close to her ear. "Just don't tell me you need a drink to take the edge off."

/////////////////

Flora pulled off onto one of the desolate side roads that ran perpendicular to Main Street. The neighbourhood was on the fringe, lacking in colour and life. There was only one other car around, a pristine red Nissan with valid Ontario licence plates parallel-parked ahead of them. She saw that someone was slumped in the passenger seat, either sound asleep or wasted.

"I'm going to go poke around a little," she told Murray, who was still on hold with Children's Aid. So far he hadn't gotten very far. Something about the case files being sorted differently back in 1976. *Yeah, likely in brown paper boxes stacked roof-high in some suburban warehouse*, she thought.

While Murray hung back, she stepped out into the sunshine and sauntered up the first weed-ridden walkway to a basic no-frills bungalow, one of the few along this desolate stretch that actually looked lived in. She pressed the buzzer and heard it chiming on the other side. Then she heard the shuffling of elderly feet. A curtain was yanked back, and a wrinkled face scowled at her through a dirty windowpane.

A moment later the door creaked open, and a gnarled old woman in a floral muumuu appeared. "Thought you were that fella from Stats Canada back to hassle me again," she said, glancing at the police cruiser out on the curb. "What can I do for you, officer?"

"I'm just patrolling the neighbourhood, ma'am, looking for a suspect who lives somewhere in this block of houses. Goes by the name of Clive Berringer. Any chance you know him?"

"Never heard of him. But then again, I'm not too sociable these days. Can't say I know a single person who lives around here, not anymore," she croaked.

"Well, there's a chance he grew up in one of these houses, raised by a single mother. Were you here that long ago?"

"I was, but my memory isn't so good. Let me see, now. Seemed there were always kids coming and going." She scratched her whiskered chin as she peered out at the stark, treeless street. "A long time ago, a boy lived in that house with his mother," she said, pointing. "Or maybe it was that one. In any case, they sure don't live in it anymore. Everyone's gone. Most of these places are empty, tagged for demolition. Some new mall development coming next fall, we've been told."

"Well, thank you, ma'am, I appreciate the effort. Now you go ahead and get back to enjoying your day."

Flora raised her hand in a parting salute and hurried back down the walkway.

/////////////////////

Abeer rounded the corner of his second block. He wished that he'd tried a little harder to resist Neil's plan. So far he'd only encountered two homeowners, a crotchety old lady who'd deeply resented the invasion of privacy, and a rough-looking character in a soiled wifebeater who'd called him "Punjabi" before slamming the door in his face. All the homes in between were unoccupied. At least it seemed so from their boarded-up exteriors.

He looked across the street and noticed an unmarked laneway that cut through a row of backyards separated by wire fences. What caught his eye was the garage at the very end of the lane. The door was half raised, and inside he could see the rear end of a shiny black automobile. It was too new, too nice, for this ragtag neighbourhood.

His spine tingled as he considered his next move. Should he go back and tell Neil about the car, then have Neil notify the police? Or should he first take a quick stroll down the lane — a reconnaissance mission, so to speak — and get a closer look at the vehicle's make and licence plate? That might be the more efficient thing to do. Though his instincts told him to abort mission and sprint in the opposite direction, Abeer decided to carry on.

A few more steps wouldn't kill him.

/////////////////////

Ellie could tell that Clive was beginning to tire of her teasing and stalling, flirting and withdrawing. But the way he'd been kissing her, his mouth gorging on her face with the reckless incompetence of a drunk teenage virgin, had filled her with utter revulsion and she'd felt the urgent need to make it stop. Now she was at risk of making him angry.

"Take off your shirt, or I'll take it off for you," he whispered in her ear, nuzzling her neck and running his tongue along her jugular, over her chin, and across her mouth.

Ellie had been forming a plan. She was hedging her bets that the drawer she'd almost opened moments ago contained an assortment of utensils. Forks, knifes, scissors — anything she could plunge into his gut before kneeing him in the scrotum and making a screaming run for the door. If she could just keep him occupied a little longer, hold his attention where it was, then there was a chance she could ease the drawer open, dig out something useful. But what if the drawer contained nothing sharp — or what if he again caught her in the process? He'd be furious, and the jig would be up.

"Just kiss my neck a little longer," she breathed, the thought of failure causing her to hesitate. She couldn't squander another precious opportunity.

Clive's hands were planted on the counter, away from the edge of the drawer. But Ellie worried about that squeak. She'd have to yank it open ever so slowly, moan loudly in his ear at just the right time. "Yeah, that's good … I like that," she said, thrusting her hips into his midriff as she carefully made her move.

Miraculously, it worked. She was able to gain just enough clearance for her fingers to dip inside and forage around. As Clive gnawed on her neck, she fumbled with unseen items, desperate to find a useful weapon. But at first graze, there was nothing but lightweight plastic junk.

She was about to give up, to try forming a Plan B, when her fingers made contact with something cold and substantial. On one side was a clunky, ragged cube. Her heart raced with adrenalin as she took hold of the vintage meat mallet and readied herself to slam it into Clive's skull.

///////////////////

Flora figured she'd skip the houses in between and hit the last one on the street. It was one of the two homes the elderly lady had identified as having possibly belonged to a single mom with a son. It was definitely neglected, with boards over the windows and a yard full of dead grass and blooming weeds.

Flora went up the walkway, noting a prickly feeling on her skin. It was the sensation she got whenever trouble lurked in the form of a nearby assailant. She was never wrong about these things — her sixth sense was what had gotten her where she was today in a profession that hadn't been very accepting of her vagina. Of course, the silent consensus around her was that she *must be* a closeted lesbian. She wasn't, though. In fact, nothing turned her crank more than a virile young stud like Murray. The bigger and dopier, the better.

She searched in vain for a doorbell, then resorted to knocking on the decaying slab that acted as a front door. She struck it a few times, but nobody responded. The place had to be vacant, yet still, she sensed that she wasn't alone, was being watched. She rattled the door handle and noted resistance on the other side, as though the door had been barricaded shut. She'd do a little walkaround, see if there was a functioning entry point elsewhere on the building.

/////////////////////////

Clive covered Ellie's mouth and pulled her to the window. Holding her tight, he carefully nudged back the drape. "Fuck," he said under his breath. "We've got company."

Ellie felt a rush of hope, a certainty in her bones that Clive had glimpsed the police, that the house was surrounded by an armed SWAT team and that she'd be saved momentarily. And then, as he yanked her to a new spot, she lost her grip on the mallet … Ellie watched, horrified, as the mallet tumbled to the floor, and Clive's eyes filled with silent rage.

"What are you up to?" he whispered, bending down to pick it up.

"Just in case we need it … to get past them," she said.

Thankfully, Clive didn't have time to question Ellie's sincerity. He was too fixated on whatever was happening outside the window. Suddenly there was another rapping, this time at the side entrance directly in front of them. Clive pulled Ellie into his chest and stared at her threateningly. She knew she had to stay quiet, otherwise he'd reach out and snap her neck, but holding in her screams was the equivalent of torture; she could feel her inner shrieks practically bursting from her pores.

The door handle jiggled. Clive kept hold of her, his eyes sharp, his flexed biceps like boulders. After that came a sound that robbed Ellie of all her hope, drained her of all her bravery: footsteps receding down the walkway. Then, silence.

Clive released her from his vice-like grip. "There's been a change of plans." He raised the mallet and smashed it against the table.

Ellie felt faint and was temporarily blinded as he unlocked the door and muscled her out into the searing light.

There was no one outside.

//////////////////////

Abeer was halfway up the laneway when his nerves kicked in, and he began to question his sanity. Out of nowhere, one of his mother's favourite proverbs came to mind, one of the pithy truisms she loved to recite whenever opportunity and happenstance aligned: "Danger should be feared when distant and braved when present."

He took a breath.

The sun shone at an angle, reflecting off the metal door and casting a heavy shadow on the car's licence plate; that meant he'd have to get right up close to make out the plate number. But he had a bad feeling about it, a feeling that he was entering perilous territory. Abeer wasn't accustomed to being afraid. He'd lived a secure, happy existence raised by two doting parents and a good-natured older sister. Confrontation was rare in his world. Danger, even rarer.

His hands were trembling, his armpits sweating. He took another deep breath. He'd come this far; all he needed to do now was to get a closer look at the car and take note of the make and licence plate so he could report his findings to the police.

Easy-peasy, he told himself.

Cautiously, he approached the vehicle, shielding his eyes from the sun with his hand. When he was nearly close enough, he suddenly heard a door slamming, footsteps coming in his direction. With no other hiding place available, he scurried into the garage and crouched in the darkest corner.

"Don't piss me off," a male voice said. It was deep and husky. Terse.

Suddenly, Abeer wasn't alone. A woman was thrust into his sight. She was slim and athletic, scantily dressed, with sandy hair cropped at the chin. It took him a moment to realize that he was looking at his sister-in-law, Ellie. The man who followed after had urgency in his eyes and chiselled, too-perfect features — exactly as Neil had described Clive.

"Get in the car and stay quiet," Clive said, pushing Ellie into the passenger seat and slamming the door behind her. Abeer knew he needed to think fast, couldn't let them drive away.

Frantically, he scanned the heaps of rubbish around him and eventually located the only object with real damage potential. A shovel. He lunged at Clive from behind, slamming the metal end against his head with as much force as he could muster, nearly enough to knock the powerhouse of a man over.

Nearly, but not quite. Instead, Clive staggered back, clearly rattled, and swung at Abeer with the mallet. Flashbulbs ignited in Abeer's vision as it struck him in the face. He collapsed into a cluster of trash bins.

////////////////////

Flora was making her way back to the cruiser when she heard a loud clatter. It came from somewhere close by, likely the property she'd just checked. She turned and sprinted back toward the bungalow with her pistol raised, then crept up the walkway, and edged her way around the side of the house.

As she neared the backyard, a black car tore out of the garage. She strained to catch a glimpse of its occupants as it bulleted past. A man — dark features, big-boned, handsome. A woman — stunned but alert, chin-length hair. It was Clive and Ellie, she knew it without a doubt.

She got on her radio and called for backup as she memorized the licence plate of the car, which had looked like a Mazda6. With help on its way, she headed toward the back alley and heard a moan coming from the garage. Raising her gun, she leaned under the door and spotted a man lying on the concrete floor. He was barely conscious and visibly wounded. Blood seeped from his mangled face.

Flora rushed to his side, tried to rouse him from his semi-conscious state. "Sir, can you hear me?" she said taking his hand and squeezing it. "Sir, help is on its way, but I need you to stay with me … I need you to tell me your name. Tell me what happened."

"Uhhh … uhhh," was all he could say.

She came in close, inspected his battered face. "It's okay. You're going to be okay," she said. But it was too late. He'd already slipped away.

///////////////////

Around the corner, less than two blocks from the alley, Neil, too, had been drifting in and out of consciousness. Hot, blistering pain lanced through his body, screaming of an infection.

He was asphyxiating, unable to fill his lungs. In an instant, he woke completely and threw open the car door, hung out his head. Gulped in as much air as he could get. He tried to focus his eyes on the pavement below — on the hot asphalt and the tiny ants moving over it. He just needed to cool off, catch his breath, then he'd be all right.

A noise caught his ear: the escalating roar of a car engine. He raised his head and saw a black sedan speeding in his direction, about to run the stop sign. He locked eyes with the driver — dark eyes he knew all too well. Eyes set in a stolen face. Then he shifted his gaze to the passenger, a woman stricken with fear.

Ellie.

But she didn't see him; they were moving too fast.

Neil cried out her name as the car shot past. He tumbled onto the pavement and watched it screech around the corner like a dragster. In the blink of an eye, it was gone.

Ellie was gone again.

CHAPTER 24

Flora tapped on the hospital room door. When no one answered, she stormed in anyway. Neil was lying on his back in bed, his eyes glassy, his complexion sapped of colour. He was awake, but he was lost — and for good reason. Not only was his wife still out there at the hands of a lunatic, his friend and brother-in-law, Abeer Singh, had been brutally attacked. Struck in the face with a meat mallet, Abeer's cheekbone was shattered. The doctor said he'd likely need several rounds of reconstructive surgery, and even then, there was a good chance he'd be permanently disfigured.

"Knock, knock," Flora said solemnly as she approached his bedside. "Anything else you want to tell me ... Adam?"

As much as she felt sorry for Neil, she was sick and tired of his meddling and suspicious of his intent. Naturally, the man was distraught. But his refusal to co-operate combined with his mysterious past made Flora wonder what exactly he was hiding.

Neil blinked and struggled to sit up. "What's that, Detective?"

Flora crossed her arms and stared down at him. "Your name used to be Adam Neil Hughes. Why'd you change it?"

"That was thirty years ago," Neil said, readjusting himself with a wince. "My parents' idea to set me on the right path. I'd been hanging around with some bad kids. They wanted to make sure I got into a good school, that I —"

"Was untraceable?"

"No, of course not," Neil snapped, which bothered her. "I mean, you traced me, didn't you? Look, it was all done legally. They just didn't want my old delinquent friends to find me. My parents had ambitions for me. They were real hardasses ... and thank God for that, because I got to start over in a new place, buckle down, and make them proud. Trust me, that has nothing to do with what's happening now with Clive. Speaking of which, any news on where they are?"

Flora maintained her unflinching eye contact, crossing her arms. "Not yet. But we did get a match on those plates. The car belongs to some guy by the name of Trevor Glover. Lives in an apartment building in East York."

"The bouncer?" Neil perked up.

"Just what bouncer are you talking about, Neil?"

He looked away and shook his head ruefully. "I'm sorry. I should have mentioned it. I found him on Facebook. He used to work at Andromeda as the bouncer back when Clive was a bartender there."

"Jesus Christ, Neil. I thought I told you to stop snooping around."

"I know. Honestly, I forgot about it. I messaged the guy last night, but he never responded. I thought he was a lost cause. You have his address, right? I assume someone's out there apprehending him?"

Flora stared at Neil in disbelief. His audacity was incredible. Ignoring his question, she said, "You know, it annoys me to no end that you didn't trust me to do my job in the first place. Your brother-in-law could have died today. *You* could have died ... which is why if you do not co-operate from this moment on, I will have no choice but to detain you. Your part in this investigation is to be truthful and comply with everything that I ask. Nothing more, nothing less."

"I will comply from now on, Detective, I promise," Neil said earnestly. He swallowed hard. "Actually, there's something else I need to tell you. I probably should have mentioned it sooner."

"Oh, what's this now?" She stared down at him, bracing for a doozy.

"I ... had an affair. It happened three months ago. Just a one-night stand with someone I met at a conference in San Francisco. Her name is Mia Jones. There's no connection to what's happening here, but I thought you should know. Truth is, it was a mistake, and I wish to hell that it never happened."

Flora was quiet for a moment. Her tolerance for Neil's antics was coming close to breaking point. Still, she wasn't all that surprised by the confession. Marriage was tough — the world had taught her that, but her job had hammered it home. "Does your wife know about this … mistake?"

Neil sighed, averted his gaze. "I think so. Mia sent me a text message right before Clive came and took Ellie. It was just a coincidence, bad timing. But now she's out there … thinking I don't love her."

"Well, thank you for your honesty. That wasn't so hard, was it?" Flora smiled icily while making note of the woman's name. She didn't let on, but this new piece of information gave rise to a new question: Was it possible Ellie and Clive were in on this together?

///////////////////

Laura was storming down halls like a rabid dog, her unwashed hair scraped back in a messy bun. So far she'd only encountered dimwitted numbskulls who shrugged off all her questions, not having the authority to utter a single peep that wasn't nebulous or completely devoid of useful information.

How was it that no one could tell her anything she didn't already know? Her husband was laid out in one room recovering from a shattered cheekbone while her brother-in-law was confined to another, missing a finger and a toe. Meanwhile, her little sister had been kidnapped by some psychotic bartender who used to gawk at her … and the maniac was still at large! It was preposterous, all of it.

Laura arrived at Neil's room just as a mousy-haired detective was coming out. She immediately pounced on the detective, throwing her six-foot frame in front of the smaller woman, whose face reminded Laura of an angry ostrich. "Listen, I want to know who's in charge of this investigation, because whoever has been calling the shots needs to be fired. Now, I'm sure you're working to the best of your abilities. But from my perspective, everything about this incident has gone from horrible to fucking disastrous … and that man is still out there with my sister. I'm losing my shit here."

The detective lifted her hands and placed them up on Laura's lofty shoulders. Laura could see her own annoyance reflected back at her in this woman's eyes. "I appreciate your frustration, ma'am, but we are doing the best we can. We are currently in pursuit of your sister's captor and are honing in on their precise whereabouts now."

"Honing in? Jesus Christ!" Laura stomped her foot, exasperated. "It's been twenty-four hours. This is Canada, not the fucking Ivory Coast! We're talking about one mental case in a Mazda carrying a meat cleaver. I don't understand why your band of merry idiots is unable to intercept and capture him."

She immediately realized that she'd gone too far and felt tears welling in her puffy, bleary eyes. She knew Abeer would be disappointed with her for unleashing her old-school temper, for being so blatantly disrespectful to the authorities. Frankly, that was what stung her the most: the thought of disappointing her husband.

"Look, I didn't mean what I just said. It's just … they mean the world to me. All three of them. I can't lose them, do you understand?"

"No harm done, ma'am. Just please do me a favour. You seem like a woman who knows how to impose her will. So, I'm going to ask that you stand out here — or, better yet, pull up a chair — and do not let Neil Patterson set foot outside that room. If you can keep him contained, we'll be a lot better off, and hopefully I won't find myself back in this damn hospital. Can you do that for me?"

Laura nodded.

"Good. Now, please excuse me while I go catch our bad guy. Toodle-oo!"

//////////////////

It had been a few hours since their hasty exodus from Rockdale. They'd been travelling the same northbound highway unhindered like an arrow aimed straight at God's Country. By this point, they were well beyond the cottage towns — Bala, Port Carling, and all their trendy like. Places where privileged city folk went to "summer."

"Hey," Clive said, jerking Ellie's shoulder. "You awake?"

She was propped against the passenger door, as far from Clive as she could get. "Yeah … I really have to pee."

"Well you're in luck, because so do I."

Ellie tilted her head toward the window, looking out at the passing scenery. Sheer, grey rock and towering evergreens appeared as colourful, distorted blotches in her eyes. Not a restaurant or gas station in sight. "Aren't we going to stop somewhere with a real toilet?"

"Do you see any creature comforts around here, princess? Sorry, but you'll have to cop a squat at the side of the road."

Clive eased the car onto the gravel shoulder and shut off the engine. With a vulgar grunt, he hoisted himself out of his seat, stepped outside, and came around to the passenger door. "You can piss right there. I promise I won't look," he said, yanking her out by the hand.

Ellie felt a rush of blood hit her in the back of the eyes as she stumbled over and squatted where he'd told her. Though she hated the thought of relieving herself in plain sight of Clive, she knew resistance was futile, and her sense of shame was rapidly dwindling. Besides, she really had to go.

As the warm fluid trickled out of her, she stared at her filthy bare feet. Found herself wondering about her faceless rival for Neil's affections — MJ, the buxom young beauty whose panties were likely in a twist because Neil hadn't responded to her texts. Of course, Ellie didn't know if MJ was young and buxom or not, but the sad-face emoji and that demanding, flirty tone certainly fit. Young, buxom, and bold. Someone who hated to be kept waiting.

She wondered how they'd met, how they'd made their mutual attraction known. On an airplane? At that tech conference in San Francisco? She wondered if Neil had been the pursuer or the one pursued. Was it possible that Eddie, Neil's unscrupulous work crony, had had something to do with the whole thing? She'd never trusted Eddie. Never approved of his treatment of women as conquests, to be used and tossed aside like trash. Perhaps Eddie had noticed MJ dining with a hot friend and convinced Neil to be his wingman — only somehow, Neil had wound up being the one who scored.

Ellie held back a sob as she remembered their last night together, the way Neil had made her feel so enraptured, so adored, as though no other woman in the world had ever existed. She felt a wave of heartache, a heavy sense of betrayal. She needed to confront Neil and demand he tell her the truth. But would she ever get that chance? Or would she die not knowing why he'd demeaned their love, cheapened something as rare as what they'd had? Certainly, their love had shape-shifted over the years, evolving and redirecting, falling dormant, then flourishing again. But no matter what, it had always been there — the safe, cushy underpinning of their lives. The beating pulse within her.

Ellie finished up, sidestepped her puddle, and yanked down her tiny skirt. She could feel Clive's eyes on her exposed behind.

Then she heard him zip up his fly. "Let's hit it. Next stop, the Sands Inn Motel. Maybe they have a honeymoon suite. What do you think, honey?"

//////////////////////

Flora was back at the station awaiting the arrival of Trevor Glover, the three-hundred-pound former bouncer whose visible epidermis was completely covered in tattoos. Not that she had a problem with tattoos. But his all seemed to have a sadistic theme — bleeding eyeballs, demonic corpses, and such. In her humble opinion, anyone who went to the extreme pain and expense of permanently branding themselves with images so twisted they could turn a child into an insomniac for life probably had a screw or two loose.

As she poured herself some hours-old coffee, she spotted Officer Murray in the distance, his mouth set in a thin line. "Hey, Murray!" she called, intercepting the young officer, who did a prompt about-face. "Where's Glover?"

"He's here, in your office," Murray said. "Claims he's innocent, of course. Says he has no knowledge of anything unusual. Just that an old buddy of his needed a car."

Flora took a deep breath and finished fixing her coffee. Then she headed off to question the only living soul who appeared to be on friendly terms with Clive Brown, or whatever handle he'd been using at the time.

She pushed the door wide open with dramatic force. The huge man snapped at attention, taking her in with clear, sober eyes. She always liked to see sobriety reflected back at her. Most of the people who sat in that chair could barely stay sitting in it, let alone speak without slurring, drooling, or yakking all over themselves.

"Mr. Glover, thanks for joining us on this fine summer afternoon," she said, chipper as a kindergarten teacher.

The man was momentarily speechless, caught off guard by the sight of her. But Flora was used to that by now. At five-foot-three and fifty-five years of age, most of the men she questioned looked at her like she'd just wandered through the wrong door, or come to drop off paperwork. But that first impression never lingered for long. Flora had a commanding voice and she damn well knew how to use it.

"So," she went on, pulling up the chair opposite him. "Explain to me how a wanted fugitive sought for three counts of murder, aggravated assault, and, if we're lucky here, *just* a kidnapping, has disappeared into the wild blue yonder in a black Mazda6 registered to you?"

Glover rubbed his face and heaved an impatient sigh. "Listen," he said, "like I just told that hotshot rookie out there, Clive called me a few months ago, right after he was released from prison. Said he needed help rehabilitating himself, getting sorted, you know? But I wasn't exactly equipped to offer much help in that regard. I live in a one-bedroom apartment in a piece-of-shit highrise. Still, I owed him. He … well, let's just say he took a lot of heat for the team back in our Andromeda days."

"What do you mean, took heat?"

"Look, it's all ancient history. That being said, Clive did the honourable thing and refused to implicate anyone but himself in all those drug allegations — not that I had anything to do with it," Glover said, raising his hands innocently. "Still, the investigation could have ruined lives, set us all back, you know? So, it was a real upstanding thing to do. Anyway, out of gratitude for his being so gentlemanly, I helped him out, loaned him a car. Last time I'd seen him, he was in prison and real broken up about his mom's death. I felt bad for the guy."

"So, let me get this straight," Flora said, leaning in closer. "You hadn't seen or spoken to this old work colleague for over ten years. He gets out of prison and you go ahead and give him your car?"

"That's right. My brother owns a used car dealership."

"Did he say where he was going?"

"Just back home to where his mom used to live. He was all bent out of shape about missing her funeral. Figured he wanted to go home, tie up loose ends. She was a drug user, from what I know, in real rough shape when they found her corpse up in Sudbury. Anyway, I swear on my own mother's grave, I never knew he was going to kidnap some chick or kill a pair of seniors."

Flora took a gulp of coffee. "What else can you tell me about Clive? Did he have any friends or family members aside from his mother?"

Glover shook his head and twirled his ginger beard into a twisted point that reminded her of a devil's horn. "Other than that one visit to prison, I never saw him outside the bar," he said. "He was a loner. He may have had other people in his life, but he sure as hell never mentioned anyone to me."

"How about the Patterson woman? Do you know if they kept in touch?"

"Honestly, I couldn't tell you. I've seen her picture on the news, and truth is, I don't remember her. Lots of beautiful girls came through those doors. Back in the club's heyday, they were a dime a dozen. But I highly doubt a woman of that calibre would give Clive the time of day. He was a freak. Had a bad energy, you know? Not exactly Prince Charming, even with his new mug."

Flora had to admit, the more she learned, the more unlikely it seemed that Clive and Ellie were in cahoots. A loner drug dealer who'd spent ten-plus years in prison did not make for a good eligible bachelor. It seemed far more plausible that this was a straight-up case of kidnapping by a sexual predator. There were no phone records to suggest the two had ever been in touch. Nothing aside from some unverified interactions over a decade ago at a now-defunct dance club.

Unless the forty-year-old mother of two was a drug user, and Clive had been her supplier. But by all accounts, Eloise Patterson had a squeaky-clean reputation and not a single skeleton in her closet.

"Any chance you've got an idea where he might have taken her? Any secret bunkies I don't know about?" she asked.

Glover shrugged. "No clue. He liked watching the ladies dance, though. If I were a betting man, I'd say you might find him at a strip club. Then again, he's got his own lady now, so that changes everything, doesn't it?"

Flora hated to admit that it did.

CHAPTER 25

If Clive could do over one year of his life, it was 2004, the year his mother died and his efforts to become the man she'd wanted him to be had gone squirrelly. His transformation had been interrupted by a take-down he hadn't seen coming.

The truth was, he'd been guilty as sin. By late 2003, he'd developed quite a booming side business dealing drugs at Andromeda. He'd begun the small enterprise all for her, all to keep Brenda well-supplied and comfortable. Andrew Muir, the club owner, had turned a blind eye. He quietly reaped the rewards as Clive's illicit trade brought in a whole new calibre of customers, the kind with deep pockets and money to splash around. Everybody, including the bouncers, had benefitted.

But then Clive went and got himself busted by an undercover cop. That was the cataclysmic error that triggered his downfall and tore apart his new and improved identity. He'd only just gotten his surgery. Girls had only just started to cast their eyes his way. His mother had only just started treating him with a modicum of respect and appreciation. And then, *poof*, it was all gone. He'd been whisked away, locked up, never to see Brenda or his object of desire again.

In fact, the last time he'd seen Ellie was the night she'd sent Neil that Heineken, and boy, had that ever burned him. It made him blind with rage. Trusting her and delivering that fucking beer in the first place had been another pivotal mistake. Still, he'd never expected her to end up marrying him. Who in their right mind would have seen that coming? In the weeks and months afterward, he kept hoping she'd return, fall in love with the new face he'd had sculpted just for her. But she never did come back, and Clive got sloppy.

The worst moment was finding out that his mother had died of an overdose while he was incarcerated. It was all his fault. He hadn't been there to minister to her needs, to feed her the life-sustaining substance under his watchful supervision. Trevor Glover was the one who broke the news to him shortly after her death in November. Said her body had been discovered up near Sudbury, in some roadside motel. That part had baffled Clive, because he couldn't imagine why she'd gone up there in the first place. She'd never been to Sudbury. Hated nature, so far as he knew. Plus, she'd been such a recluse those last few years, barely able to set foot out the front door. Then, suddenly, off to cold, blustery Sudbury? None of it made any sense. He'd spent weeks reeling with sadness and confusion, unable to accept the bitter reality that she was gone for good, and that he was to blame.

At the time, he felt like his heart had been ripped out of his chest and stomped on. Felt like he'd been dumped, deserted. Orphaned, like she'd always threatened. Once the haze of disbelief lifted, the animal rage set in — fury over the world's consistent cruelty toward him, the genetic weaknesses he'd been born with, and the hard knocks he'd endured ever since.

But he wasn't going to be a victim anymore. No, he was going to emerge from his old sorry self and flower into something bigger, stronger. Someone she'd be proud of. Someone who deserved his strong man's name.

And that was when Clive Rutger Brown's real transition began.

/////////////////////

Ellie saw the flashing motel sign up ahead and felt her familiar panic set in. It was go time. Time to put on her battle face. Prepare for whatever horror was next.

Clive still had the meat mallet resting against his thigh — the very weapon she'd failed to employ when the moment had first presented itself. Instead, she'd armed him, given him something to smash against that poor man's face back in that garage.

This time she had to do better.

She closed her eyes; tried to draw strength from thoughts of her children. She tried to conjure them in full sensory detail. But, distressingly, she seemed to be unable. Try as she might, she couldn't see the flecks of gold in Mikey's blue eyes or the wispy tips of Beth's long, full lashes. Her mind was too unsettled, jumping in every direction at once. Was this a symptom of that knock to her head? It was possible. Seeing as how Clive had thumped her unconscious, she was lucky to have any wits about her at all. But the nausea and the dizziness were unrelenting. Her only coping mechanism was to keep her eyes shut.

She felt the car decelerate, heard the crunch of gravel beneath the tires. Her pulse quickened and a helpful surge of adrenalin shot through her. She lifted her eyelids a crack and caught a glimpse of a waxing moon that a day ago, she didn't think she'd live to see. It was hard to believe that a full rotation of the earth had elapsed since she'd last seen her husband — strapped to a chair, blood leaking from his hand and his foot.

The memory sickened her.

"Wakey, wakey," Clive muttered, smacking her on the knee. "You know the drill. Stay where you are, I'll come get you out … and don't do anything to make me angry."

Ellie forced a smile. "I'll be good, I promise."

She had to shift back into character, convince Clive that he could trust her again. They were about to enter a public space, where normal people would be present. Addressing each other in normal ways. *Not chopping off each other's fucking fingers.* She'd already managed to fool him once, convincing him that she'd snatched that mallet for their joint protection against the police, and if he believed that, then surely she could fool him again.

Only this time, she'd have to lay it on thick. She had no choice. Who knew if there'd be another chance?

Clive pulled her out of the car and shepherded her into the motel foyer. Ellie was certain that alarm bells would go off for someone. She was barefoot, for starters. Then there was the matter of her unseemly appearance. She doubted even a strung-out prostitute would enter a public establishment looking as rough around the edges as she did now. Someone was sure to notice her fearfulness, question Clive's manner, and take appropriate action. That's was what normal people did.

She was disheartened at first to see that the office appeared to be empty. Then, to her relief, she spotted the greasy mullet of a young male clerk who was slouched behind the check-in counter watching a YouTube video on his cellphone.

Clive tapped the ledge, jerking the young man to attention.

"Can I help you?" he asked.

"You sure can, Kenny," Clive said, noting the kid's nametag. He was in hyperconfident boor mode, and Ellie wasn't sure if that was a good or a bad thing. "We'd like to check into Room 118, please."

The clerk raised an eyebrow and smirked at Clive. "Um, okay. But are you sure you want that room? I can offer you something a little nicer. A room with a king-sized bed, perhaps?"

"Nope, that's the one I want, and I'm paying for it with cash."

"Have it your way," Kenny said. "Here are your keys. There's a vending machine outside to the left. You can get your coffee right here in the morning. The ice machine is over by the first set of stairs. Other than that, there's a diner about a mile up the highway. Nothing else until Sudbury. Enjoy your stay."

Ellie stared desperately into Kenny's shifty, unobservant eyes. Clive grinned and tugged her toward the exit.

///////////////////////

As an employee of the Sands Inn Motel for just over two years now, Kenny was used to the occasional oddball coming in, waving dollar bills and requesting to sleep in that godawful room. He'd been told it was part of some kind of "deathbed tour" on the website known as *Morbid Dreams*. Twisted as it was, people paid good money to travel to random destinations and stay where someone had been slain or had otherwise died heinously. In the case of Room 118, it was the latter. *Sickos*, he thought as he pocketed the cash.

But, to each their own — and the money would go to good use, he figured. Anyway, what did he care if some heroin-infused junkie had died in that room, likely on that very bed? Cheap as all hell, there was no way the proprietors of the motel had swapped out the mattress for a new one. Which was precisely what drew in the *Morbid Dreams* freaks and paid for his cellular data overages.

He watched them leave, noting with disgust that the woman wasn't wearing any shoes.

///////////////////

Flora found it absurd and distressing that in three hours' time there hadn't been a single sighting of the black Mazda6 carrying Clive Brown and the missing Patterson woman. It was unfathomable that he'd managed to get away, to escape Rockdale at breakneck speed without anyone noticing a goddamn thing. Of course, there was a decent chance he'd ditched the car and stolen a replacement vehicle by now. Or that he was holed up in a new location. But where?

She tried to imagine what kind of destination would entice a confused, dangerous man like Clive, a wanted fugitive with a scantily clad victim in tow. Tattoo man had suggested they search the strip clubs, and Flora had figured that wasn't such a bad idea. She'd dispatched a request to have every girly establishment in a two-hundred-mile radius identified and searched, but so far, no promising leads had been churned up.

There was one thought niggling around in her mind, and that was Clive's seemingly profound attachment to his unfit, drug-addled mom. For a boy who'd been removed from her inept care and forced to live with foster parents in an unfamiliar town, he was surprisingly loyal. Hell, he'd even gone and tattooed her name on his arm. The more she thought about it, the more it became disturbingly clear that Clive was a man motivated by his mother's affection, even though she was dead and twelve years buried.

This led her to another idea. It was a long shot, but at least it was a shot. If Clive's first instinct was to take

Ellie to Rockdale, where it had all begun, was it possible he was now taking her back to where it all had ended?

Sudbury. Trevor Glover mentioned that the woman had died in Sudbury. The question was, where?

/////////////////////

It was just after 8:00 p.m. when Neil finally convinced Laura to let him out of his hospital room. He wanted to see Abeer, needed to know his brother-in-law was going to be okay. Laura agreed to push Neil down the hall in a wheelchair, but on one condition — that he keep his ass firmly planted every second of the way.

They found Abeer sitting up and alert. His face was swollen and disfigured, his eyes two gashes in bloated purple flesh. Neil could see precisely where the meat tenderizer had punctured his skin, branding his face with its sharp metal teeth.

"I'd smile if I could," Abeer said through clenched jaws, "but I can't ... so you'll have to take my word for it that I'm happy to see you."

"Abeer, I'm so sorry ... I don't know what to say," Neil answered, fighting tears. "I made a seriously bad call. I was so selfish. I should never have sent you out there like that."

Abeer cleared his throat. "If I recall correctly, you told me to go knock on doors and act like a government dork, not sneak down back alleys and swing shovels at people. I did this to myself. But," he said, looking over at Laura, "do I regret it? Buddy, I saw her. And I came so close to bashing that motherfucker over the head. So, no, I don't regret it. At least now we know she's alive, and we're that much closer to finding her."

By now, Laura could no longer hold back her brewing storm of emotions. "Baby, you were so brave! I'm so glad you're going to be okay," she cried, throwing herself at Abeer's chest. "Ellie will be okay, too. They'll find her, I know it. They have his licence plate now and they know what he looks like. They even know his fucking name. Of course they'll find her. It's only a matter of time."

Neil nodded, but didn't have the energy to console Laura, to show solidarity with what she'd just said. He wasn't sure if she believed it herself, or was just trying to remain positive. But Ellie had been missing for more than twenty-four hours. Statistically speaking, that was bad news.

"She looked scared, but not hurt," Abeer continued, struggling to enunciate through his injuries. "I got the sense he was hustling her off to a new hideaway, maybe. She looked different, though. Her hair was chopped short and a few shades darker, and she was wearing a tight skirt and clingy top."

Neil's blood simmered, his heart hammering with rage. Why had that depraved lunatic dressed his wife up like that? Was he turning her into his personal sex slave? Forcing her to do unthinkable things, filthy sexual acts that she would never be able to recover from?

Abeer's expression changed, and he looked regretful he'd said anything. Neil realized he was visibly fuming. He loosened his fists and took a deep breath.

Always the empathetic one, Abeer back-pedalled and said, "I got the impression that the outfit was for camouflage, to throw off cops who might be looking for them." He cleared his throat. "The good thing is she didn't appear to be injured."

Not on the outside, Neil thought. On the inside, she might be wounded in ways that she could never get over.

That included his own betrayal of her, with Mia.

CHAPTER 26

Clive unlocked the motel room door, then hesitated. His hands were sweating, his heart furiously racing. They'd stopped back at the car to collect his mallet and his all-important bag of goodies — he was excited to share them with Ellie. They were the tools that would bring them all together, in one permanent place.

But suddenly, Clive couldn't move. Perhaps he'd been a little too eager to see it, this long-imagined room where *she* had passed to the other side.

Brenda. The woman who'd given him life. Who'd sacrificed everything to raise him on her own after his no-good sperm-donor of a dad had deserted her.

Brenda. The most captivating, explosive person he'd ever known. A rare, sensual being who brimmed with passion, volatility, grief, and fury.

Before Clive had met Ellie, Brenda had been the only one who mattered, the only one who inspired him to transform into a better man. Only Brenda had seen his true potential, what he could become, thanks to her vital motherly coaxing. And he, in return, was her only champion. Her flesh-and-blood creation who saw into her soul and appreciated her greatness, despite what others said. *All those fucking simpletons who tried to brainwash me!*

"Clive, baby," he heard Ellie say. She was standing next to him, peering through the open door. He was holding her wrist, squeezing it. "I'm hungry. The clerk mentioned something about a diner up the road. What do you say we go check it out?"

But Clive only heard the word *baby*. It bounced off her pretty wet lips, breaking his trance and causing a stir in the crotch of his pants. Suddenly his mind was off Brenda, off the hamburger and French fries he'd been ravenously craving. Now, all he wanted was to get her down on that bed and ravage her. To trace his tongue up her legs, starting at her dirty little toes and licking his way up to that sweet spot he'd yet to touch. He wanted to smell her, get inside her, and really feel her. But he wanted to go long and slow. Not rush it. Relish every moment. Savour her.

"No," he said, nudging her into the fusty room. "I've got something better in mind."

"Really?" He could feel her body resisting, and he didn't like that. "It's just … I want this moment to be special, and I think a G and T would help me. Come on, what do you say?"

Clive had heard all this before and he wasn't going to be fooled again. The way she'd behaved back at Dewy's — shooting glances at Randy — well, that had triggered a domino effect of trouble. Because as much as he'd tried to be the nice guy, feed her a few drinks to help her take the edge off, he'd ended up losing his temper. Bludgeoning that asshole and leaving an unnecessary trail of blood for the police.

Since then, he hadn't known whether he could trust her or not. She'd been throwing out loads of mixed signals, sometimes sexual ones like she wanted him to touch her, other times signs of fear and loathing. Sometimes even disgust. It made him wonder if she was just pretending to love him. Toying with him, like a cat batting around a field mouse.

He took her by the back of the neck and pulled her in close. "What exactly are you up to?" he asked, his lips brushing hers.

"Nothing, Clive. Like I said, I'm just hungry … and thirsty."

"Well, lucky for you, there's water inside." He wrenched her into the room and shut the door behind them. Locked it with the slide bolt, then the chain. "Go freshen up in the bathroom. I'll be waiting for you out here. And Ellie … I have a little surprise for you."

///////////////////

Back at the Maplewood OPP station, Flora decided to follow her hunch and get on the horn with the police division up in Sudbury. She figured it was worth looking into, this loosely formed theory of hers that he might be going to where his mother had passed away. While death records were being searched, along with the area's motels, bars, and girlie clubs, she and Murray struck out on the road. It would be a three-hour haul, perhaps a pointless one, but at least they could explore her hypothesis on route. Murray, as always, would be a good listener.

Flora yawned and rubbed her eyes as they hit the northbound highway. She was beyond tired. Too tired for rational thought. She'd entered that hyper, twitchy state in which she was unable to settle her mind, to harness her inner calm. There were things jumping out of the shadows, faces in her periphery. A dreadful feeling that if she didn't catch their bad guy real soon, there'd be more bloodshed, and this time that blood would land squarely on her shoulders.

She cringed, imagining the heat they'd feel from both her superiors and the public at large if she didn't catch this guy before another victim ended up dead. In her mind's eye, a swarm of angry citizens surrounded her, shouting blame and accusing her of incompetence.

"Hey Murray, do you ever see faces that aren't even there?" she asked her companion, who was driving and whistling mindlessly.

"Only after a few too many pops," he said.

Oh, to be young again.

//////////////////////

Locked in the bathroom, Ellie found herself thinking about the time she and Neil had first met at Andromeda

— how, as cliché as it sounded, she'd felt electricity. Truly, she had never been so drawn to another human being in all her life. Initiating contact had been such a rush — not to mention its eventual outcome. It was as though she had always been fated to send Neil that beer, and he was fated to accept it.

But now, held captive in this squalid motel with dread seeping into her bones, she was struck by the irony of it all. That night she'd also made her offhand remark about George Clooney, just to get Clive off her back. Instead, it had fuelled his resolve to be with her. To transform himself into the man she wanted. To hunt her down and steal her … from her home, her family, her life.

Her mind was spinning as she considered how far-reaching the consequences of that blip in time had been, setting her up for the very best in her life — finding love and happiness with the man of her dreams — and the very worst — being raped and killed by the monster of her nightmares.

It was crazy. *Inconceivable.*

And now, as Ellie faced her own looming mortality, uncertain whether the love of her life was lying dead in some morgue or not, she felt a brief appreciation for her captor's madness. Madness had its advantages, after all. It released the thinker of responsibility, of restraint, and permitted that person the freedom to just be. Guiltless.

She stared at her own peaked face in the mirror, her dyed sandy hair and tired blue eyes, but she was considering Clive, analyzing him. He was a man of many facets, many oddities. He could be fiercely present one moment, then drift away, unreachable, the next. Where did he go? What alternate universe drew him away?

She suddenly remembered the tattoo on his arm of a woman's name, Brenda Brown. A deceased wife, or mother? At some point Clive had said something about "becoming the man she wanted me to be." Since Ellie's concussion, all their exchanges had bled together into a single dark cesspool. But now those submerged details were beginning to surface with clarity.

Whoever she was — wife, mother, or unrequited love — Brenda Brown was at the centre of this morbid, miserable mess. Undoubtedly the inspiration for her newest tawdry look.

///////////////////////

Clive could feel himself beginning to lose control. Gripping the bedspread in his hands, he fought to keep from crying, but the image of his poor, sick mama had taken over his mind. He saw her all alone, jacked up on heroin. Convulsing, and eventually dying.

But why? Why had she come all the way up to this arbitrary dump on the outskirts of some remote nickel-mining town? He gathered the slippery fabric in his hands and squeezed as hard as he could until his fingers turned deep purple and a blood vessel nearly popped in his eye. But he managed to dislodge a new thought.

He lessened his grip as the repressed memory flooded back. Clive saw himself, a scrawny boy with bony knees sitting on a beige corduroy sofa next to his mom and that Children's Aid heifer, Miranda. The image was as clear as anything. So clear, in fact, it seemed to be playing out in real time. Miranda's podgy cheeks in stark contrast to Brenda's dull, limp jowls. Brenda opening her mouth and uttering the string of words he'd forgotten until this very second: "Clive's dad was just some idiot hotel manager from Sudbury. Just some random nobody who never mattered a single fuck …"

Except maybe he had mattered. If she'd come all the way up here in her final days of life, then likely he'd been more to her than just some sperm-donor who'd knocked her up. Maybe Brenda had loved him. This realization filled Clive with a tremendous sadness, and he started to sob, right into the very place his doomed, ill-treated mother had taken her last lonely breath.

/////////////////////

Ellie heard Clive weeping and pushed open the bathroom door. At first she just hovered there, confounded. It was surreal to see him like that — her brawny captor, rotten to the core, bawling into a bedspread like a broken-hearted child.

Clive glanced up. Quickly wiped away all traces of his grief. "I was just thinking about someone," he muttered.

"You mean … Brenda?"

When she said the name, Clive's entire countenance changed, his eyes and face noticeably brightening. Ellie recalled the bar incident back in Rockdale, the way

Clive had hectored that poor bartender into admitting he knew Brenda before promptly bludgeoning him to death. But this was Ellie's chance to dig a little deeper, to absorb Clive in the memory of someone who was obviously integral to his fucked-up story.

"You miss her a lot, don't you," she prodded gently.

Clive sniffed. Nodded his head.

"Brenda was … your mother?"

He nodded again. "She died a long time ago. I couldn't be at her funeral."

"Oh, I'm so sorry," Ellie said.

"I should have been with her, I should have taken better care of her. It was my fault she died. I'm a terrible son."

"No, Clive, you can't blame yourself. I'm sure you did the best you could."

Ellie watched incredulously as Clive's eyes filled with tears. She knew she needed to keep him preoccupied for as long as possible while she figured out a new way to escape. Stall and form a plan. But then, suddenly, it was too late. She saw the abrupt change happen before her eyes — darkness and rage replaced what had just seconds before been shame — and Ellie became deeply afraid.

If I scream, will anyone hear?

Clive threw the bedspread aside, stood up, and puffed out his chest.

"Take off your clothes," he growled.

"What?"

"You heard me."

Ellie took two steps back. "Hold on, Clive, I …"

But he didn't wait for her to comply. He came at her, grabbed her by the arms, and threw her down on the bed. Suddenly she was sprawled out on her back, watching in terror as Clive got on his knees and started sucking her toes. Then he pulled her ankles apart and began running his tongue up her bare leg, around the curve of her knee, until his face was almost between her thighs.

Ellie was desperate to stop him, desperate to redirect his aggression. But he was too strong, too sexually charged. It was as though he'd grown eight times bigger since the mention of his mother's name. And now, with Clive's hands locked around her legs like restraints, his coarse whiskers rubbing against her flesh, Ellie felt defenceless. On the verge of the very thing she feared most. Being raped.

Then, she had a thought. A vision so clear it might have been beamed down from somewhere above. She was going about her resistance all wrong; there was another approach Clive would respond to. The control she'd been seeking all along could be achieved by letting it go.

"Stop touching me right now, you filthy piece of shit!" she yelled with such rage that spittle flew from her mouth and landed on his face. "You heard me. Get the fuck off me now, damn it!"

Clive froze. Fell silent and pulled away. Ellie continued scowling at him with profuse hatred, and he stared back at her with wide, childlike eyes. To her amazement, he turned his head away in what seemed to be a show of submission.

"Now, you listen to me," she went on, summoning her angriest mom voice, "I don't know who you think you are, but unless I ask you to put your hands or your mouth on me, you are not to do it, ever! Do you understand me?"

Clive nodded, his countenance so altered, so deflated, that Ellie could scarcely believe what she was seeing. Was this some sort of game? A bizarre role-playing fetish? Whatever it was, she needed to keep the harsh mama routine rolling for as long as she could. She'd spank his bare ass, if she needed to. Anything to ensure that the power remained in her hands, and that her hands eventually found their way to the mallet.

But just as Ellie was feeling confident about securing the upper hand, Clive did something so unexpected that it shook her to her core.

He raised his thumb to his mouth and sucked it.

CHAPTER 27

Murray and Flora had been on the road for nearly two hours when they pulled into a gas station for a pit stop. Just as Flora was coming out of her stall, her cellphone rang. It was Patterson.

"Hello, Neil. Everything okay?" she asked, her tone flat but with a hint of empathy. She figured he'd been through enough already, didn't need any more of her condemnation or sass. Sure, he'd broken the law — he'd purposefully set out to hunt down a suspect with the likely intent to kill — but seeing as that lunatic had hacked off his finger and toe, then made off with his wife, she could let it go. At least while she had bigger fish to fry.

"I'm fine. Just checking in to see if there's been any progress," Neil said.

He sounded sedate. *Too much morphine*, Flora surmised.

"Nothing firm to report just yet. But I did have a nice chat with that bouncer, Trevor Glover. He gave me a few ideas about where they might be headed."

"Where?" Neil asked, perking up.

"Now, now, fool me once, shame on you — fool me twice, shame on me," she said, tucking her phone under her chin so she could squirt fluorescent-pink soap into her hands. "When I have any solid information to share with you, you can trust that I will share it. For now, I need you to sit tight, remain at the hospital, and behave yourself."

"Detective, please ... I swear to you, I will not interfere. After what happened to Abeer, I just can't risk endangering anyone else. Plus, I'm a wreck ... my foot is infected. From what they're saying, I'm going to be laid up here for a while. I just can't handle not knowing where she is."

She chuckled as she strode out the door. "Spare me, will you?"

Just then, Murray surprised her from behind. "Hey, I've got the Sudbury Chief of Police on the line. Says he needs to speak to you about a possible Clive sighting."

She scrambled to cover the mouthpiece of her phone. "Gimme a sec, will ya, Murray?"

Then to Neil, she said, "I'll call you back with an update in a bit. Get some sleep, do you hear me? And remember, this time I'm serious. You leave that hospital, you're going to jail."

She signed off with her trademark. "Toodle-oo."

///////////////

Ellie tried to shake the feeling that she was hallucinating. Before her eyes, Clive was sucking his thumb like a little boy fearing punishment. Ellie had finally tapped into the weakness that she'd been looking for: Brenda.

Clive's mother was a nasty, abusive bitch, and Ellie needed to emulate her.

"You're a bad boy, Clive, do you hear me? Mama is very angry with you!" she shouted, her fists raised in the air, scowling hatefully. "You're pathetic! A pathetic, worthless son, and I wish you'd never been born!"

Clive's eyes were downcast, his shoulders stooped in submission. Ellie shuddered at the incongruous sight of this huge man acting like a toddler, but she managed to tear her eyes away from him long enough to take stock of the room. She had to find the mallet.

Then something shiny caught her eye. It was leaning by the door, just five steps away. Tugging down her skirt, Ellie marched past Clive, desperate to keep her gaze steady and her nylon-thin illusion of dominance intact.

Three more steps, two more steps ...

She was almost there when Clive clued in to what was happening. He sprang up from the bed, his fingernails scratching at her calves. Ellie jumped away at the last second and succeeded in grabbing the mallet.

"Stay away or I'll kill you, I swear to God," she said vehemently.

But Clive looked anything but afraid. Pure venom shot from his eyes, and Ellie knew that despite her momentary advantage she would be no match for whatever hell he was about to unleash next.

"You fucking ungrateful bitch," he seethed, his hateful gaze piercing the air between them. "Turning on me after everything I've done … after all the years I spent protecting you, making things right for you, for us …"

Ellie was beyond the point of hearing, of processing anything Clive said. She was desperately trying to figure out what to do, with how to get around him and unlock the barricaded door.

"That fucking dick, that spineless *twerp*," he went on, spitting globs of saliva. "Gets everything handed to him a silver platter while I get nothing, no one. Well, I don't think so! And you … so forgiving, so willing to forget. Acting like nothing ever happened, like he didn't destroy your life and fuck with your family …"

Clive's crazy eyes suddenly shifted away from Ellie and onto the crumpled bag on the floor. Though it looked no more threatening than a child's packed lunch, she knew better. She knew it contained something cruel and unusual. Something to be frightened of.

"Let me go, Clive. Please, let me go and I'll disappear … I'll —"

Clive let out a sharp laugh. "Sorry, Ellie, but that's not possible. We're not finished our game yet. In fact, we're just getting to the best part, the part I've been waiting for." He flexed and curled his fingers, his grin fading as he looked back at the empty bed. "You see, that's where my mother died. Right there in that very spot… and my biggest regret is that I wasn't by her side. I wasn't there to comfort her, to help ease her into the afterlife. But I can make things right. I can be there this time … for you." He stepped toward her. "Everything will be all right, I promise. All your pain will be gone, and finally you'll be free. Free of the pain *he* caused you. Don't you see? All that pain you've been carrying around will be gone, and you can be at peace knowing that I was there. The man you've always wanted … always wanted me to be."

Ellie felt the blood draining from her face as Clive's intent became clear. He was going to pump her full of heroin, recreate his mother's gruesome death. It was all starting to make a twisted sort of sense, like some textbook Freudian psychic unravelling. All this time Clive had been confusing Ellie with his mother and Neil with his absent dad. That explained the hatred toward Neil, the obsession with her, the lust and longing. The incongruous references to some deep sorrow he'd saved her from…. It was all fuelled by his own incestuous need to make amends with his past. A warped reckoning that had nothing to do with her or Neil.

"You're sick, Clive," Ellie said, the mallet raised high as she slowly backed away. "You need help. You're confused … confused about who I am, don't you see? I'm a married woman. Someone you don't even know. You need to understand that. You need to see that I'm not your mother — I'm not Brenda, and Neil's not your dad."

She gave him a tender look, tried to subdue him with all the phony empathy she could muster. Then she took her chance and sprang at him, clobbering him on the side of the head with bull's eye accuracy.

Clive's eyes rolled back as he began to fall, grabbing her hair and pulling her down with him. She hit the floor shockingly hard, and his dead weight made it impossible for her to move, to breathe. As he twitched and moaned, fighting to recover, she managed to wiggle out from beneath him, scramble to her feet, and fling herself at the locked door. She could sense him behind her rubbing his eyes, shaking himself awake, and she knew she had only a few seconds to release the bolt and unlatch the chain.

Clive was in the midst of staggering to his feet when Ellie finally got the door open and ran screaming into the parking lot. But she mistakenly turned left instead of right and found herself fleeing into the woods. Dark woods thick with branches. Woods that led to nowhere.

Barefoot and half-naked, she ran, stumbling and picking herself up multiple times as she ducked under branches and leapt over fallen logs. She kept going for as long her lungs could stand it. Behind her, she could see Clive lumbering along, and she knew her energy was dwindling fast — she needed to find a place to hide.

She knew that the highway was to her right, and there was a diner about a mile up ahead. Still, the smart thing to do, she decided, was to go a little farther and take cover. Watch for Clive to pass her by. Then she could circle back to the motel and call the police.

When Laura discovered that Neil was missing from his room, she rolled her eyes and huffed in frustration. Then, trying to give him the benefit of the doubt, she reasoned that he'd probably just gone off to take a leak, or maybe he was wandering the halls to stretch his legs. Of course, given that there was a toilet in his room and that Neil had suffered a non-medical toe amputation, neither of these possibilities made much sense. Laura shook her head.

She was exasperated, her brain and her emotions on overdrive. She didn't have kids of her own. Loathed the idea of motherhood, in fact. Frankly, she wasn't good at taking care of other people's needs. Her parents and Evelyn were much better at crisis management, but they were all off together on a month-long Mediterranean cruise, oblivious to this entire fucking catastrophe. Oh, how she longed for them now! How she wished they could all be together so she could lean on them, concentrate on coping with her own crushing grief.

But then her eyes fell upon her purse lying open on the side table, and she was whipped into a frothy rage. She let out a loud string of curse words. Her car keys were gone. She took a breath, calmed herself, and yanked out her cellphone, thinking even as she dialed that Neil wouldn't possibly be dumb enough to answer. But it turned out he was.

"I'm sorry, Laura," Neil said, pre-empting her tirade. "I know you're pissed off, and rightfully so, but I won't be swayed. I need to do this."

"Do what, exactly?" Laura yelled into the phone. "Steal cars and get in the way of police investigations? You're being a stubborn jackass, Neil! Not only are you acting unlawfully, but what you're doing is dangerous. Ellie's not just your wife, she's my sister — one of the remaining two I have left — and I will not let you jeopardize her life for some dumbass machismo, do you hear me? Now turn my fucking car around and get your ass back in bed."

"I would never do anything to put Ellie in harm's way," Neil fired back, his tone deep and resolute. "I just need to be there for her. Look, I can't explain how, but I know that she needs me ... and I promised her I'd always be there for her."

Laura went silent. Then she cursed again. "Of course I get it, but that's not how these things work. Jesus. For starters, you're not trained for this kind of shit. You're upset, I get it, but that's not enough. This guy is a murderer ... and you're not. You're *good*. And let's not forget that the cops have guns. You don't!"

"I'm just going to Sudbury. There's been a sighting and the police think she could be there. I'm just driving up so I can be with her when they find her. That's it. Please just do me a favour. Tell Abeer that I'm grateful for his friendship and I love him, okay? And Laura ... Ellie's going to be fine, just like you said."

Neil hung up the phone.

///////////////////

Flora's bowels compressed as the Sudbury Police Chief droned on about his Clive sightings, or lack thereof. The sweep of all hotels, motels, and drinking establishments within city limits had turned up only one suspect, then quickly snowballed into a "giant clusterfuck," as he'd put it. He explained that they'd stormed into some seedy adults-only club and mistakenly hassled an innocent bystander who was there incognito, on a tryst. Turned out the man was some highfalutin investor in town to consider a multimillion-dollar real estate opportunity. To make matters worse, the aggressive takedown had been captured on video, and the footage had already gone viral.

It was a clusterfuck, all right.

Flora felt sick as she hung up the phone. Sick and tired of dealing with all the bullshit that went along with her thankless, high-stakes job. Was she wasting valuable time on combing some northern nickel-mining town that might be totally irrelevant to the case? For a moment she considered telling Murray to turn back for the station, forget Sudbury altogether. But then she shook off the impulse, figuring it was best to persevere. They'd come this far, and sadly, her instincts were all they had going for them.

"We sure are in God's Country now," Murray breathed, oblivious to her mental strife as he gazed appreciatively at the scenery. "I can see why people choose to live up here, to get away from it all."

Flora grunted her agreement, but she wasn't in the mood for small talk — or for basking in the breathtaking view. She'd been up for two days straight, her brain on overdrive, firing incomplete thoughts in multiple directions at once. She'd depleted every ounce of fuel she had left, even what little was in her reserve tank. No human of any age, not even a young buck like Murray, could function rationally without shutting down the system for a quick reboot at some point.

"Hey, what do you say we take a short hiatus … hit the next motel we come to, and have ourselves a cat-nap?" she proposed.

Murray yawned and flashed her a silent thumbs-up. Then he turned his attention back to the transient land-scape, wondering if there were any motels between nowhere and Sudbury, anyway.

///////////////////////

Clive couldn't see his target, but he knew she was out there a few yards ahead, hidden in the shadows of the trees. He figured she was aiming for that diner, the one she'd been so hell-bent on going to earlier. The clerk had said it was a mile up the road. But it was dark, and his head was pulsing with pain right where Ellie had cracked him with the mallet. The trees were swirling, making him dizzy. Not that a little pain or dizziness would stop him from finding her. On the contrary, it was helping to fuel his rage.

Enough is enough. The game is over, Clive thought as he trudged along at a half gallop. At this point, all he wanted was to catch her and punish her. To squeeze the life out of her for foiling his plan and making such a fool out of him. He could hear Brenda cackling and howl-ing at his incompetence, at his failure to be a real man. Killing Ellie would be a cathartic climax to a drawn-out botched mission.

"Oh, Ellie," he sang, imagining her pretty blue eyes dripping in fear, "I know you're out here. I can smell you. Come out, come out, wherever you are!"

Clive stopped and listened, though he figured she wouldn't respond. *The rotten bitch!*

A distant turkey vulture whined. Leaves rustled in the wind. Besides those sounds, there was only the infuriating drone of mosquitoes. Clive carried on, his agitation mounting as the unseen ends of branches snagged his clothes and scratched his exposed skin. Even more bothersome were the damn mosquitos feasting on his sweaty neck. He smacked one dead right on the cheek, and the impact of his hand awakened a surge of pain that cut like molten streaks of white light through his tender brain.

"I'll find you, Ellie," he whispered. "Even if it takes all night."

////////////////////

Ellie held her breath. She could see Clive's outline skulking toward her, the only thing moving against the silhouette of the trees. Any other time, she'd be jumping and swatting at the stinging mosquitos, but right now, her survival depended on keeping perfectly still. Clive was dangerously close. One mistimed inhale would be enough to give her away.

She assumed that Clive was headed for the diner. If he kept his bearings for a little longer, stayed his current course, there'd soon be enough distance between them that she could make haste in the opposite direction, run like hell back to the motel, preferably without him knowing she was doing it.

She could hear him cursing and muttering and guessed he was in a fair bit of pain. Told herself she just needed to stay hidden, keep quiet, and wait. Wait for him to pass, then run. But the tree trunks were playing tricks on her, bouncing noise in every direction. She felt a surge of panic when his shape was no longer visible. It was as though he'd disappeared into thin air, and any second, he'd reach out from the darkness and grab her.

She looked toward the glow of the motel, which was still faintly visible in the far-off distance. Then she looked the other way, due north, presumably toward the diner. She considered running for it, but felt beholden to her plan, as though giving in to impetuousness might bring about her downfall.

A snapping twig a few feet away caused her to jump, leaping into motion like a terrified deer. It was nothing, a mistake, but now she had no choice but to keep on running. She was lighter and faster than Clive, but he'd be more determined than ever to catch her.

Something caught her foot. An ensuing pain shot through the length of her leg and up into her hip. Ellie shrieked. She'd planted her bare foot down on a spike of wood, and the jagged shard had been driven straight through her instep like a stake. It was stuck there, causing searing pain as she tried to hobble on, inadvertently pushing it in even deeper.

"I heard that!" Clive yelled from the near distance. His savage cackle bounced and swirled through the trees. "Is that blood I smell?" He sniffed the air wildly. "Boy, you've really fucked yourself now. Do you hear me, Ellie? You're fucked!"

CHAPTER 28

Flora and Murray spotted a dingy-looking motel from the highway. The Sands Inn Motel, it was called. They weren't about to be picky, especially since it appeared to be the only game in town. Plus, they were closing in on their destination. Only fifteen miles to Sudbury, so they could rally quickly if need be.

As he drove into the parking lot, Flora took stock of their desolate surroundings, noting the mostly empty stalls in the parking lot. A sigh of relief escaped her. She might have bawled like a baby, right there in the presence of her hunky subordinate, if she'd have been faced with a *No Vacancy* sign.

As Murray steered them into the nearest open stall, Flora squinted over at the three parked vehicles at the far end of the lot. Only one of them, she noted, was black. Maybe it was a Mazda; it was tough to say in the diminishing light. She'd wander over and have a look after they'd checked in. *Wouldn't that be something*, she told herself. *Too good to be true.*

They climbed out of the car and shuffled into the office, abruptly awakening the clerk, who'd fallen asleep at the counter. "Welcome to the Sands Inn Motel," he said, trying to sound spry. "I'm Kenny. May I help you?"

"Two rooms, please, Kenny," Flora said. "Quiet ones, if possible."

"That won't be a problem," he replied, rubbing his eyes and casting a glance at Murray, who was outfitted in full police uniform. "You two here on duty?"

Flora shook her head. "Just stopping in for a rest — unless we get lucky." She nudged her tall companion and snickered to herself.

Kenny blinked at her in confusion. "Here are your keys," he eventually said, doling them out. "There's a vending machine outside to the left. You can get your coffee from that table in the morning. The ice machine is over by the first set of stairs. Other than that, there's a diner about a mile up the highway, and nothing else until Sudbury. Enjoy your stay."

They left the office and trudged down the walkway toward their respective rooms.

"Well, have a good rest," Murray said, arriving at his door.

Fitzgerald nodded and kept going, the black car in the distance calling out to her.

Just in case, she told herself.

She stepped down off the walkway and directly into a cloud of midges. Flailing her arms, coughing and sputtering, she continued cutting a path to the far side of the lot. Turned out the car in question *was* a Mazda. She checked the licence plate. Rubbed her eyes and checked it again.

They're here. This is real …

She unclipped her flashlight and beamed it inside the vehicle. It was empty. She rushed back to the motel and pounded on Murray's door. The lights in his room instantly flared on, and a second later he was standing in the doorway, staring down at her.

"You won't believe this … Clive, he's here. The car is here." She pointed across the lot with her flashlight. "He could have ditched it, I suppose, stolen another one. I'll go glean whatever I can from that dopey clerk while you call for backup … just in case."

Just in case was becoming her mantra.

Flora dashed back to the office and tore inside to find Kenny already fast asleep at his post. She pounded on the counter with her fist. "Wake up, it's an emergency!" she shouted. "I need to know if a man and a woman checked in here today at some point before us. Both white, approximately forty to fifty, both attractive. Likely about two or three hours ago."

The kid was tongue-tied, still half-asleep. "Yeah." He blinked. "I guess they were what you'd call attractive, but they were kind of weird. I don't know. She had no shoes. They're in Room 118. I remember because —"

"Thanks," she said, cutting him off and nearly bumping into Murray as she flew out the door. "Room 118. Let's go."

////////////////////

Ellie's plan to flee back to the motel had backfired. Even before she'd impaled her foot on that piece of wood, the forest had presented a series of natural barricades that had forced her to stray off course. Now she was deeper into the woods, deeper into the darkness, her bearings completely lost. And Clive was still coming after her.

Ellie looked toward the horizon and noticed a clearing of some kind up ahead. The sky was fractionally lighter, though still quite dark, and there were no obstructions in the form of tree branches. A lake, maybe? She limped toward the opening, too afraid to move in any direction but forward.

Fighting her way through the tangle of branches, she emerged with a terrible fright. The clearing wasn't a lake or a swamp, but a sheer drop-off, and she'd almost gone right over it. Clutching onto some branches, she leaned out to see where the steep rockface led, but the slope staggered as it sank toward ground level and prevented her from glimpsing the bottom. She could tell from the expanse of treetops before her that there was land below, not water.

No one could make that fall, she decided — not without snapping their neck and shattering every bone in their body along the way. Not even a freak of nature like Clive.

///////////////////

The door to Room 118 was wide open, and no one was inside. The only indication that someone had been in there was a ruffled bedspread and a discarded lunch bag on the floor. Flora picked it up and emptied it out onto the bed. A vial of powdered heroin and assorted drug paraphernalia tumbled out. She looked at Murray, mystified.

Outside, the scream of approaching sirens indicated that the backup Murray had requested had arrived. "Let's go," Flora said. "If they're on foot, they can't have gotten very far."

Kenny was in the parking lot capturing the spectacle with his cellphone when Flora came out and slapped the phone from his hand. "What else is around here, Kenny? Any bars or restaurants?"

She figured if Murray was right about Clive's motives back in Rockdale, perhaps he'd taken Ellie to a public space here — another mission to show off his pretty treasure.

"Like I told you, there's a diner about a mile up that way," the clerk said, pointing north. "Other than that, there's only these woods for miles around." He waited for her to turn her head before bending down to pick up his phone, muttering something about filing a complaint.

"Doubt they would have walked all the way to that diner when the car is right there," Flora said to Murray. "Unless they stole a new one." She glanced back at Kenny, who looked at the handful of parked cars and shrugged. Then she peered at the ridge of trees. She couldn't imagine having to seek refuge in such a terrifying place. "Could be she got free from him and ran like hell to hide. Murray, why don't you do a preliminary search of the forest there, see what you can see. I'll join you once I've updated our new arrivals."

Murray nodded and leapt into motion, igniting his flashlight and cutting a path into the forbidding darkness.

//////////////////////////

Neil was in Laura's MINI Cooper, a little shy of halfway to Sudbury, when the radio station issued a breaking news report on Ellie's abduction. He cranked the volume.

"*The suspect, known to police as Clive Berringer, who is wanted in connection with the murder of Maplewood retirees Jake and Nella Palmer and the disappearance of forty-year-old Toronto native Eloise Patterson, is still at large as the search throughout central and northern Ontario continues. Patterson, the missing mother of two, was last seen Monday in a black Mazda6 leaving the town of Rockdale with her alleged kidnapper. Her husband, Neil Patterson, is said to be in hospital with life-threatening injuries. The police are asking anyone with information to contact the hotline ...*"

Neil squeezed the steering wheel and let out a series of anguished cries, caught between immense relief and bitter disappointment. The "breaking news" hadn't contained a single new detail. Hadn't even mentioned the related murder of the bartender, Randy Miller.

He wiped his eyes with his shirt. Refocused on the open road. Tried to convince himself that Ellie was still alive. Ellie, love of his life and mother of his children. Homemaker by default, whose publishing company had upended through no fault of hers. Why hadn't he encouraged her to try again, start something new? No, instead, he'd cheated on her. *What a fucking asshole!*

Neil ran his good hand through his hair, resisted the urge to pull it out. He swallowed what little saliva was left coating his throat. Felt deeply alone.

Suddenly, he thought of his kids at camp and desperately longed for them. He hoped they'd been spared the knowledge that their mother was missing and their father tortured. Then he thought of his own dad in Winnipeg, realizing he hadn't even bothered to call him. He picked up his cellphone, held it for a few seconds, then dropped it back on the seat.

He was just about to switch off the radio when another announcement came on, this one about a highway closure fifteen miles south of Sudbury. No specifics were given, just a general statement advising commuters to avoid the area until further notice.

Neil put the pedal to the metal. There was no doubt in his mind that the closure had something to do with Ellie.

///////////////////

Ellie was crouched behind a stump, holding a long, jagged stick — her intent to snag Clive's ankles and send him over the cliff. *Easy*, she told herself as the plan played out in her mind. She had to do this successfully. If she failed again, she would die. *This is it.*

She heard Clive approaching, his heavy boots tromping toward the clearing, his lungs wheezing for air. It sounded like he was going fast. Fast enough that maybe his momentum alone would be enough to take him over the edge. Send him plummeting straight to his death. But tripping him would be her insurance policy.

Then, suddenly, he was propelling through the branches toward her. Ellie raised her stick as planned, caught his ankles, and sent him flying into the void. For one surreal moment, everything was quiet. Her relief was uncertain. It was too dim to make out where he'd landed, or even if he'd gone over the edge at all.

She took a step forward, then paused. The silence was chilling.

She took another step. This time a shadowy form lurched up from the ground and grabbed her by the foot. She fell hard onto the rock, her stomach smacking the surface with such astonishing force that she couldn't breathe.

"Got you!" Clive roared, pulling her close. He flipped her onto her back and buried her beneath his weight. Ellie opened her eyes and saw his flared nostrils, his enraged eyes inches from her face. She was pinned, flattened against the rock. There was no way she could wriggle out from under his crushing girth.

"Tell me my name," he said, his eyes two angry slits, his breath hot on her face. But Ellie couldn't breathe, let alone speak. "Tell me my name!" he demanded again, and this time she managed to say it. Clive grinned, ramming his mouth onto hers and kissing her so aggressively, she thought she might suffocate. She had to get him off her or she'd pass out.

Fighting to remain conscious, she somehow managed to slide her arm out from under him and feel around for her dropped stick. No luck. She raked the ground for something, anything she could use to daze him, but found only loose pebbles and rocks within reach. Still, she took hold of the biggest rock she could find and waited until Clive was swept away in the kiss. Then she clamped her teeth down on his tongue until she tasted blood; it filled her mouth and trickled down the sides of her cheeks as Clive screamed. She brought the rock down on his cheek, smashed it against the bridge of his nose, again and again, until he recoiled, sputtering blood and incoherent threats.

Ellie scrambled to her knees, tried to get away. But Clive was too quick, diving at her sideways and knocking her flat a second time. They were just a few feet, if that, from the edge, but Clive was too enraged to notice. With his fists clenched and his mouth oozing blood, he rose before her and let out a gurgling roar. Ellie took advantage of the moment to haul back both legs and kick him in the knees, throwing him off balance and sending him staggering backward. Then, he was gone.

Ellie sat up, stunned. Panting. Her lungs were on fire. She gulped in as much air as she could. The taste of blood filled her mouth — Clive's blood. She spat it out and managed to stand up, blinked several times in hopes that her eyes would better adjust to the light. Finally, when she was ready, she took hold of some branches and leaned out, catching sight of a fallen log. But it wasn't a log. It was Clive, dangling from the edge by one hand, his fingertips nearly touching her bare toes.

"Ellie ... help me ... give me your hand," he pleaded, his voice thin. Desperate.

She couldn't see his eyes, but she could imagine them — wet with fear, imploring her to save his life.

"After everything I did ... to set things right ... to get back at him ..."

Clive was half crying, half whimpering, still confusing Neil with his deadbeat dad. But Ellie said nothing as she stared down, unable to move. It was a strange place to be — on top, looking down. The one in control, her tormentor begging for mercy. Mercy for the man who'd sliced off her husband's finger and toe, who had threatened to rape and kill her. The man who'd bludgeoned a bartender to death and murdered her elderly neighbours. It was so strange to feel sorry for that man, to feel remorse for what she was about to do.

And she hated him for that. Hated that he would die, while she spent the rest of her life saddled with the knowledge that she'd killed him. Willfully. Not in a frantic moment of self-defence, but looking down at him and letting him fall. Helping him along, even.

"Maybe fingers are more important than you thought," she said coldly. She bent down and began loosening his claw-like grip. One by one, she unhinged each finger, all the while ignoring his escalating pleas. And then, in a flash, he was gone, slipping from sight, bringing a shower of pebbles and debris down along with him.

When all the dust had settled, Ellie fell back on her haunches and tried to catch her breath, let her surreal victory sink in. Unconsciously, she let out a long, pained howl that carried over the treetops and echoed back at her in ethereal, diminishing bursts. As soon as she was able, she stood up, wincing from the pain in her foot, and stole a final glance over the edge. Then she turned to hobble home.

The question was, home to who?

CHAPTER 29

Officer Murray was about half a mile into the woods, shining his torch on what appeared to be fresh footprints. "Detective Fitzgerald," he called out, "better come see this!"

Flora followed his voice and the flicker of his flashlight. A few minutes later she was staring down at two sets of human tracks. First, small barefoot tracks. The second, imprints of large, man-sized boots.

"Come on, let's move," she said.

Not far ahead but still out of sight, Ellie was stumbling along through the wild terrain, still in a haze of shock. She felt vaguely confident that she was moving in the right direction. Her senses were deadened to the bugs and branches, her bleeding foot numb to the pain. She had outlived Clive, and now nothing in these woods would get in the way of her getting out of them.

When she saw the lights, her first instinct was to duck and hide until she was certain it wasn't a trap. But then, something about the way the bright beams sliced and weaved through the maze of trees felt like salvation, like a lifeboat searching for survivors in an ocean fog, and she knew they were meant for her.

"I'm here!" she yelled, "I'm okay … I'm right here!"

///////////////////

Forty minutes later, Ellie found herself alone in a motel room nearly identical to the one she'd just escaped. Same bargain bedspread, slightly different pastel art.

She was dazed. Disoriented. Depleted.

She looked around at the tacky decor and longed for her children. Longed for Neil and the normalcy of her life back before any of this had happened, before everything had taken such a violent, unfathomable turn. She still didn't know if Neil was dead or alive. She hadn't been able to face the truth, and so she'd refrained from asking the question. She just needed to decompress. Take a few moments to collect herself. Pretend that he was okay, that someday they'd forget about Clive, and that MJ had never existed.

She turned to the mirror and barely recognized her own reflection. She was filthy, ragged, in clothes that hugged her every curve, scarcely providing any coverage. How she longed for her tracksuit and a decent bra and underpants. Big old granny ones that stretched up over her navel and would make men turn away, limp. She wrapped herself in the polyester bedspread and stepped outside into the presence of Detective Flora Fitzgerald. The tiny woman's face was a comforting sight to behold, and Ellie couldn't resist leaning into her wiry arms for a hug.

"It's okay, you're safe now," Fitzgerald said, patting her on the back. "You know, I've met a lot of married couples in my lifetime, but none quite like you two. He's a committed fella, that Neil."

Ellie stumbled back, searched the woman's face. "Are you saying he's alive? Is Neil alive?"

"Alive? Are you kidding me? Nothing could stop him. He managed to jump out a second-storey window, severed digits and all, without breaking his legs. Then he somehow tracked you down to Rockdale. He'd make quite a detective in another life … and that brother-in-law of yours, Abeer, he'd make a great sidekick. He took an awful wallop to the face, but he'll be okay."

Ellie gasped. "That was Abeer? Oh my God, I had no idea."

Fitzgerald was just about to answer when she became distracted by the sight of a small blue car turning in to the parking lot. She rolled her eyes and muttered something about having ordered a road block.

"Anyway, Mrs. Patterson," she continued, "I'll need to take you to the hospital when you're all set. We just have to get you officially checked out and document your condition. You say you weren't raped — please excuse the harsh language — which is a good thing, and other than a concussion and that piece of wood stuck in your foot, you're pretty much injury-free. I'm both amazed and delighted."

"Yes, I'm fine. He didn't …"

This time Ellie's attention was caught. Someone was approaching from the parking lot. She could hear the distant clip of footsteps hurrying toward them. Then a man emerged from the shadows. Her heart swelled. For a moment she couldn't breathe.

"Ellie!" Neil shouted, his face suddenly bathed in light. "Ellie, I'm here!"

The most intense emotions she'd ever felt washed through her and seemed to turn her into a liquid state. Her knees buckled, but Neil's arms flung around her just in time to hold her up. Only then did Ellie manage to choke out his name.

////////////////////

Flora was speechless as she watched the reunion unfold with disbelieving eyes. She couldn't fathom how Neil had managed to track them all the way to some random motel in the middle of nowhere. She wanted to be angry at him, wanted to cuff the back of his head for being so defiant, so unmanageable, but given the heartfelt nature of the circumstances, she refrained.

Instead, she turned to give them some privacy. In doing so, she spotted a team of officers trooping out of the woods, with Murray leading the way. He looked solemn, but still Flora remained hopeful as she strode toward him, expecting to hear that Clive had been found dead.

As she got closer, the look in Murray's eyes told her something else: Clive hadn't been found dead. In fact, he hadn't been found at all.

////////////////////

Neil sat in the corner as the nurse completed Ellie's physical examination, as photos of her injuries were taken, marks and abrasions logged. Aside from a concussion and the injury to her foot, she was mostly unscathed, a fact that stupefied Neil, who'd naturally presumed the worst — that Clive had violated her in unthinkable ways, that the damage would be ruinous, and life as they knew it, over.

Yet there she was, the same buoyant, pragmatic Ellie. Polite and co-operative, wearily going through the motions because she knew she needed to, yet somehow a hundred times stronger than before, for she had been the last one standing.

Of course, brave appearances aside, Neil knew that Ellie would need support, that she was bound to have nightmares, trust issues, post-traumatic stress. Hell, so would he. Then there was the matter of Mia, something they had yet to address.

After the nurse left the room, Neil hobbled over to join his wife on the bed. He sat beside her and took her hand. "You are amazing. I always knew it, but this goes way beyond heroics, this is … I don't know … super-human stuff."

Ellie sighed, too wiped out to acknowledge Neil's compliment. "I'm just lucky. He was deranged, so I was able to manipulate him."

"Fucking deranged is right," Neil said, the anger clotting his throat. "It killed me to think of you alone

and scared, how he had you … that he could have …"
His voice trailed off and he wiped his eyes with his
sleeve.

Ellie squeezed his hand. "But I always knew I'd get
home. I always believed that you'd escaped that fire and
gotten free. It was like …" She paused. "Well, like my
sister Bethany was there, feeding me strength, coaching
me along. Weird, I know."

Neil looked at her despairingly. "I'm going to be
there, too, Ellie, you can count on me. Whatever it takes
to get through this, I'll be right there with you."

Ellie pulled her hand away and gaped at him. Her
lip quivered and she said, "Does MJ know that?"

Neil lowered his head and began to openly weep.
When he was able to pull himself together, he turned and
looked her square in the eye. "Mia, her name is Mia …
and she was the greatest mistake of my life. You're all that
matters to me, Ellie. Nothing matters to me but you and
the kids. I'm so sorry for what I did. I'll do whatever it
takes to make it up to you."

"I don't know, Neil," Ellie whispered. "At this point
I don't know what it'll take. I guess only time will tell."

Before Neil could respond, Detective Fitzgerald
appeared in the doorway. "Sorry to interrupt. Is this a
good time?"

"Of course," Ellie replied, wiping her eyes. "Whatever
you need, Detective."

"Well, I'm afraid I've got some bad news." Fitzgerald
walked over and faced them, her tight smile degrading
into a frown.

"What is it? You're scaring me," Ellie said.

"It seems Clive didn't die out there after all. In fact, there was no sign of him beyond some scuffed moss and a few footsteps that didn't lead anywhere. He must have landed in such a way that he wasn't critically injured."

"But that's impossible!" Ellie yelped. "Did you see that cliff? It had to be eighty feet to the bottom!"

"Look, I'm as shocked as you are. But we're doing what we can. There are cops and dogs scouring every inch of those woods as we speak, and a couple of choppers, too. I promise you, we're not going to stop until we find him."

"This is unbelievable!" Neil said, jumping to his feet. "I mean, what are we supposed to do, just go on with our lives until you catch this psycho? Just carry on like he's not out there planning his revenge?"

"I don't have a great answer for you just yet, Neil," Fitzgerald said calmly. "I'm still optimistic that we'll have him before morning. If not, we'll keep watch over you, make sure you're protected, until —"

"Until what? He's behind bars? Dead?" Neil pressed. "What happens if you never catch him? What happens if a month or a year from now he's still on the loose?"

"That's not an outcome I'm prepared to consider," the detective answered. "Clive Berringer, or Brown, or whatever identity he concocts for himself next, *will* be found. And he will be punished for his crimes, I can assure you of that."

Neil glanced at Ellie and realized his outburst had been a mistake. She was trembling, visibly gripped in terror all over again. He reached for her and drew her into his arms. He wanted so badly to shield her from any more pain.

But in his mind, dread flickered.

Dread that a new phase of hell was just beginning.

PART THREE

MERCY

CHAPTER 30

Ten Months Later

"Michael! Beth! Come downstairs this instant!"

Ellie was standing at the foot of the steps, her hands planted firmly on her hips. Beneath her was a trail of mud tracks that extended from the front door to the refrigerator. Michael and Beth appeared on the landing wearing matching looks of bewilderment. Ellie pointed to the mess on the floor, and the air filled with myriad excuses, loud proclamations of innocence, and raucous finger-pointing.

"Should I pull out your shoes and compare them to the footprints?" Ellie asked, breaking up their high-pitched squabbling.

"Yes," Beth said. "Yes, you should."

"But ... but," Michael piped in, "You told me to do it ... you told me to get you a cookie. And ... and ... my shoes had double knots ... and you wouldn't untie them ..."

"Enough," Ellie said. "You can both clean it up. You know where the mop is."

Beth rolled her eyes and pushed in front of her little brother. "Thanks a lot, buttface," she said, marching toward the utilities closet.

Ellie had to hold back her smile. Beth, who'd been doing the "holier than thou" routine lately, reminded her so much of Laura at times, it was uncanny. Laura ... who would be arriving in less than an hour with Abeer for dinner. She'd been so attached at the hip to Ellie lately, needing perpetual reassurance that Ellie wasn't dead, or about to die anytime soon.

As the kids mopped the tiles, Ellie emptied the dishwasher. She looked out over the back deck at the lush, green garden that had sprung to life out of nowhere. It seemed she could finally look out the window and not instantly be reminded of *him*. Of meeting him in the woods that morning, or serving him steak dinner that night. Of hearing his voice when she bent down for that spice jar, the way he'd said "I love your ass" before covering her mouth with a toxic cloth ...

Ellie shook the memory away. Carried on with her chore. She was getting good at that — shaking off the bad stuff. After ten months of intensive therapy (both couples and crisis recovery), even Mia Jones was beginning to fade into the backdrop.

The truth was, she didn't want to think about MJ anymore. Didn't want to feel the bitter pang of deceit, the resentment. Quite simply, she couldn't cope with the undoing of her marriage. Not now. Not when security and normalcy were her foremost needs and desires. Sure, she'd done her covert research, trolled the dark-haired beauty on social media and judged her for wearing too much makeup, but above all that, she didn't doubt Neil's love. Truly, she didn't. Nothing solidified a ten-year marriage quite like overcoming a trauma of mammoth proportions.

Sometimes she did question their decision to keep the cottage, but that had been a decision of her own making. Neil had wanted to sell it, urged her to embrace a brand-new start. But Ellie had refused. She had grown too attached — and the practical, logical part of her brain convinced her that by staying put, they'd be sticking closest to the officers who were most equipped to protect them. Since last summer, patrol cars were always in the vicinity, always on the lookout.

She also liked being next to a busy construction site. The Palmers' land had sold remarkably fast, and now it belonged to a friendly couple with a dog and a gaggle of kids. They were loud and boisterous. A textbook happy family. Resonances of normal life always seemed to be emanating through that dark acre of trees. Lively aural reminders that the world was spinning, as it should. That people were good, that all neighbours needn't be feared.

"Ellie?" Neil called as he barged through the door, his arms laden with groceries. Hamish leapt to his feet and skittered over to greet him.

"Daddy!" Michael yelled. "I thought you were going to take me with you?"

"Sorry, bud, just a quick mission today. Next time," Neil said, whisking over to the counter and unloading the merchandise. He was wearing his new prosthetic finger. It was remarkable how true to life the fake digit appeared. Same skin colour, slightly diminished grip ability. "I picked up more of the usual. Steaks, fresh basil, field tomatoes, a baguette … Laura eats meat again, right?" Neil asked, extracting four individually wrapped butcher parcels from his supplies bag.

"Yup, seems she's foregone her allegiance to veganism," Ellie said. "Guess I'm not too surprised."

Neil glanced at her. "Surprised? Are you kidding me? It would take an iron will to keep up that lifestyle."

Ellie snorted. "You have met my sister, haven't you? Willful is her middle name."

Hamish was whining and yelping by the back door, pacing its length with unusual agitation. Neil went over and peered outside. "Damn," he said. "Looks like another one of those diseased raccoons has dropped by for a visit. If you call animal control, I'll go see if I can trap it in the garbage bin."

"Okay," Ellie said, concerned. "Just, please try not to get rabies, okay? We've got company arriving in less than an hour." Her tone was jokey, but she was dead serious.

Neil went out to the deck to deal with the raccoon. Meanwhile, Ellie searched for her phone. She had the number saved in her call history. This was the third time in three months they'd had to trap one.

"Kids, stay inside while Daddy gets rid of that thing … and don't let Hamish out," she reminded them, thinking of the time he'd run over to the Palmers'. The furry mound. The broad-brimmed hat …

"Uncle Aby!" Michael squealed, wrapping himself around Abeer's slender legs. "Daddy had to trap a raccoon today. It had a disease called distemper. It was blind and had gross yellow stuff around its eyes. We've caught three of them now."

"Welcome to the country," Ellie sang, swooping in and relieving Laura of one of her many bags. "Never a dull moment here in the outskirts of Maplewood."

"I don't know how you do it, Elle-belle," Laura sighed. "I mean, really … why don't you just stay in the city where there aren't so many wild beasties lurking in the shadows?"

"Yeah, no diseased raccoons in the city," Abeer said, rolling his eyes. "No rats, no pigeons, no pit bulls. Speaking of killer dogs — hello, Hamish."

Abeer got down on his knees and ruffled the dog's head. Ellie noticed that her brother-in-law's face looked much better since his latest round of surgery. The skin wasn't smooth or flawless, but she had to agree with Laura: the indentations gave him a degree of character. A rugged, dangerous quality.

"Actually, I'm thinking of starting a little side business," Neil piped up. "Not to brag, but I am getting pretty adept at wrangling woodland creatures into cages."

"Blind, dying ones anyway," Ellie quipped. "Not to deflate your ego. Speaking of which, Neil is very excited to be serving up his world-famous succulent steak for dinner … so Laura, a heartfelt thank you from all of us for accepting meat back into your life."

"Hold the gratitude," Laura said. "After all this talk of sick raccoons, I think I've just reconsidered."

After a brief stopover in the kitchen for a round of wine, the group spilled out onto the back deck to enjoy the last hours of sunlight. It was a perfect summer evening aside from the bevy of blackflies. No one spoke about Clive — it was the cardinal rule of their monthly get-togethers. Though he was always the elephant in the room, the absent spectre that frightened Neil and Ellie equally, they'd each vowed never to mention his name, particularly in the presence of the kids.

Actually, Neil was of the opinion that Clive was dead, and even though Ellie would require cold, hard proof to believe it, she took silent comfort in his theory nonetheless. He'd formed it after reading about an unidentified man having been pulled from a remote lake east of Sudbury sometime in the late fall. According to news reports, the corpse had been too badly decomposed for the forensics team to identify him, but given the proximity to where Clive had disappeared and the computer rendering of a large, sturdy male, it made sense that Clive had been too injured, too weak to escape those woods alive. Detective Fitzgerald couldn't confirm or deny it, and she advised them to exercise extreme caution until the precise moment that she could. In the meantime, Ellie clung to the hope that her family was no longer under threat.

"Anyone up for more vino?" she asked, topping up all four glasses before a single response was issued. "You're spending the night here, aren't you?"

Abeer turned to Laura, who looked taken aback. Eventually, she heaved a theatrical sigh and said, "Hell, why not? One night in the country might be cleansing. But I draw the line at one."

///////////////////

The next day, Ellie didn't think her houseguests would ever leave. Her head was splitting from all the red wine and she wanted nothing more than total silence and a long, solitary nap.

"Michael, come down here right now, please!" she yelled, feeling as though she were in a time warp. Somehow, she was staring down at the same mud tracks she'd ordered the kids to clean up yesterday. Only these seemed to originate from the back door. Which made more sense. It was the more direct access-point to the cookies, after all.

Michael came to the staircase and peered over the bannister. "What, Mom?"

"The floor," she said, pointing at the mud. "You forgot to take your dirty shoes off again."

"That wasn't me! I haven't even been outside yet," he protested. "Beth was the last one to come in. Why don't you blame her for a change?"

Ellie sighed. "Mikey, do me a favour … just come down here and clean up the mess. I myself have just finished vacuuming, doing the dishes, and changing all the sheets. I'm done with the housework. Officially off duty, okay? And remember, it's raining out there. So, if you are going out to play, please wear your boots and be sure to take them off when you come back in. Got it?"

"Yes," he said, tromping off angrily. He was wearing his bright red Avengers T-shirt, the threadbare favourite that was ruling the spring rotation.

Ellie hated sounding like an annoying, nagging taskmaster, but she was tired of cleaning up after everyone else. It was time to kick up her feet and recuperate from an excessive night. Beth had taken Hamish over to play with the neighbour's dog, and Neil was out running an errand. Other than Mikey, the place would be quiet, and she could always count on her cellphone to keep the boy busy for an hour or two.

"When you're done cleaning the floor, my iPhone is on the couch. It's all yours, buddy. Don't wake me unless it's an emergency, got it?" She climbed the steps to the sanctity of her bedroom and closed the door behind her.

Tucked in bed, Ellie promptly fell into an exhausted sleep. But like most of her sleeps in the months since Clive, it was fitful. Wrought with fear. Fear of a dark, looming presence.

CHAPTER 31

Neil was just pulling out of the lumber yard when his cellphone chirped out the familiar ringtone he'd assigned to one vital contact: Detective Flora Fitzgerald.

"Detective, how are you on this fine, soggy day?"

"Hello, Neil. You out there chasing bad guys for me?"

"Nope, today I'm building something very special for my beautiful bride. A sauna for our upcoming eleventh anniversary."

"Oh, how nice of you. A handyman, too, I see. Anyway," she began with a sudden edge to her voice, "I've got some news, so hold on to your hat. It seems that body they fished out of the lake last autumn wasn't Clive after all. It belonged to a hunter, an American fellow who was reported missing last July."

Neil felt his jaw tighten and his pulse begin to race at the mention of Clive's name. He pulled off onto the shoulder so he could listen without distraction.

"And there's more," Fitzgerald went on. "A man fitting Clive's description was spotted in an old blue pickup truck at a gas station just west of Toronto a little over two hours ago. The attendant called him in after he tried to use an invalid credit card. There was an altercation and he fled without paying for his gas. Turns out the credit card he'd tried to use belonged to that dead hunter."

"Wait," Neil said. "Are you saying Clive killed that hunter last summer and has been using his identity ever since?"

"It appears that way. The police are in pursuit of him as we speak, and I'm sure they'll have him in custody any minute now. I'm assuming you're up here in Maplewood for the weekend?"

"Yeah, we're here. I'm just out picking up some plywood, but I'll be home in twenty minutes."

"Good. You and your family should stay indoors until I confirm that we've nabbed him. In the meantime, I'm sending Murray over to keep watch."

"Of course. Thanks, Flora."

Neil hung up the phone and quickly dialed Ellie's number. It seemed to ring endlessly before finally clicking into her voicemail. He hit call-end and tried it again, only this time Michael's muffled voice answered.

"Hello?"

"Hi, Mikey, is Mommy there?"

There was prolonged silence, and Neil realized his son had pressed the speaker button so he could continue playing his game on the phone.

"Mikey, did you hear me?"

"Yeah."

"I asked if you could put Mom on."

"No."

"Why not?"

"She's sleeping."

"Could you wake her for me, please?"

"No way!" he said. "I'm not getting in any more trouble. She keeps blaming me for things I didn't even do. She told me not to wake her unless it's an *emergency*."

Neil sighed and thought about the risk level. It was low. The police were actively pursuing Clive down the highway and Murray was headed over to keep watch. "Listen, I'm on my way home. Just stay inside and lock the doors, okay? Tell Beth to stay inside, too."

"Yeah."

///////////////////

Michael heard his dad's voice somewhere in the back of his mind, but he wasn't finished playing his game yet. He just needed to keep focused until he finished slaying all the creepers. It was a mission that required his full attention — the methodical bludgeoning of a swarm of pixelated monsters. Then, once he'd finished, he leaned back proudly to reflect on his accomplishment.

But what was it he was supposed to do?

He thought long and hard until the instruction finally came to him. *Lock the doors.* He'd been told to stay inside and lock all the doors.

Just as he was about to slide off the couch and fulfill the unusual request, a voice spoke. "Hi, Mikey, remember me?"

Michael was startled, but not exactly afraid, because the man *was* familiar. He'd definitely seen him somewhere before, he just couldn't remember where or when. Also, the fact that he was standing right inside their kitchen, smiling in such a friendly way, meant that he must have dropped by for a visit.

"I'm sorry you got in trouble for my mess," the man said, pointing to where the mud splatters had been. "I owe you big time for that. Do you like ice cream?"

Michael nodded.

"Great, I was about to go into town and get some. I told your dad, Neil, and your mom, Ellie, that I'd pick some up for our dessert tonight, but, silly me … it slipped my mind until now. Want to come into town and help me choose the flavour? Or maybe you should run upstairs real fast and wake your mom up, ask her for permission?"

Michael considered his best course of action. He knew he wasn't supposed to talk to strangers and that he should never get in a car with one, but this man wasn't a stranger. He was standing in their house, and his parents had invited him to dinner. Plus, his mom was in such a bad mood. He didn't want to get into trouble again. She'd distinctly told him to only wake her if it was an emergency, and ice cream definitely wasn't an emergency. "Okay, I'll come. By the way, what's your name?"

"My friends call me CB — and you're my friend, aren't you?"

Michael nodded and yanked on his boots. "Can we get chocolate ice cream?"

Ellie jerked awake and looked at the clock. She'd only been asleep for less than ten minutes, but something didn't feel right. There was a prickly sensation under her skin. A hot worry.

Where was her family?

Beth was next door, Mikey was downstairs, and Neil was at the lumberyard, she recounted to herself. Feeling somewhat mollified, she untangled herself from the sheets, rose from bed, and plodded over to the window. It was still drizzling out. Grey and misty. A bona fide miserable spring day. But at least all the precipitation would be good for the garden, her practical side reasoned.

Everything was quiet when she made her way downstairs. Ellie spotted her phone on the couch, the screen lit up with whatever game Michael had been playing. She looked over at the sliding door and noticed his boots were gone. *Off to the neighbour's*, she told herself. He'd likely taken the road, too — a practice that made her uneasy, given his distinct lack of street smarts. The boy was bright in so many ways, but anticipating danger wasn't his forte.

Feeling an urgent desire to find him, to find both her children, she pulled on her rain slicker, threw on her sneakers, and made her way outside.

///////////////////

A few miles away, hunkered at her desk in the Maplewood OPP Station, Flora was grappling with her own unsettled feelings. She got up and paced. Wondered why Murray still hadn't come back from his lunch. No one took longer to scarf down a sandwich than he did.

Last she'd heard, their fugitive was roaring westbound in an old Ford pickup truck with a fleet of cruisers in hot pursuit. A real high-speed chase — not something first responders in these idyllic parts were used to. Still, it was beyond her comprehension why they hadn't caught him yet, particularly given the reported age and model of his vehicle.

She huffed impatiently. Just then her phone buzzed, and she scrambled to answer it, nearly toppling her water glass in the process. "So, what's the status?"

"Wasn't him," the officer from the neighbouring jurisdiction said.

"What?"

"It wasn't your man. It was a decoy, some guy named Trevor Glover in a Chevy, not a Ford. Says he refuses to speak to us without his lawyer present. So the guy we're after is still out there —"

"Fuck," was all Flora could say as she armed herself and headed for the door.

"Michael! Beth!" Ellie called, rounding the corner into the neighbour's driveway.

Behind the new house she could see a flurry of little bodies and two beige dogs bounding and cavorting in the tree-trimmed enclosure. She took a breath and told herself she'd just been paranoid; her children were fine.

Everything was normal. There was nothing violent in the works.

"Hi, Mom!" Beth shouted, waving at her from the backyard.

Ellie smiled and beckoned her over. As Beth trotted toward her up the stone footpath, she looked at the property and shuddered. She hadn't seen it up close since that night, back when it still belonged to Jake and Nella Palmer. She tried to dispel all thoughts of Clive — of being tied to the bed as he groped her breast, of him hacking off Neil's finger and toe — but it was hard to quell those disturbing memories. The new place was practically a replica of the old one, aside from the happy shrieks and giggles emanating from the back lawn.

"Hi, sweetheart, I just came by to make sure you were having fun. Is the boy with you?"

"Yeah, he's playing fetch. He gets along great with Daisy."

"No, not Hamish ... I meant Mikey."

Beth looked at her funny. "Mikey's not here. I thought he was home with you."

Ellie felt her heart palpitate. Worry must have instantly shown on her face, putting her daughter on edge. "Mom, relax. He's probably just skipping rocks at the lake. I'll come help you look."

They jogged back to their own property along the road, then split up. Ellie barrelled down to the shoreline, while Beth checked the woods behind the deck. A few minutes later they reconvened in the house. Both of them had been shouting his name to the point of hoarseness. Ellie tried to stay calm as she picked up her cellphone and called Neil.

"Thank God you answered. Mikey … we can't find him. He wasn't next door with Beth and he's not down at the lake."

"Honey, calm down. I just spoke to him ten minutes ago. He was playing a game on your phone."

"Yeah, well, the phone's in my hand and he's not here."

Neil went silent for a moment. "Okay, just keep looking for him while I call the police. Search everywhere … the water, the woods, all along the road. I'll be there in ten minutes. And Ellie … everything is going to be okay. Detective Fitzgerald called. I'll fill you in when I get there."

//////////////////////

Michael was in the passenger seat, sitting atop a rusty old tackle box in his friend CB's vintage-1970s Ford pickup truck. He liked sitting up front, being propped up so high that he could actually see out the windshield. Normally he wasn't allowed to sit in the front seat at all, but this truck didn't have any back seats — just the flatbed — and as much as he wanted to ride back there, CB said it was too wet and slick with fish guts.

"So, where should we go for that ice cream?" CB asked, smiling down at him.

Michael took a closer look at his face and suddenly he remembered where he'd seen him before. It was on Netflix.

A movie they'd watched just recently about some futuristic civilization. Michael felt excited, suddenly, because not only was he riding in the front seat of a pickup truck, but the driver of that truck was somebody famous. Someone his parents knew, but had never mentioned before. He wondered why, especially the night they'd watched the movie on Netflix. Unless he wasn't the same guy but just happened to look an awful lot like him. But that would be weird. And just like that, Michael's excitement transformed into a feeling that something wasn't quite right.

"You know," he said. "I'm not that hungry for ice cream after all. I think I should have asked my mom for permission. I'd like to go back now if that's okay."

"So, you don't want to go with me anymore?"

"Nah, I think I should go home."

"How about this: we call your mom and ask her if it's okay for you to come with me. Would that make you feel better?"

"Um, maybe. Do you have a phone?"

CB opened the glove compartment and pulled out a cellphone. Michael, who'd been drilled on his mother's telephone number practically since birth, took it and punched in the digits.

"Hi, Mom," he bellowed, relieved to hear his mother's voice. "Guess what … me and CB are in his pickup truck going to get some ice cream. We're going to bring some back for dessert tonight. I wanted to ask you, but you were asleep and you said to only wake you if it was an emergency. Then CB said I could use his phone to call you … which is what I'm doing now."

"Mikey ... sweetheart," his mom said. She sounded uncomfortable but not angry. "Please put CB on the phone, okay?"

"Okay, bye, Mom," he said, handing the phone back.

"Hello, Ellie," CB said.

Michael couldn't hear anything his mom was saying at that point, but he was relieved that she hadn't yelled at him.

"Hm, that's a darn good question," CB said. "I suppose what I want has changed a little since I last saw you. It's been a gruelling ten months, after all. Took me a while to get out of those woods. I was pretty injured out there with a broken ankle and a dislocated shoulder ... felt like my tongue was going to fall off, too. But eventually I crawled my way out. That's what real men do ... we survive." CB reached over and ruffled Mikey's hair. "Your boy here has been very good, very polite. Really looks like you around the eyes. So, here's what's going to happen. We're going to go get some ice cream, like he told you. Then we're going to play a little game. But this time, the game is just for you and me. No husband, no neighbours, no pesky law enforcement. Listen carefully. I want you to go on foot to where the woods meet the old logging road about a mile or two out behind your cottage. I want you to be there, alone, in exactly fifteen minutes. And if you thought the stakes were high last time with Neil, think again. Be there on time and alone ... or you'll regret it."

Neil and Flora pulled into the driveway at precisely the same moment, switched off their respective engines, and ran inside. Beth was crying at the back door. Neil rushed toward her and took her face in his hands. "Beth, tell me what happened."

The girl looked close to hysterics. "Someone phoned Mom's cell … it sounded like a man. He told her to do something, to be somewhere, but I don't know where. She took off that way." Beth pointed at the forest. "Whoever he is, he has Mikey … and I heard Mom call him CB."

Flora had her radio in her hand and was just about to relay the details when she saw Neil running out the door. "Neil! Get your ass back here now!" she bellowed after him, but it was too late. He was gone.

She got on her radio and informed dispatch of the situation — it appeared Clive Brown had snatched the Patterson boy, and now the mother and father had gone after them. She stressed that all of them were in grave danger, and time was of the essence.

Afterward, she looked at Beth, who was visibly trembling. "Sweetheart, I'm going to take you next door to the neighbours' place — is that okay? I promise that your folks and your brother will be back here, safe and sound, before you even know it."

Beth nodded and followed her out to the cruiser, and Flora wished with everything inside her that she wouldn't regret making that promise.

CHAPTER 32

It took Ellie exactly thirteen minutes to reach the designated location at the edge of the forest, where the old logging trail cut through. She was panting. Sweating. Pumped with adrenalin. Desperate to see her child, and enraged that Clive had taken him.

Tucking the wet clumps of hair behind her ears, she scanned the abandoned lane in both directions. She wasn't sure what she was looking for, but she took a moment to catch her breath. To calm down and think. She knew it was dire, that her baby's future was in the hands of a demon, and she knew that this time it wasn't just herself she needed to save, but the whole world she and Neil had created.

At the bend in the road, she saw something coming, heard the rumble of an engine. It was an old pickup truck meandering along at an unsettlingly slow pace. The pale-blue vehicle was swerving, zigzagging like a drunk was at the wheel. As the truck got closer, she could see that the driver was, in fact, Michael. He was sitting on Clive's lap.

Thankfully, her son's face was bright, gleeful, even, as they pulled up alongside her and Clive shut off the engine. "Hi, Mommy!" Mikey shouted through the open window. "Isn't this so cool? I'm driving a real pickup truck. Well, steering it — I can't quite reach the pedals."

"That's great, baby," Ellie said. She felt like her head was in a bubble, like she was floating a few feet off the ground. "Why don't you hop out now and come to me."

"Now, now, Ellie," Clive said, leaning out. They were face-to-face for the first time since she'd released him off that cliff. "I'm the one giving the orders, not you. We had a deal, remember? Mikey has reached the end of his fun-filled adventure. *Finito*, as they say."

Her heart seized. "But you said —"

"What did I say, Ellie? That we'd be together forever? That we were kindred souls? Did I ever say anything about biting my fucking tongue off or smashing my nose with a rock?"

"Clive, I'm sorry. I was scared after what you said, about what was in the brown bag …"

Clive wagged his finger at her like a scolding father. "No, no, no," he mocked. "I won't hear your excuses. Because now I know the truth. I know that you were always lying to me … that you were never the woman I thought you were, that you never deserved my mercy, the gift of my revenge. And I can't say I'm happy about your new look." He reached forward and pulled at a tuft of her hair. "But don't worry, I've lowered my expectations of you. Your hairdo no longer matters."

Mikey was looking straight ahead and Ellie could see the mounting fear in his eyes as his innocent mind grappled with Clive's transformation from friend into foe.

"I followed your rules, now you let him go," she said, trying to keep her own fear from showing.

Clive sighed and patted her son's shoulders. "Hey, kiddo, she's right. Moms are always right, aren't they? Seems the time has come for you to hit the road. We had fun, though, didn't we? Now you hop on out and skedaddle straight through those woods over there." He pointed vaguely in the direction of their cottage.

Mikey didn't move at first. Then he looked at Ellie imploringly and said, "I'm not leaving without you. I can't leave without you."

"Yes, you can. It's okay." Ellie got down on her knees and beckoned him out of the truck. "Come on now, sweetheart, come to me."

With tears streaming down his cheeks, the boy finally relented and unlatched the door. He dove at Ellie, whose knees were entrenched in a dirty puddle. "Listen to me," she whispered in his ear. "All you have to do is cut straight through those woods. I made a trail for you with my feet. Just follow it back to the cottage. But you have to tell Daddy something important for me. You have to tell him I'm in an old, light-blue pickup truck with New York licence plates. Can you do that?"

Mikey nodded. "But I don't want to leave you. I want you to come with me."

"I know, baby. That's all I want, too. But right now, I can't … so you have to be brave. You just have to know that I love you very much and I'll be coming home just as soon as I can, okay? Go on … run!"

Ellie shooed the boy along, watching him scurry into the trench with a combination of sadness and relief. Then he disappeared into the tangle of branches, a blur of flaxen hair, and was gone.

For a moment, she didn't move. Couldn't.

A flash of sheet lighting lit up the sky, followed by a crack of thunder that roiled to the east. The clouds were ominous, dark as death, and Ellie thought back to the day of Bethany's crash. That had been a day much like this one.

A day fit for a tragedy.

////////////////////

Neil was crouched at the treeline, silently watching as Mikey left Ellie and disappeared into the woods. He felt rage fill his veins, an animal instinct to attack. But he had nothing in his hands to attack with, and Clive was stronger — he was smart enough to recognize that. Which meant he needed a plan. He had to come in fast and hit Clive hard. The dirtier, the better.

Crawling on his stomach, he began searching the ground for anything that might penetrate skin. Shards of glass, sheet metal, a rusty can.… Hell, this was an old logging trail; Neil was sure he'd find a discarded relic at some point.

But there was nothing. Just rubble and debris.

He descended into the trench between the woods and the road and hastily combed the weeds for a weapon.

When nothing turned up, he resorted to the only thing he could think of, unbuckling his belt and taking the well-worn leather strap in his hands.

///////////////////

"It's time, Eloise," Clive said, almost tenderly. It was as though he felt her pain, understood her grief as a mother. Then his tone changed. "Get in the truck right now, or I will hunt him down and rip his little blond head off with my bare hands. Do you hear me?"

Ellie pulled herself up out of the mud. She could no longer see Mikey, but she wasn't worried about that. She knew he would find his way home, eventually. The question was, would she find her way back to him? To Neil and Beth? Could she be lucky enough to escape this savage twice?

Wet and trembling, she walked around the front of the truck and climbed into the passenger side. Clive stared at her with wild animalistic eyes. Eyes that burned with rage and arousal. He grabbed the back of her head, tightened his grip, and said, "You really pissed me off, Ellie! I'm deeply upset about all the shit you've put me through. I mean, is this the thanks I get for everything I've done for you? For trying to set things right? For trying to give you peace and happiness and the love of a real man?"

"Clive, I —"

"Shut up! Shut the fuck up."

He turned away from her, reached down, and revealed the blood-smeared blade he'd been concealing on the far side of his seat. Ellie recognized it immediately.

It was the one he'd used on Neil. The sight of it made her sick. Dizzy. He leaned over her and pressed its tip against her cheek, his eyes bloodthirsty.

Then Ellie saw something — Neil, his face blurring past the open window, his hands gripping a leather belt. The belt jutted forward, wrapping around Clive's neck. Squeezing. Squeezing with such force that Clive's face went purple, his eyes frantic as he dropped the knife and tried to break Neil's hold.

Ellie was in shock as she took in the horrifying scene. Her husband's warped features, Clive's face choking grotesquely, his bloated eyes locking on hers as his expression shifted from panic to rage. She had to get the knife, but it had fallen somewhere on the floor. To retrieve it would mean crawling over Clive's lap and rifling around by the pedals. She was terrified of going near him, but had no other choice.

Then, it was too late. The moment was gone. Clive unlatched the door and tumbled from sight. She could hear a scuffle, Neil howling in pain. She leapt out of the truck and sprinted around to find Clive on the ground wrestling the belt from Neil's hands. Neil, struggling to hold on with his prosthetic finger. Clive, easily taking possession, kicking him in the gut with unchecked rage, then staggering to his feet as he snapped the belt in the air and prepared to lash it against Neil's face.

Ellie ran at Clive, launched herself onto his back. But her weight, her flailing hands, were ineffective. Clive reached around, grabbed a fistful of her T-shirt, and flung her violently to the ground.

"Well, isn't this lovely," he hissed, his skin blotchy. "Just look at us three all together again. You know, I'm not sure which one of you I'd rather kill more … actually, I'm lying. Neil, you should have been dead a long time ago. As for you, Ellie, what kind of a woman *chooses* to be with a man like that, after everything he did to you? I really want to know. Why don't you go ahead and enlighten me with your dying words?"

"Clive, listen to me," Ellie said, squinting up at him through the hard, spitting rain. "Neil is not your dad. You're confused about who he is … who we are."

Clive cackled at that, lowered the belt, and said, "Jesus, Ellie, it seems you're the one who's confused, not me. You think I think Neil's my dad?"

Ellie locked eyes with him as he towered overhead, hoping to sway him with empathy. "I think you wish your life had been different … I think you were hurt and you're trying to make amends for what you did, and what your mother and father did to you."

"Hold up, hold up a sec," Clive said, crouching over her, his impatience mounting. "It seems you've forgotten a few integral details of our story — like the part about Neil fucking up your life and destroying your family. That's why we're here, Ellie, to make amends for that."

"You mean Neil's affair with MJ?"

"No, not fucking MJ!" Clive shouted, the whites of his eyes showing as he flogged the belt viciously against his own denim-clad leg. "I'm talking about *the girl*."

Ellie couldn't see Neil from where she lay, but she could hear him shifting in the mud behind her. Which meant that he hadn't been beaten unconscious, and he could hear Clive, too.

"Wait a second," Clive said. "Are you completely clueless about this, Ellie? Because I'm starting to get the impression that Neil never told you."

"Never told me what?" she cried. "Please, Clive, what's this about?"

"Well, what do you know," he said, glancing over at Neil with a wide, shit-eating grin, his cleft chin dripping with rain. "And here I thought you knew. Knew all about the shameful part your dirtbag husband played in your sorry little upbringing."

There was a long moment of silence. Ellie couldn't decide whether Clive was churning out utter nonsense — the empty ramblings of a madman — or if she was about to find out something true, something unbearable.

"Oh, what was her name again," he went on, thwacking his forehead with his knuckles. "It's been so long and I've been so distracted — not that that's any excuse. I should never have forgotten her name. Jeez, Ellie, I suppose you deserve some credit. This name game shit is harder than I thought."

Clive went blank for a moment, then beamed at Ellie with unreserved glee. "I've got it! I knew I'd never forget. Still, my humble apologies, wherever you are ... *Bethany Anne Blakely.*"

CHAPTER 33

"So," Clive said, his rain-soaked shirt clinging to his barrel chest, "I guess now we've established that our little triad originated a long time ago, back when we were all just innocent little sprogs. Well, some of us were innocent ... isn't that right, Neil? Or should I say *Adam*?"

Neil was speechless, his face draining of blood as Clive carried on spewing words that felt like bullets ripping into his chest.

"Moving out of province, changing your name like that ... it was an effective strategy for a while. Wasn't enough to throw me off your scent completely, though. I got older, more able. Learned to use a computer. Never forgot your rich daddy's licence plate, you see."

Clive paused and looked down at Ellie, who was splayed out on her back in front of him. "And you. Seeing you at Andromeda that night — what an awesome chance encounter that was! It was the first time I saw you as the woman you'd become. You reminded me of *her* ... the way you danced ... and I guess I got waylaid, a little sidetracked from my original goal of rectifying things with Neil there."

Neil trembled. The dark sky was spinning over him.

"But back to that morning ... it had been raining, much like it is right now," Clive remarked. "And Mama, well, she was all strung out, likely hadn't slept in days. We were headed into the city for a pickup. She was showing me the ropes, you see, training me for my future responsibilities. We turned a corner and that minivan appeared. It all happened so fast ... the screeching tires, the crunching metal as the two vehicles collided head-on. Somehow, I'd managed to grab the wheel and veer us out of the way. But the other guy hadn't. No, not the little turd in the snazzy Audi, who smashed right into them. He just stalled there for a second, then squealed off like a bat out a hell. I caught a good look at him, though. Some pre-teen kid. A rich brat who shouldn't have been behind the wheel of his daddy's fancy car in the first place. A kid I'd later come to learn was called Adam Neil Hughes ... a.k.a. *that guy.*"

There was hammering in Neil's ears, a rush of blood so intense he could barely make out what Clive was saying. *No, this isn't happening,* he told himself. *It was all just a mistake ...*

"Later on, I heard that two people had been killed in that crash. A mother and a daughter," Clive said, rain trickling down his face like liquid streaks of light. "But one young passenger survived. Bethany Anne Blakely. Aged twelve. A promising young figure skater. Heard that she'd snapped her spine and had severe brain damage … that she'd never walk or speak again. You know, it really tore me up. The fact that some asshole, some *twerp* with no moral decency had damaged an innocent girl that way. Turned her into an invalid. Some kid who'd likely been handed everything on a silver platter. A brat who'd never suffered a second in his charmed, cushy existence. So I vowed to find him and make him pay for his sins. Get retribution for what he did."

By this point Neil had gone numb. He tried to move, but couldn't summon the strength to complete the task he'd been preparing to do all along — to spring up from the ground and tackle Clive. Instead, as long-buried memories came flooding back, Neil turned his head and threw up.

Is it true? Was all this happening because of one unlucky instant a lifetime ago? *His* accident, the one he barely remembered and never spoke about to anyone? Had he really been the driver of *that car,* the one that had fatally struck the Kendalls' minivan, permanently marking Ellie's life — her whole family's life — with unspeakable grief?

He tried to recall the moment with more clarity, remember how exactly the frantic scene had played out. But he'd suffered a bad concussion that day, and ever since then, there'd been nothing but haze and uncertainty. Only foggy, ill-formed memories. What he did know was this: at the time of *his* accident, he'd been heading to a girl's house with a six-pack of beer. Not drunk driving, but distracted by youthful excitement, nonetheless.

He remembered something coming at him, a vehicle entering into his lane, and then the feeling that he couldn't stop. Afterward, he'd been so afraid of his parents, about what they'd do to him for taking the car, that he fled the scene as fast as he could. Fled, and hid the truth for days. Then, when his parents finally returned from whatever lavish trip they'd been on and found him holed up in his room, a battered, terrified wreck — the Audi's front end bent and twisted in the garage — they had of course been furious. Furious at first, then surprisingly calm. And secretive. Always whispering behind closed doors. Plotting his punishment.

He was on lockdown, of course. Grounded with no TV, no access to the outside world. Then, a few days later, they'd made the shocking announcement that they were selling the house and moving to Winnipeg. Neil was going to start all over using his mom's maiden name; he'd never speak to his old friends or classmates again. Either that, or they'd ship him off to military school (or better yet, *jail*) and be done with him. And so, being fourteen and stupid, he'd gone along with it. Never questioned their motives or their radical plan to start over. He just knew that he'd driven illegally, smashed up his parents' beloved Audi, then fled the scene of an accident. That he'd better do everything they said, or else …

But his parents had known the truth, had seen the devastating headlines about the hit and run crash that had ended two lives, broken a child's spine. Of course they knew …

//////////////

Ellie was in shock. She felt like she'd just borne witness to the heart-rending moment of impact when innocent lives had been taken, setting off a domino effect of suffering that could never be undone or forgotten. She felt immersed in her parents' grief — as a mother herself now, she knew she would never have been able to bear it.

Had Neil been the one who'd done all that to them?

"I remember once, when I was a kid about Mikey's age," Clive said, his voice carrying through the rain, "a baby swallow hit the side of our house. It was badly injured, but still alive. It upset me that this precious creature with wings that could fly had been rendered useless just like that. It was so pathetic, the way it looked at me. And I knew what I needed to do ... show it mercy. Snap its little neck in two. It felt so good, Ellie ... it felt so right. Anyway, when I eventually found out that the girl who'd survived that accident was in some long-term care facility, hooked up to machines that were keeping her alive, I knew she needed to be shown mercy, too. That was the reason I'd witnessed that crash — so that I could be the one to set things right. Only killing her wasn't as easy as killing that little bird. It took me some time to get up the courage, you see. For three years I went there regularly ... and sometimes I'd see you there, Ellie — you and your grieving family. This one time, you were all by yourself. No parents, no sisters. You were growing into a pretty teenager by then, and when I watched you talk to her, when I saw the false hope in your eyes, I knew it needed to be done. I knew I could be the one to spare you the perpetual grief ... and set both you and Bethany free. Because that girl, that thing in the bed, needed mercy. But everyone else was too damn selfish to grant it to her."

"You didn't," Ellie seethed. Tears were streaming down her face, and her fists were clenched so tight, her knuckles were white. "You had no right to kill her. It wasn't your choice!"

"But I had to do it, Ellie. I had to. And you know what? She was relieved. She wanted it that way. It was written in her eyes as I placed the pillow over her face, as she slipped away without even a struggle. And Neil? It took me a while to find him, but I never gave up my search. Eventually I tracked him down at some engineering firm in Toronto, lured him to my bar, gave him the drink he was *supposed* to drink, the one that would have ended it all," he said, visibly angered now. "You see, Ellie, you weren't supposed to meet him like that, sending him that beer and messing with my plan. But you did, and ever since, all of this has been a huge fucking waste of my time. And I'm sick of it. Sick and tired of you and your ingratitude, your constant interference. So it's game over, Ellie. The game is finally over."

Clive raised the belt over his head and looked down at her with savage eyes.

Ellie raised her arm, preparing to be lashed — but the lashing never came. She looked up and saw that Neil had surged up from the ground and somehow grabbed hold of the belt. He was weaving the leather strap around Clive's hulking neck. But she knew he wouldn't have the power to finish the job.

Forcing herself into action, Ellie scurried over to the truck to find the only thing that could stop him. She flung open the door and felt around the pedals, catching the sharp end of the blade with her thumb. Blood pulsed and splattered on the upholstery as she fought to dislodge the knife, eventually succeeding just as Clive was breaking free of Neil's chokehold.

Ellie raised the knife and ran at him, releasing a guttural scream as the blade penetrated his flesh and planted into his abdomen. She scurried away, tripping and falling next to Neil.

For a moment no one moved. Clive's arms extended like wings as he gaped down at the knife protruding from his stomach. Neil and Ellie both watched as Clive teetered there, as he slowly extracted the blood-soaked blade, raised it, and prepared to retaliate.

//////////////////////

Finish her, Twerp. Be a real man and finish her. If you'd only listened to me all along.... Did you really think she'd love you? Kill her!

Clive was gripped with shame. His humiliation so raw, so biting, that the only way to stop it would be to heed his mother's orders. All around him, he could hear her shrill laughter, Brenda's scathing howl throbbing in his ears. And Clive knew Ellie was to blame — she, his imagined soulmate, had made a mockery of him and destroyed his efforts to make his mama proud.

"Yes, Mama."

Clive smiled. It would be the perfect exodus. A poetic finish to their tumultuous, soon-to-be legendary love story.

He took a step forward, his face twisting up into a demonic grin. But then a sharp sound blasted — the unmistakable crack of gunfire.

One single, piercing shot.

Clive didn't feel the bullet bite into him at first, but then he looked down and saw the hole that went straight through his ribcage, just above where the knife had slashed into his gut. His eyes went cloudy, then he buckled — first to his knees, then face down into the mud.

//////////////////////

Detective Fitzgerald lowered her weapon and jogged over to Clive's body, squatted, and felt for a pulse. The rain was coming at them sideways, stinging their eyes like tiny shards of glass. Ellie watched, breathless, as the scene unfolded in slow motion, as she struggled to come to terms with the heavy ache and profound release that were playing tug-of-war on her heart.

"He's gone," Fitzgerald said, releasing Clive's limp hand. Then she stood up and surveyed the crime scene, as though mentally replaying the steps and counter steps that had led to the gruesome outcome. "Wait, where's your boy?"

"He … I sent him home through the woods … I've got to find him," Ellie said, her motherly instincts jolting her back into a ready state.

"I'm coming," Neil said, stepping into her view. His eyes were red and inflamed. Until then he'd been outside Ellie's periphery. A presence she couldn't bear to face.

Fitzgerald hesitated, then nodded them on as a blaze of sirens sounded in the distance. "Go get your son. We'll come find you shortly."

Neil took the lead into the woods as Ellie nursed her bleeding thumb, winding it in her wet shirt. Neither spoke. No words could penetrate the storm of relief, uncertainty, shame, and betrayal that hung like an iron curtain between them. Silence was better. But when Michael's red Avengers T-shirt came into view, they both shouted his name, the only word that still had any weight.

Michael stopped, searched for them through his locks of wet hair, then tore back and launched himself into Ellie's open arms. "I don't like CB anymore," he wailed into her chest. "He's not really our friend, is he?"

"No, he's not our friend," Ellie told him. "But the good news is, we'll never have to see him again."

"Where did he go?"

"Oh, he's with Detective Fitzgerald now," Neil said, bending down and stroking his son's hair. "CB is gone from our lives forever."

After a few minutes of gently debriefing the boy, delicately deflecting his questions so as not to trauma-tize him permanently, they started off for home. But just as they set out, they heard something. The rustle of leaves. Footsteps moving in their direction. Neil put an arm out and gestured for Michael to be still. It sounded like panting, heavy feet loping toward them.

When Hamish sprang into view, followed in short order by Beth, everyone gasped and came together in a desperate huddle. Beth was sobbing, muttering apologies for having gone against Detective Fitzgerald's orders, and Ellie couldn't help but think, *Like father, like daughter*. "It's okay," she told her. "She'll understand. I promise, everything is going to be okay."

As she heard herself saying these words, as she knelt in those woods with her children and felt Neil's arms wrapping around her, she hoped more than anything that they'd be true. That Neil was the man she wanted him to be, the man she knew him to be — a man who'd made some mistakes.

But the longer they stayed in that close-knit huddle, the more Ellie felt that she couldn't stand the weight of his touch, his tears, and soon she wanted nothing more than for him to be gone.

Gone, away from her and her children.

CHAPTER 34

Nine Weeks Later

Ellie stepped out onto the deck, savouring the last bit of sunlight that filtered through the steep bank of towering evergreens. Hamish was staked in the yard, snoozing under his favourite tree. The flowers as bright as she'd ever seen them. The air was heavy, her mind quiet, her dread less pervasive than usual, and Ellie knew that ready or not, there could be no more dodging the bullet.

Since Clive's death, Neil had been living in the city, and she at the cottage, the kids moving between them as was logical. School had been out for a few weeks, and so they'd mostly been living with her. But now they were off at summer camp, and boy, did she miss them. Their boisterous energy, their neediness. The sense of normalcy they brought to her permanently altered world. There was no time to lament the past when there were so many present needs to attend to.

Since they'd left for camp, she'd felt so alone, so vulnerable. Even suffered a few panic attacks, which she supposed was only natural. Sometimes she'd see Clive's chiselled jaw or hungry eyes staring back at her through the window. Streaks of blood on knives that weren't even there.

Neil, though — according to what she'd heard from Laura, he'd been teetering on the edge of sanity, contending with wounds far crueler than her own. Wounds with the power to infect one's soul. Guilt so potent it could seep into your bones, feed a noxious vine that would steadily grow until it choked the life right out of you.

This made Ellie terribly sad. She'd heard from her parents that he'd paid them a visit, confessed everything he knew about the accident that had crippled their darling child. She'd also heard he'd been in to see Detective Fitzgerald — that he'd badgered and begged her to throw him in jail. Apparently Flora had received his confession with a great deal of consternation, the stickler for justice in her likely at odds with her desire to help this poor, cursed family out. So, straying from police protocol, the detective had nipped Neil's confession in the bud and sent him home. Spent the better part of the night poring through the collision reconstruction report that, it turned out, supported Neil's hazy recollection of the Kendall vehicle being in his lane, likely due to poor visibility.

But even Ellie knew that failing to remain at the scene of a fatal accident carried a serious penalty. She knew that a life sentence wasn't likely, but it wasn't out of the realm of possibility, either. That's why she was relieved to learn that Flora had advised Neil to consult with a lawyer before taking any more rash, irreversible steps.

Meanwhile, the only thing Neil could do to atone for his sins was to bare his soul to those victims' families. It was likely the hardest thing he'd ever done, forcing a remarried widower and grandfather of three and his former in-laws to relive that brutal moment — to hear that he was the man who'd crashed into their minivan and bolted from the scene like a coward. But his admission of guilt had been received with a good deal of sympathy (and God-fearing forgiveness) with Laura summing up the general consensus thus: it had been a terrible accident. Neil had been just a kid. Any punishment he deserved for running had already been doled out in spades. He'd suffered enormously at the hands of Clive. Endured an unholy nightmare. Lost a finger and toe. He'd never walk right or sleep soundly again. But most importantly, three decades had elapsed since those loved ones had died, and nothing would bring them home.

As for Ellie, she wasn't there yet, wasn't so ready to offer forgiveness to the man who'd once been her husband. For he'd become a stranger, an imposter. A man named Neil with thinning chestnut hair. Same eyes, same nose. But not her man. Not her Neil. His birth name was Adam Neil Hughes, for God's sake. *But of course,* Ellie thought, remembering Clive's cryptic comment, that he didn't know Neil from Adam. It all made crazy-perfect sense.

Ellie took a deep breath and released it slowly. That was how she did most things these days — slowly. Day by day, minute by minute. Methodically coming to terms with her new reality. Taking thoughtful stock of her then and now. She'd survived extraordinary pain, felt a darkness within her she never wanted to feel again. Now, healing was all she had left to do. Healing in whatever form, whatever timeframe she needed to become whole again.

Helping her in that regard was the one person who'd seemingly helped her all along, giving her strength when she'd needed it most ... Bethany. Sweet Bethany. "Oh Very Young," as Cat Stevens sang. Ellie would never hear that song again without thinking of the sprightly sister from her youth, the girl who'd only danced on this earth for a short while before a great bird stole her away. Clive had been a monster, the very essence of inhumane, but she couldn't help but wonder if he hadn't done one thing right: he'd released Bethany from her pain. Shown her mercy, as he'd put it. Not that she condoned what he did — but that was what Bethany would have wanted, Ellie was certain of it. So certain, in fact, that she decided never to tell anyone about it, to let her parents go on thinking that Bethany had left her body on her own terms, with God showing her the way.

A swallow chirped overhead, and Ellie looked up at the burnt-orange sky, imagined Bethany's lucent form dashing across the horizon. Lovely, athletic Bethany, with her soccer cleats and long braided hair, a resilient life force kicking the winning goal, cheering triumphantly as golden dust trailed behind her. She blew her sister a kiss, then turned and went inside. Neil would

be arriving at any minute. The time had come for them
to talk.

///////////////////

Neil got out of the car to the sound of Hamish yelping in
the distance. He looked timid. A frail shell of his former
self. Ellie immediately saw him as that fourteen-year-
old kid scared out of his wits. The rattled teenager who'd
fled the scene, concussed and confused, not knowing
the severity of what had just occurred. He should have
known, should have stayed. Should have figured out
that his snake of a father, a criminal lawyer, had broken
the law to protect him. Should have, but didn't, and his
entire future thereafter was entwined in the aftermath.
He was forever linked to the saddest, most devastating
moment of Ellie's life.

And somehow she'd ended up married to him.

"Hi, Ellie," Neil said solemnly, coming up the steps
to where she stood on the front porch. No bags or supplies. Ellie had never seen her husband walk through
the door looking so naked, so transitory. Like a visitor
popping around for a coffee.

He entered the cottage and took a deep breath,
appearing to hold in the clean woodsy air for as long as
his lungs could stand it.

"It's good to see you," Ellie said.

"It's good to see you, too."

An hour breezed by as Neil got reacquainted with
the dog, as Ellie updated him on property maintenance

matters — the trees that needed felling and the handful of shingles that had been torn away by the recent
windstorm. After touring the exterior, they strolled over
to the picnic table, where Neil apprised Ellie of similar
banalities — the mould he'd discovered on the basement
tiles and the new lawn furniture he'd purchased for their
back stoop at home. ("Home," he'd said, the word slipping out. Ellie noticed he was careful to use the word
house from that point onward.)

"It's getting to be dinnertime," she eventually said.
"Why don't you stay? We'll make pasta."

"Really?" Neil said brightly. "I'd love that. But only if
you're sure you're okay with it."

"Why not? You can make your world-famous mar-
inara sauce," she winked, then regretted being so cava-
lier. Hoped she hadn't sent the wrong message.

They went inside to prepare dinner. Ellie tossed a
salad, then excused herself to take a shower and throw
on some clean clothes. She had to admit, it felt nice. Safe
and comfortable to have Neil back in her company, in
the cold, empty space around her where the air felt all at
once too thin and too dense to breathe.

When she returned to the kitchen, Neil was standing over the stove stirring a pot of homemade sauce. The
scent of oregano and white pine candles hung in the air.
He didn't notice her watching him as he licked his prosthetic finger and wiped onion-induced tears from his
eyes. In the background, Van Morrison crooned about
strolling his merry way and drinking the clear, clean
water. The candles' muted shadows danced on the walls.

"Care for some wine?" Ellie asked, brushing past Neil with the corkscrew. "I know it's a long drive back to the city. You could always spend the night here … sleep on the couch?"

Neil looked surprised. "I'd love that," he said.

Ellie poured two generous glassfuls, then took a seat at the kitchen table. As Neil got settled opposite her, she saw him glance at her hand, sensed his longing to reach for it, to touch her. It had been a while since they'd made any physical contact. Nine weeks, to be exact, since the day Clive had died and Ellie decided she couldn't stand the thought of Neil being anywhere near her, unable to subdue the hatred that had swept through her so intensely, the surge of disdain for the only man she'd ever loved so truly, it hurt.

"Listen," she said, the memory of that moment making her feel cold all over again. "I know you weren't responsible for Bethany's death, and I know you can't undo the past and make it all go away. But Neil, I can't make it go away, either. Too much has happened, too much has changed. I mean, Jesus Christ! Our entire lives, our whole marriage — it was all because of Clive. He was the reason we met at Andromeda. He brought us together. And then there's the matter of your parents — what they did was terrible and unforgivable!"

She was shouting now, letting all her pent-up anger loose. As damaged and fragile as Neil had become, she knew he needed to hear it. Needed to understand the depth of her bitter pain, the unspoken trauma she'd been struggling to process along with her brutal kidnapping.

"They broke the law, Neil! Even if your dad still won't admit it, they did."

"I know," he said, his face weary. Devoid of hope. "I just wish I had been smart enough to know it then … to have done the right thing instead of being such a coward."

Ellie shrugged and chewed her thumbnail, a nervous habit she'd long ago kicked but that had come back with a vengeance. They were quiet for a while, then Ellie broke the silence and said, "Well, looks like you're setting the record straight now. And that's very admirable. Stupid, but admirable."

Neil was staring at the ground, his eyes rimmed with tears. "No punishment in the world could be worse than this … than just knowing what I did, that I … " His voice trailed off, then he glanced up at Ellie with a look so woeful it almost broke her heart. "The truth is, I don't blame you for hating me, for wanting me out of your life and the kids' lives. The fact that you're even talking to me after everything I've done … and everything *aside* from the accident … well, it astounds me." He turned to her, this time boldly taking her by the hand. "But, Ellie, I need you to know that I love you … I love you more than anything, and I'll do whatever it takes to make you happy again. I'm not asking you to love me back. Hell, I'll go to jail, face the consequences I should have faced thirty years ago, if only you'll just … believe in me."

Ellie heard her husband's words, truly heard them and tried to let them filter through her toughened heart and make a genuine impact. Sway her.

Of course she didn't want him going to prison. Of course she didn't want her children growing up without their father. But how could she believe in him after everything they'd been through? Bethany … Mia … Clive?

She was tired of the heaviness, the sadness, the fear. She was tired of feeling trapped, a victim. Clive was dead and gone, a fact that brought her immeasurable peace, but the trail of indignities he'd left behind would endure, perhaps forever.

If she let it.

Behind them, Van Morrison's ballad faded out, and a new song began. This one upbeat, sultry, fun. Ellie felt sidetracked by the song, the familiar guitar riff prompting an unexpected blast of emotion that rose from the pit of her stomach and practically knocked the wind out of her. It was the feeling of being home. Home in her skin and the very air they breathed. Home in the faces of their children and their uncarved future. It occurred to her suddenly that all those years ago, when she'd first spotted Neil and sent him that beer, he hadn't come along and saved her. She'd come along and saved him.

"Hey, what's wrong?" Neil said, frowning.

"Nothing's wrong. Why?"

"Suddenly you look … different."

"Oh."

There was a prolonged silence, then Neil cleared his throat. "Look, if you're uncomfortable, I can head back to the city. Give you your space."

"No!" Ellie barked, her tone so imperious it surprised even herself. "I mean … I just think we should talk more. About other things, besides *that*."

"Okay. So what do you want to talk about?"

She looked away and shrugged. Felt her face turn red, followed by an unforced smile. The song was still playing behind them. Given recent events, it should have made her cover her ears in revulsion. But instead, Ellie found herself more and more caught up in it, moved by the exultant joy it triggered, the warmth that spread to her fingers, her toes.

"Actually, I don't want to talk," she said.

Neil sighed. "Thank God, me neither."

"There is something I'd like you to do … if you don't mind."

"Sure, do you want me to fix something?"

"Actually … I'd like you to dance."

Neil shot out a laugh, dismissing the odd request as a joke. She'd never told him about that degrading moment in Clive's kitchen, the impromptu performance he'd demanded of her and how the memory of Neil had empowered her through it. She grinned at him unflinchingly, making clear that her odd request was real. Neil wasted no time jumping to his feet to deliver his best Mick Jagger impression.

It was awkward at first — hell, he looked ridiculous — but neither of them cared. Ellie whooped and laughed, and all the tension lifted from the room. It even lifted from her stiff, heavy shoulders that felt like they'd been carrying the burdens of two, if not three, lifetimes.

And then they danced. Threw off their shackles and danced like no one was watching. Ate pasta, drank wine, and set their sad story aside. There were no promises, no lies. No kids or moral obligations. No guilt or reconciliation.

Just a sky full of stars, and a sleepy dog at their feet.

Just a man and a woman, taking it one day, one moment, at a time.

ACKNOWLEDGEMENTS

There are a number of individuals I'd like to thank for their help and support as I endeavoured to write this book. Getting it published was the dream ... and I'm proud to say the dream came true, thanks to these instrumental players:

First, there's my agent, Bill Hanna, a smiling force of nature who is forever undaunted in the face of rejection. Thank you for believing in my book.

Also, a huge thanks to Allison Hirst, Jenny McWha, and the talented team at Dundurn Press. I'm thrilled to be on this book journey with you and look forward to many more.

Behind the scenes, there's my fabulous author dad, Ron Base, who kept me laughing when I wanted to cry and soldiering on when I wanted to give up.

To my trusted beta readers — Joel Ruddy, Kathy Lenhoff, Nikki Hewitt, Anne Cooney, Lisa Cullingworth, Rachel Brown, Erin Grinnell, and Amy Schwalm — thank you for suffering through those (awful) first drafts and filling me with the courage to go on. And thanks to Luke Schwalm for the invaluable legal insight.

To my husband, partner, and best friend, Brad — oh, the countless hours you've endured, listening to me blather on about this book. Thank you for your patience and your willingness to keep listening. Marrying you was the best thing I ever did!

To my sweet sons, Nate and Cohen, thank you for referring to me as an author long before I deserved the title. I can finally sleep knowing I've earned it.

And above all, I'd like to thank my incredible mother, Lynda Schwalm, who not only read the manuscript a good dozen times, but caught typos in every single draft. Thank you for your unwavering support, your passion for reading, and for never giving up on our dream.